Dedicated to G.A.M and M.L.M: The two people that brought me into this world and taught me the power of kindness, compassion, forgiveness, and hope.

To my wife and children: You inspire me each day to be the best man I can be. Thank you for your patience, love, and your ability to endure my never-ending bad dad jokes. I love you more than anything else in this world!

toddgrayauthor@gmail.com - 2021

Chapter One

The Dreaded Mom-velope!

"How can a guy get some decent shuteye around here with all that banging going on in the kitchen?" grumbled Nate from the top of the stairs.

Standing at the stove, Kate, looked over her shoulder at me and smirked. "Run for your life Tate, the morning grump-a-lump has finally awoken from his beauty sleep," she announced, just as Nate stumbled into the kitchen in his red and white striped pajamas.

"What are you two varmints doing up so stink'n early?" asked Nate.

"And good morning to you," replied Kate, turning off the hot stove. "So nice of you to grace us with your presence before noon."

"You can't rush the first day of summer vacation, I always say," chuckled Nate as he fumbled for a chair at the kitchen table.

"Apparently not," replied Kate grabbing a clean plate out of the cupboard as Nate slumped down into the chair next to me.

"I can't wait to spend my first day of freedom hanging out in my undies and playing video games *all day long,*" said Nate sounding a little more enthusiastic, "but I kinda wish Amanda were still here because the only thing missing from this perfect summer scenario is a purse full of delicious candy!"

"Yeah, too bad," said Kate sarcastically as she walked over and plopped a pile of warm chocolate chip pancakes and crispy bacon strips in front of us. "No more Amanda and no more sugar highs for you, I guess."

"Well, that's no fun!" complained Nate as he reached over and snatched three pieces of bacon from off of the plate.

"And neither is your ADHD when you're all sugared up," complained Kate.

Spearing two face-sized pancakes with my fork, I dredged them with sweet sticky maple syrup, recalling the day, about nine months earlier, when Amanda Wellington first came into our lives.

Even though Amanda insisted we call her "Nanny Amanda," she wasn't very good at doing anything nanny-ish. In fact, except for feverishly texting her boyfriend in between naps on our sofa, Amanda didn't do much of anything at all when she was on duty. However, unlike some nannies that are practically perfect in every way, Amanda was virtually perfect at sugaring us up. Whenever Amanda wanted us to stop harassing her, which was quite often, she would wearily roll over on the sofa, grunt like a sleep-deprived sloth, and feebly point at her overflowing purseful of goodies.

In order to get a crunchy caramel chocolate bar or a handful of Glacier Mountain Jellybeans, which happens to be our favorite form of high fructose corn syrup, we just had to annoy her incessantly until she'd let us raid her candy stash.

It wasn't until about six months into Amanda Wellington's Rein of Sugar that Mom realized that Nate and I were, as she put it, "getting a little husky." When Amanda finally fessed up to being a sugar pusher, she was promptly replaced with our more responsible, yet bossier, thirteen-year-old sister Kate, who was now feverishly dictating her summer decree.

"...and furthermore, before you play video games, you and Tate have a list of required chores to complete," instructed Kate as she sat down and poured herself a glass of milk.

"But that's not how I imagined we were going to spend our first day of summer vacation," complained Nate as he picked up another piece of bacon, sniffed it, and then plunged it into his mouth.

"Well, I'm sorry, but you've got no choice because Mom and Dad left me in charge for the whole summer, so what I say goes," replied Kate not really sounding sorry at all.

Nate plopped a pancake onto his plate and then bent over and sniffed it. "Okay, okay, hold on to yer' britches Li'l

Mama Overlord. We know we have to do thy bidding," Nate replied dutifully as he poked the pancake with his finger.

"That's more like it," glared Kate over the rim of her cup.

"You can start the day off by cleaning up your bedroom, then move on to the downstairs bathroom, and then-"

"And then Tate and I will pick up the dog poop, wash and dry the dog, trim the dog's toe nails, take the dog on a walk to the park, teach the dog how to speak Latin, and-"

"We don't have a dog, you big doofus!" interjected Kate.

I almost choked when Nate stuck out his tongue and looked over at me with crossed eyes just as I folded an enormous syrup-soaked pancake in half and pushed the whole thing into my mouth.

"Slow down, Tate!" barked Kate. "You remember Mom's number one rule at the kitchen table, don't you?"

With my mouth full of pancake, my cheeks bulging out like a greedy gerbil, I slowly shook my head back and forth, carefully breathing through my nostrils.

Nate quickly popped up out of his chair and raised one finger high into the air. "Tate-er-tot, I shall remind'eth thee rule number'eth one...Thou shalt not die at the breakfast table," he declared in his best scholarly accent.

"Which means, don't shove a whole pancake into your mouth all at once," finished Kate. "Otherwise, you could choke to death."

Nate grinned as he plunged his fork into a mass of crispy bacon strips, drenched them with maple syrup, and shoved them all into his mouth at once. "Amd defimitwy dom't eet wike thwis!"

"I swear…if you two numbskulls didn't have someone to look after you," said Kate shaking her head, "you'd have been in a sorry state a long time ago."

"I know, Mini-Boss Mama," replied Nate as Kate fetched a carton of orange juice from the fridge and two cups from the cupboard. Pouring the cups half full, Kate carefully placed them in front of us.

"We appreciate you, we really do," replied Nate as he grabbed a chocolate chip pancake, rolled it up, and dunked it into his cup of orange juice. "And we'll happily do thy bidding as long as you provide us with delicious sustenance like this," said Nate shaking the orange drippy pancake at Kate.

"That's gross," griped Kate, "Use a fork, would you?"

"Forks are for dorks," giggled Nate as he shoved the whole drippy pancake into his mouth, "beshides, woo shwoold twy it, it tastes'em mwore dem-whicious dishway!"

I couldn't help but smile as a gloppy piece or pancake, dripping with sticky maple syrup, hung from Nate's lower lip.

"Gross piggy!" snapped Kate as she picked up a hand towel and threw it at Nate.

"I'm blind! I'm blind!" shrieked Nate when the towel landed over his face.

"I'm not so sure why Mom and Dad wanted to have twins anyway," muttered Kate under her breath.

"I don't think Mom had much choice," replied Nate, wiping his mouth on the hand towel.

Getting up from the table again, Kate placed her now empty cup into the dishwasher. She then grabbed a large manilla envelope from off the counter and slid back into a chair directly in front of us.

"What ya got there?" asked Nate, reaching over to pour more orange juice into his cup.

Kate cleared her throat but didn't say a word as she laid the envelope on the table in front of us.

"Is that what I think it is?" asked Nate eyeing the envelope suspiciously.

"It's just another mom-velope, that's all."

"Oh no," whispered Nate under his breath.

"It may not be *that* bad," replied Kate, unconvincingly.

"All mom-velopes are bad!" yelped Nate, smacking his forehead with his hand, "every single, last one of them."

I scowled at Nate and ran my pointer finger across my throat.

"Tate's right," said Nate looking at me and then over at Kate. "I think we are about to die a very painful death."

Kate reached over and patted the envelope. "You're being a little dramatic, don't you think?" she asked.

"Mom's devious," replied Nate throwing his arms up over his head. "She can't be trusted...that's all."

Kate sat up straight and looked over at us with a serious expression. "Remember, I'm in charge while Dad's away on his business trip and Mom's at work, so whatever you say about Mom kind of applies to me too, so be nice."

"I know what you're trying to say," replied Nate standing up and pointing at the mom-velope, "but, I say we tear that thing up into itty bitty pieces, burn them, and then bury it all in the backyard."

"Again, with the dramatics," scowled Kate.

"How could I not be so dramatic? Don't you remember last summer's mom-velope?" shrieked Nate as a piece of chewed orange pancake shot from his mouth and landed directly in the middle of the sealed envelope.

"Rule number two, say it, don't spray it!" yowled Kate. "Now you've gotten your mouth muck all over the mom-velope."

"Well, I guarantee that slobbery bit of pancake is a big improvement compared to what's actually inside!" cried Nate.

"I'm sure it's not as bad as you're making it out to be, scowled Kate."

Nate threw a half piece of chewed bacon onto his plate and then stood up in his chair. "Are you kidding me! I mean, think about it!" shouted Nate, running his fingers through his short brown hair. "There's got to be a corny-lation between Mom's previous mom-velope and why Tate suddenly stopped talking last summer. It was just *that* upsetting!"

Kate chuckled, "You mean correlation?"

"That's what I said," muttered Nate flopping down in his chair and crossing his arms in front of his chest, "corny-lation."

Kate reached out and picked up the envelope and shook it until the orange slobbery bit plopped onto the table. "That's probably not why Tate stopped talking and besides, we can't just get rid of it, even if we wanted to," replied Kate.

"Go ahead open it up then," said Nate, placing his elbows on the table and his hands on his chin. "It's your death."

Taking a deep breath, Kate slowly ran her finger under the flap of the sealed envelope and peered inside. "I'm sure it'll be good this time," she whispered as she reached inside the envelope, withdrew a handwritten letter, and laid it upside down on the table without looking at it.

"It's going to be another special family virtual summer trip," sputtered Nate. "I'm sure of it."

"Let's try to be a little optimistic for once, shall we?" replied Kate, "...but for the record, I agree that last summer's mom-velope was a doozy."

"Yeah, that little 'summer vacation surprise' consisted of writing twelve reports on unique places to visit in Colorado. And if that wasn't bad enough, she forced us to research lame locations, like the giant forty-foot fork in the middle of nowhere and the antique washing machine museum that contains over one thousand vintage washing machines," said Nate scrunching up his face and throwing his arms high in the air. "I mean, who wants to wear clean clothes anyway, for crying out loud? It's summer vacation!"

"And we didn't get to personally visit any of those sites either," moaned Kate, sounding a bit deflated.

"It was just Mom's evil plot to get us to do homework over summer vacation," moped Nate, "and I'm sure she's at it again."

I slumped back in my chair, folded my arms across my chest, and scowled angrily as Kate glared down at the letter.

After a few anxious moments passed, Kate finally took in a deep breath and said, "Well, we have to take a look some time."

"Careful," pouted Nate, "It's probably booby-trapped."

I held my breath as Kate cautiously picked up the corner of the letter as if it were some dangerous creature lying in wait to bite her and inject her with deadly venom.

"I'll read it first, just in case," said Kate opening up the letter and laying it down in front of her.

"Please don't be more homework," whispered Nate. "Please don't be more homework."

I crossed my fingers, legs, and eyes for good luck, but it didn't appear to be working because Kate's facial expression became more and more uneasy as her eyes moved across and down the paper. Once she finished reading the letter to herself, Kate exhaled, rolled her eyes, and then tilted her head as far back as her neck would allow.

"What? What?" blurted Nate. "You're killing us! What does it say?"

Kate held the letter out in front of her. I sat up on my knees as Nate snatched the letter from her hand and began to read it out loud.

Dear Kids,

I'm sorry to spring this surprise on you, but I have run out of options for you three this summer. As you know, Dad's on his emergency business trip for another two weeks and my work has me completely tied up...

"Here it goes," frowned Nate. "First comes the guilt trip and then, KA-BOOM...tons of summer homework!"

I reached over and patted Nate's head. He flashed me a quick nervous grin and then went back to reading the note out loud.

...and with such short notice, I haven't been able to arrange for another nanny to look after you this summer. After much thought, your father and I don't feel that it would be fair or safe for Kate to have to watch you 24/7.

Nate stopped reading and looked up at Kate with an unsure grin. "I'm not sure what you're going on about because I think not having a babysitter or nanny this summer is a fantastic idea! We'll have all kinds of freedom. Tate and I can guzzle gallons of warm maple syrup for breakfast, eat enormous bowls of brown sugar for lunch, shave our heads and eyebrows, use our bedsheets to repel from the roof, and-"

"Just keep reading," sighed Kate, "because like you said, Here comes the Ka-Boom."

Nate read on.

...So, Dad and I have decided to send you to Camp Crusader for two weeks. Your grandfather will be by to pick you up in a bit. I've left out three pieces of luggage in my bedroom along with packing lists. Boys, please make sure to bring everything on the list, including more than one pair of underwear. Sorry, that this is so sudden but have a good time, stay safe, and remember we love you!

- Mom and Dad

Nate haphazardly folded up the note and laid it back on the table.

"You're right, Kate, this *is* horrible!" exclaimed Nate. "How could she expect us to pack more than one pair of underwear? I mean, one pair of undies is plenty for two weeks!"

"Way too much information," groaned Kate as she reached over, grabbed the letter, reexamined it, and flung it back onto the table.

"That's me," giggled Nate, "Too-much-information-Boy!"

"I just can't believe that she's sending us away to camp," said Kate, looking and sounding irritated.

"What do you mean? It'll be great," grinned Nate. "We have never been to camp before. There'll be swimming, archery, arts and crafts, skydiving, underwater basket weaving, explosives training, and-"

"It's Mom and Dad's old camp," interrupted Kate.

"So, what's wrong with that?" asked Nate. "No arts and crafts?"

"Camp Crusader is where Mom and Dad first met," said Kate stuffing the letter back into the manilla envelope.

"And your point *is*?"

"And my point *is*...Don't you remember hearing stories about what Mom and Dad did at Camp Crusader?"

Nate looked over at me for help, but I just shrugged my shoulders because I had no idea what Kate was going on about, either.

"Of course, I remember," replied Nate looking around the room, trying to avoid Kate's irritated glare. "Mom and Dad had a great time at camp...playing in the green grass and sparkling blue water, climbing in the tall trees, playing in the brown dirt...and-"

"And what else smart guy?" asked Kate, her angry scowl turning into an amused smirk.

"There were kids, there at camp...ones with faces and mouths...and these kids, they ate breakfast, lunch, and dinner...and the sun was there...and rocks...and oxygen..."

"You don't have a clue, about Camp Crusader, do you?" grinned Kate.

"Not the foggiest," chuckled Nate. "But how do you know about their camp?"

"Well, I only remember because when I was younger, I used to bug them constantly about going to Camp Crusader," Kate replied.

"So, why'd you stop pestering them?" asked Nate.

"Mom and Dad finally explained to me how they started attending Camp Crusader when they both turned nine," said Kate.

"Tate and I are nine and a half, so what?"

"Well, I finally stopped bugging them when then they told me about some of the so-called fun things they did at camp like Identifying animal scat through sight, sound, touch, and taste, Algae gathering from Lake Crusader, and capture the flag."

"Nothing wrong with capture the flag," replied Nate cheerily.

I patted Nate on the back and gave him big thumbs up, excited to play a round of capture the flag because being sneaky and quiet was my specialty.

"Well," said Kate, "It isn't much fun if the losing team is forced to clean the grungy camp toilets with their toothbrushes."

"The sound of that gives me a bad taste in my mouth," said Nate slumping down in his chair, "...literally."

I let out a big sigh, fell back into my chair as well, and looked over at Nate.

"It appears both Tate and I are out because even we have our limits," said Nate frowning at Kate. "*So*, how do we get out of this?"

Kate turned and looked over our heads and out the front window.

"The letter said that Grandpa is going to pick us up soon, so I'm not so sure we can do anything about this," replied Kate.

"Sure, we can!" exclaimed Nate, "We can run and hide before Grandpa shows up. He's old and almost blind. It'll take him a week and a half to find us, and by that time, summer camp will almost be over."

"Too late for that Young'uns," said Grandpa silently sliding into the kitchen on four mint green tennis balls attached to the bottom of his walker. "I've been here the whole time, so I heard everything...Nate."

I looked over at Nate and smacked my face with my hand. He was so busted, again!

"Wow, it appears Grandpa is better at hide-n-go-seek than he looks because we haven't even hidden yet, and he's already found us," chuckled Nate.

Grandpa smacked his lips, adjusted his thick oversized glasses, and slowly sunk down into a chair next to Kate.

"Listen Kiddos...camp isn't all that bad," said Grandpa. "Besides, Kate left out some of the fun things we did at camp. "

"She did?" asked Nate sounding more hopeful. He leaned across the table, placed his hands on his chin, and listened intently.

"Yep," replied Grandpa smacking his lips, "I personally thought the rash competition was particularly fun and exciting."

"How is getting a rash, a competition?" asked Nate.

"Or fun?" mumbled Kate.

Grandpa's eyes grew wide behind his thick glasses as he stared off into space. "Well, to be a part of the rash competition, you had to strip down to your skivvies and then go streaking through the woods in the middle of the night, wearing shoes of course, because who knows what awful things you might step in!"

"Gotta have shoes," giggled Nate, "I mean, it'd be pretty embarrassing if you didn't have those on, for heaven's sake!"

Grandpa cleared his throat, glared at Nate over the rims of his glasses, and then continued, "And then you leap with gusto into the first pile of poison oak you find and roll around in it like a pig having a grand time in the mud!"

Kate frowned, "And why in the world would anyone want to do that?"

"And how do they declare a winner?" asked Nate.

"That's simple, the camper with the largest patches of hives wins a trophy," replied Grandpa licking his lips and adjusting his glasses again. "And boy oh boy, you should have seen where I ended up having the biggest rash...It was all over my b-"

"Way, way, way too much information Grandpa!" roared Kate, putting her hands over her ears and clamping her eyes shut.

"I was just going to say on my back that's all," replied Grandpa looking over at Nate. "What'd she think I was going to say?"

"Oh, you don't want to know," replied Nate, winking repeatedly at Grandpa.

"Why are you winking so much?" asked Grandpa. "Got somethin' in your eye?"

Nate reached over and patted my shoulder and sighed. "I hate to say it Grandpa, but this camp doesn't sound like fun at all. It sounds more like a way to torture kids."

Grandpa slowly blinked his eyes behind his large glasses and smirked, "Well, I guess kids these days just don't know how to have a good time because I enjoyed Camp Crusader and so did your parents. In fact, that camp has been showing kids a grand time since 1937, so they must be doing something right."

Kate got up from the kitchen table, opened the refrigerator, and placed the orange juice and syrup back inside. "Well, it appears we don't have much choice because Mom always gets her way," she said hopelessly shaking her head. "We better start packing."

"I'll grab some socks, a tee-shirt, a couple of candy bars, and my ninja throwing stars," said Nate standing up and pushing in his chair.

"No weapons and no candy," replied Kate.

"What about my grappling hook?" blurted Nate, "Surely I can bring my-"

"And definitely, no grappling hooks."

"You might fall out of a tree with that grappling hook contraption of yours and break a hip," said Grandpa seriously. "And then your days of doing the Watusi, or whatever dance you crazy kids are into, will be caput."

"That wouldn't be a problem Gramps because I only dance if I got ants in my pants," chuckled Nate.

Kate walked over from the fridge and knelt in front of me.

"Speaking of ants..." she said gently patting my back, "I'm sorry Tate, but no pets are allowed at camp, either."

I looked up at Kate and my heart dropped. I laid my head down on the table as tears began to well up in my eyes as Kate gave me one final pat on the back and walked over to the dishwasher. I wanted to run off, hide under my bed, and cry my eyes out because Camp Crusader sounded like an absolute horror show.

"No place for your injured lizard, turtle, or snake…" sighed Nate, "sorry about that Bud."

"I'm sure Mom'll do a better job rehabilitating your injured animals, this time around," said Kate from across the kitchen.

"The silent assassin?" gulped Nate. "Are you kidding me? Don't let that woman anywhere near your injured creatures!"

"Well, how about we call Jacob next door?" suggested Kate. "You can have him come over and take care of your patients while we're gone."

"That's a good idea, Kate," said Nate. "When we get back from camp, you can release them back into the wild, like you always do."

I picked my head up from off of the table, wiped my eyes, and half smiled at Nate and Kate because they were trying their best to console me.

"Time to get packing," said Kate as she placed the leftover bacon and pancakes in the fridge while Nate placed his dishes in the dishwasher.

"I'll locate the bazooka. I just hope it fits in my luggage," giggled Nate as he followed behind Kate up the stairs to our bedroom.

Grabbing my empty plate from off of the table, I could feel Grandpa's eyes follow me to the dishwasher. I pulled down the lid, slid out the top rack, and carefully placed my dishes inside.

"You know Tate," said Grandpa, "I think you're going to like it at Camp Crusader. The kids are really nice."

I closed the lid to the dishwasher and stood with my back towards Grandpa, my eyes beginning to tear up again. Since I hadn't spoken for a year, I had no way to explain to Grandpa about the overwhelming anxiety I felt each time I had to meet new kids.

"And there certainly are a lot of fun things to do at Camp," whispered Grandpa gently.

I blinked and warm tears rolled down my cheeks.

"They've got lots of nice counselors, too," said Grandpa, "and everyone at Crusader has unique abilities just like you."

Tiny sweat droplets broke out on my forehead. I wondered how Grandpa could know about my unique ability when I tried so hard to keep it hidden for so long. With my back still towards Grandpa, I wiped my eyes on the collar of my shirt.

"Yep...unique...abilities," said Grandpa slowly, "just...like...yours."

Taking in a slow deep breath through my nose, I stood completely motionless, hoping Grandpa would keep talking, but he didn't. So, gathering up enough courage, I slowly turned around to face Grandpa, but I was too late. Grandpa's head was tilted to one side, and he was snoring like a hibernating grizzly bear with a bad cold.

Giving up, I lumbered upstairs to face my fate. As usual, Kate managed to get all her gear efficiently rolled, organized, and packed in a short amount of time.

Both Nate and I were still sorting through our supply piles when Kate marched into our room to make our lives more miserable, by helping us pack.

"These gotta go," said Kate tossing aside Nate's baby food jar of lucky toenail clippings and a small block of American cheese he had stashed in a sock.

Nate just shrugged without saying a word about leaving behind his toenails and secret cheese stash, probably figuring it would be pointless to argue with Kate.

After Kate finished torturing Nate, she settled down next to me and examined my pile of essential sleepaway camp items. Growling like a feral cat, Kate pounced on the thick wooden broadsword I had stashed in my luggage.

"No weapons," whispered Kate, tossing it haphazardly over her head.

Unlike Nate, I was pretty furious that Kate was throwing out some of my extra camp gear. I really wanted to tell her that I was hoping to bring something to protect myself from camp bullies, but that wasn't possible, so I just sat quietly and fumed as she sifted through my gear.

Nate made a quick phone call to Jacob next door for me and then we loaded up our luggage into grandpa's trunk. With my private eye handcuffs and two smoke bombs, carefully stashed in the toes of my hiking boots, I was grateful to have snuck something past Kate's final security checkpoint.

As we climbed into the backseat of Grandpa's car, I buckled my seatbelt and looked over at Kate and Nate. I chuckled when Nate looked over at me, crossed his eyes, and stuck his finger up his nose.

"I sure hope Mom and Dad *picked* a good camp for us to attend," chuckled Nate.

Kate looked over at Nate and shook her head. "This is going to be a long two weeks," she mumbled as she laid her head back and closed her eyes.

However, as we headed off to a brand new scary place, I had a different opinion about my twin brother. As Mom once put it, as crazy as Nate was, he was the yin to my yang. And at that very moment, there wasn't anyone else that I'd rather have had by my side than my Twin Yin.

Chapter Two

Ready or Not

Being a passenger with Grandpa behind the wheel means closing your eyes and holding on tight because there is nothing scarier or more exciting than traveling in the back seat of Grandpa's 1986 gold Buick. Like riding on an out-of-control rollercoaster, we slid across the slick back seat as Grandpa zigged, zagged, bobbed, and weaved his way to Camp Crusader. After a two-hour thrill ride out of the city, and into the tall green forested mountains, the old car finally sputtered into camp.

"Well, here she is kiddos, Camp Rashy Backside," chuckled Grandpa. He turned his head around to smile at us as the car continued to slowly creep forward in the parking lot. "We've arrived safe and sound."

"Not quite yet we haven't!" blurted Nate.

"Um, you need to stop the car first," said Kate nervously pointing out the front window, "AND QUICKLY!"

"What in tar-nation are you two hooligans going on about?" asked Grandpa, slamming his foot on the brake a split second before we smacked into a tall pine tree at the edge of the parking lot.

"Whew!" exclaimed Kate slumping back into the seat. "That was close."

Grandpa turned off the engine and looked out the windshield. "Who in tarnation planted a tree so close to the front of my car?" he asked, scratching the top of his balding head.

"I know, right?" giggled Nate, reaching over me, to grab the door handle. "Crazy place to plant a tree...in nature!"

Kate sighed as she slid out of the backseat and stepped out of the car. Grandpa took the keys from the ignition, unbuckled his seat belt, and wrestled his walker out of the passenger seat as Nate flung open the door and sprung out.

Following behind Nate, I cautiously stepped onto the crunchy gravel parking lot. I tilted my head back, shielding my eyes from the mottled sun, and admired the towering giants around me. Closing my eyes, I took in a long deep breath; the powerful scent of pine tickled my nose.

"So, this is nature?" asked Nate, suddenly appearing by my side. He raised his hands to the sky and asked, "Kind of a lot of fresh air and trees, don't ya think?"

Kate hefted our luggage out of the car's trunk and exclaimed, "That's the point, goofball!"

Without saying a word, Grandpa turned away from us and began to slowly scoot his way through the parking lot, heading toward the registration table.

Keeping my head down low, I grabbed my luggage and quietly tailed Nate, Kate, and Grandpa. Pulling up to the long white registration table, Grandpa grinned up at the tall red headed girl that had bright red cheeks and freckles to match.

Smiling at Grandpa, the cheery counselor chirped, "These good lookin' campers must be your grandkids!"

"And you're super tall," said Nate looking up at the counselor.

Grandpa licked his lips, adjusted his glasses, and slowly turned his head back around to look at us. "...yep...she's a...tall one," he said.

"These two are very good at stating the obvious," replied Kate with a half-grin.

"I can see that," the counselor replied winking at Kate. "People around here call me Little Red in case you all were wondering."

"But, just exactly how tall are you?" asked Nate looking up at Little Red as she tied her short red hair back with a yellow and blue checkered bandana.

"Well, today I happen to be seven and a half feet tall," winked Little Red. "However, the big question of the day is...Do these fine young campers already know?" asked Little Red looking down at the back of Grandpa's head.

Grandpa licked his lips again and slowly turned his head back around to look up at Little Red. "...uh...nope," he replied.

"What are we supposed to already know?" asked Nate.

"No prob-lem-o," said Little Red, completely ignoring Nate's question as she snatched up a yellow pad of paper and an ink pen from off of the table. "They'll find out soon enough, won't they?" she said, not looking up at us as she hurriedly scribbled down some notes.

"Uh...yep," said Grandpa winking at Little Red. "They...sure will."

Little Red stopped writing long enough to wink back at Grandpa.

"What's with all the winking?" asked Nate looking over at Grandpa. "What are we gonna find out?"

Ignoring Nate again, Little Red tucked the yellow note pad under her arm and walked behind the registration table. "Here, ya go," said Little Red, quickly locating our name tags and handing them out to us. "Put these on."

As we stuck the nametags onto the front of our shirts, Little Red reached across the table and gently patted Grandpa on the shoulder. "As usual, your grandchildren will be assigned their temporary cabins until after they...well, you know..." she said, winking casually.

"...yep...I know..." said Grandpa, grinning mischievously.

"More mysterious winking and grinning," said Nate. "Why don't you just spill the beans already, unless you two have something nutritious to hide."

A wide sly grin spread across Little Red's face. "You caught me," she chuckled, "We are up to a lot of nutritious things here at Camp Crusader, especially at dinner time."

"I knew it!" proclaimed Nate, "They admit that they are up to nutritious activities."

"The word you're looking for is nefarious," whispered Kate under her breath.

"Be it either nutritious or nefarious," chirped Little Red, "you won't catch me ruining the surprise."

"Figures," muttered Nate under his breath.

Little Red grinned at Nate and then glanced down at her watch. "Whelp, times a ticking," she said. "Our staff will take care of your suitcases while you say your final goodbyes to your grandfather."

"Well kiddos," said Grandpa still grinning sheepishly behind his oversized glasses. "Have a great time. Enjoy your mosquito bites, rashes, ticks, rattle snakes, and tsetse fly welts."

"Bye Grandpa," said Kate moving in close to him. "Thanks for dropping us off to-"

"Camp Creepy," finished Nate.

Steadying himself against his walker, Grandpa opened his arms up wide and pulled us in for a big hug. "I'll see you all in two weeks," he said.

"Bye forever, it was nice knowing you," said Nate as Grandpa patted each of us on the head.

"Okay," replied Grandpa as he abruptly turned his scooter around and slowly scooted off towards his car. I felt anxious as I watched Grandpa load up the walker and drive off, leaving only us and a trail of thick brown dust behind.

Out of the corner of my eye, I saw Kate look over at Nate and then the two of them looked over at me. I quickly looked down at my feet, pretending to suddenly be interested in my shoes.

"I'm just kidding about the nutritious part of camp," said Nate grinning tentatively. "It's gonna be fun, especially when we get to taste bear scat!"

I looked up at Nate and gave him a big thumbs down.

"Fine," he chuckled, "then leave all those delicious critter droppings for me!"

"Looks like we're all ready to go...so follow me, troops," said Little Red, throwing a tan backpack over her shoulders. "To the Gathering Tree!"

Kate followed Red, Nate followed Kate, and I followed Nate down a wide dirt path through the center of camp. Lining both sides of the trail were a half dozen red slatted cabins with green tiled roofs. Each cabin had a large screened-in front porch with a door that opened into a large room filled with a dozen gray metal bunkbeds, all lined up perfectly in rows.

"These are the boy cabins. There are six identical cabins like these for the girls, near the center of camp," said Little Red pointing to the cabins on the right-hand side. "The six cabins all look identical inside, but they have their own unique identity just like each one of our campers."

Kate pointed to a blue hand-painted sign hanging over the first cabin door on our right. "What does volant mean?" she asked.

"That is the Volant Cabin, which means *to soar*," replied Little Red pointing to the rear of the structure. "That's why that cabin has a dozen, twenty-five-foot poles, erected behind it."

I turned and looked over my shoulder as we passed the cabin. I noticed that each bare pole stood about ten feet apart from one another, and each one had a small wooden platform on top.

"That's one weird ropes course," said Nate pointing towards the poles. "Looks like the campers in that cabin will have to spread their wings and fly up there because there's no other obvious way to get to the top."

"Precisely, but most of our newbies don't practice flying until day three or four, depending on the group," replied Little Red plainly, as if what she had just said made perfect sense.

"Good one, Red," giggled Nate as we continued down the path, past another cabin.

"I'm guessing that cabin means strong," said Kate as we walked past a cabin surrounded by two dozen pieces of gym equipment that included heavy lifting weight sets, treadmills, and rowing machines.

"You're very close," replied Little Red. "Lacertosus in Latin means strength. By the end of the two weeks, these campers will be able to lift a car with just their pinkie."

Nate let out a snort-like laugh and moved in close to me. "Little Red must be from the Pantus-on-fireus Cabin," whispered Nate as we continued down the path, "because she's pretty good at telling fibs."

I gave Nate a quick smile and then went back to memorizing our surroundings in case I had to make a sudden break for it.

Coming to a fork in the road, we veered right, which led us away from the cabins, and into a thicker canopy of tall pine trees. Walking another couple hundred yards downhill, we came to an enormous fallen log that we used as a makeshift bridge to cross over a small creek below. One by one, we carefully shuffled across the log and leapt onto the rocky pathway on the opposite side of the creek without getting our feet wet.

"So far, so good," said Little Red.

"Yep," agreed Nate. "No one's died yet."

"That *would be* a bit of a bummer because we try to keep the first day deaths to a minimum," chuckled Little Red as we squeezed onto a thin dirt path that led us into a grove of densely packed fir trees.

"I'm starting to wonder why she's *really* taking us deep into the woods," said Nate turning to look back at me.

As we continued down the meandering path deeper into the woods, the air around us felt colder and the sky above grew darker. The powerful piney scent from the trees and the chill in the air reminded me of a trip, a couple of years ago when Mom and Dad took us on a sleigh ride in the snow to chop down our Christmas tree.

"It's downright chilly in this part of the woods," said Kate looking up at the dark cloudy sky.

"I thought it was summer?" muttered Nate as we squeezed by a particularly chubby fir tree, "What strange sorcery is this?"

"It's not sorcery!" snorted Little Red, "That would be ridiculous."

"Yes, it would be," chuckled Nate.

"It's just the work of the Elemental Cabin. Their basecamp is a couple clicks from here. It's a great place for them to practice their weather-making skills because it's a safe distance from camp."

"Why do they need to be at a safe distance from camp?" asked Nate.

"Well, they tend to cause a lot of rather large explosions when they first try to create thunder and lightning," replied Little Red.

"What kind of special skill and knowledge is needed to create a violent storm like thunder and lightning?" asked Kate curiously, "Because that *does* seem to be something more like magic than science."

"Oh, you'll see soon enough," replied Little Red with a playful grin that reminded me of the mischievous Cheshire Cat in Alice and Wonderland.

Turning his head to the side, Nate whispered, "She's getting even creepier," out of the side of his mouth.

Not sure what to do, we continued to plod along the pathway behind Little Red. As we pushed even deeper into the woods, the air suddenly grew so cold that even the trees appeared to have a light dusting of snow on them. Trying to warm up, Nate pulled his arms deep inside his tee-shirt and I did the same.

"So, what's the deal with your names?" asked Little Red, seeming to be oblivious to the fact that we were about to freeze to death even though it was summer.

"Our names?" asked Kate curiously.

"Yeah, your names rhyme...Kate, Nate, and Tate," replied Little Red. "What's up with that?"

"Let's just say our parents are super busy people," replied Kate. "I think they thought they'd save some time when they had to punish the three of us all at once."

"Makes complete sense to me," said Little Red letting out a little laugh.

"That's not the only weird thing our parents do to save time," replied Nate.

"Really?" asked Little Red as she grabbed hold of a large tree branch blocking our path.

"Yeah," said Nate. "At our house, we have what we call brinner."

"You mean dinner?" asked Little Red, carefully holding the tree branch back so we could safely pass without getting whacked in the face.

"No, brinner," corrected Nate. "Every night, our mom and dad sit down to a meal of spaghetti and meatballs, scrambled eggs, sausages, and waffles dripping with sticky maple syrup."

"Now that's a weird food combination," replied Little Red, letting go of the tree branch and walking back to the front of the line.

"Dad once explained to me that having a combo meal every evening allows him and Mom to leave for work earlier the next morning because they already had a pre-breakfast the night before," replied Nate.

"A very inventive way to save time," replied Little Red.

"Yes, and weird," mumbled Kate, "but let's not get started on how they wear their pajamas under their work clothes just to save a couple minutes of changing time before they go to bed every night."

"Your parent's time-saving routines may sound strange to you, but I'd say your family sounds fairly typical...I mean, being famous super-" Little Red suddenly stopped midsentence. "Well, would ya' look at that..." she said pointing towards a narrow rocky pathway that ran down a steep incline. "We have arrived."

Nate pulled his arms out of his shirt and then scratched his head. "What were you going to say about our parents a few seconds ago? Something about them being famous super weirdos or super hippies, or super somethings..."

"Don't worry about it," said Little Red. "Just head down that hill and all your questions will be answered lickety-split."

"Lickety-split or not, Crusader sure doesn't seem like a normal camp," said Kate, looking anxiously down the hill.

"Have you ever been to a summer camp before?" asked Little Red.

"No, but this all seems pretty unusual."

"Well, if you've never been to a summer camp before, then how do you know it's unusual?" asked Little Red as she adjusted her backpack on her shoulders. "...Now, if you three will just head down that pathway to the-"

"Wait! We're going down there alone?" asked Nate nervously.

"Absolutely!" grinned Little Red. "I can't go any further, but just follow the path through the trees until you come to a door."

"A door?" snorted Kate. "In the middle of the forest?"

"Of course," Little Red said adjusting her bandana. "As you said earlier, this camp is a little unusual. Which means there are doors in peculiar places."

"But...that doesn't make any sense," muttered Kate.

"Makes perfect sense to me," chuckled Nate. "First, we'll go walking through a magical door in the middle of the forest and then we'll bake enchanted unicorn cookies and drink badger milk on the moon with a pink narwhal named Kim."

"Don't be ridiculous. You can't bake cookies on the moon," chuckled Little Red, "besides, Kim the narwhal doesn't even like cookies, she prefers lemon bundt cakes, and badger milk would probably taste horrid..."

"That's not the point," replied Nate sounding a little irritated.

"Well then, I'll catch up with you a little later after you're sorted into cabins," said Little Red, reaching out and patting Nate on his head. "Not that I have any doubt where you three will end up, being the kids of Commander Stretch and Captain Light, and all. Bye!"

Nate titled his head to the side like a confused puppy as Little Red disappeared down the path. "Commander Who's-that and Captain What's-a-ma-jig?" he asked, "Who are those people?"

"Come on," said Kate grabbing Nate's arm. "Let's just get this whole whacky day over and done with."

I reached out and grabbed a belt loop on the back of Nate's pants as Kate yanked him down the steep path towards the bottom of the hill.

"But who's Commander Stretchy Pants and Captain Dim Bulb?" muttered Nate as we slowly hobbled down the precarious path.

"Probably just Mom and Dad's ridiculous camp nicknames," replied Kate from the front of the line. "As weird as it seems to us, I believe all the counselors have them. You think that counselor's real name was Little Red?"

"No, but I think it's weird that she was acting like it's normal that a door would be standing up in the middle of the forest all by itself," replied Nate.

Kate looked back at us as we rounded a bend in the path. "I don't think she was in her right mind because if she was then she wouldn't have thought..."

"I guess we're not in our right minds either," muttered Nate, "because that sure looks like a door in front of us."

Peering around the side of Nate and Kate, I caught sight of a tall honey-colored wooden door standing upright all by itself in the middle of the rocky path. The unusual door, decorated with colorful frosted pockmarked glass windows, was impossible to see through.

"How curious," whispered Kate. "What kind of-"

"Whack job camp are we at?" finished Nate. "I know that we've never been to camp before, but this *can't* be normal," he said staring at the door.

Kate tipped her ear towards the door and asked, "What is that peculiar hum coming from behind the door?"

Nate placed his hands on his knees and leaned forward. "I hear it too. It sounds like some kind of electrical buzzing sound," he said.

Carefully kneeling on the rocky pathway, Kate tried to peer through the tiny keyhole just under the door handle. "I can't see a thing," she said, brushing the dust off her knees as she got to her feet.

"Whelp, we don't have a key..." said Nate throwing his arms up in the air. "Guess we won't be able to go through the creepy door. Looks like it's time to turn around and go home!"

"It's probably unlocked," said Kate looking back over her shoulder at Nate. "We should at least try the knob to see if it's locked, don't you think?"

"Are you insane?" asked Nate. "Who knows what's behind door number one."

"I just think we should try the handle since we came all this way."

"Let me get this straight, that freaky door in front of us is making a strange electrical hum and you want to touch it?" squealed Nate. "You have a death wish or something?"

"Come on, be realistic, Nate," countered Kate. "They didn't march us all the way out here to electrocute us to death."

"Says who?"

"Says me."

Nate took a deep breath and sighed. "Well, if you're determined to touch it, then I guess we're all going to touch it," relented Nate, "That's how Team Larson rolls."

Nate turned sideways and extended his hand out to me. I grabbed hold of his right hand while Kate grabbed hold of his left hand.

"Here goes nothing," sighed Kate as she slowly stretched her hand towards the golden doorknob.

"Careful," whispered Nate as Kate's fingertips settled on the knob.

Suddenly, Kate's long brown hair shot straight up towards the sky as if she'd just stuck her finger in an electrical socket. "Something's...not...ri..." she stammered.

"Kate, let... go...go...of the...." stuttered Nate, his short brown hair standing straight up as well.

I gasped as an intense tingling sensation unexpectedly swept through my body, from the top of my head to the tips of my toes. Startled, I looked down and saw the little white hairs on my arms moving up and down in unison.

"Let...go...of the...knob," repeated Nate.

"I, I...can't..." sputtered Kate.

"Then....tur...turn...the...knob!" stammered Nate, "Now...now!"

My whole body began to shake feverishly, including my eyeballs, as Kate slowly turned the doorknob to the right.

Without warning, the door suddenly flung wide open, flooding us with a tsunami of intense colored lights. I had to cover my eyes with my free hand because the light was so overwhelming.

Kate shrieked from the front of the line, "Hold on!" as she and Nate began to get pulled towards the open door by some unseen force.

Feeling our grip begin to loosen, I leaned back, dug my heels into the rocky path, and held on for dear life as Nate and Kate continued to slowly slide towards the open doorway.

"I can't...hold...on!" cried Nate.

Tears rolled down my face as Nate's hand slipped through mine. Together, Kate and Nate were sucked through the open door and into the lights.

Desperate, I leapt towards the open door, but a powerful pulse of white light struck me in the center of my chest, knocking me to my knees. Slumping over, I felt a tightness behind my ribcage that burned as if my heart was on fire. Grabbing my chest, I struggled to catch my breath as the door slammed shut in front of me. Frantically gasping for air, I tipped forward and succumbed to the darkness.

"Hey Dork, nappy-nap time is over," growled an angry voice standing above me. "Get off your butt and either go through the door or move out of my way."

"Wha?" I said weakly, looking up at a tall muscular boy with massive broad shoulders, a wide flat forehead, and a thick bulging nose.

"I said move it or lose it pipsqueak because Scott Sanderson doesn't want to keep the ladies waiting," said the monstrosity glaring at me from up above.

I rubbed my eyes, shook my head to clear out the cobwebs and slowly got up, feeling unsteady on my feet.

"Sorry," I muttered as I stepped back, burying myself in a fir tree so Scott could squeeze by.

Using his enormous elbow, Scott nudged me further into the tree as he walked by. "Later loser!" barked Scott, reaching out and grabbing the door handle.

It was difficult to tell if Scott was getting electrocuted because his blonde hair was already short, spiky, and standing straight up. Just as Scott disappeared through the door, I noticed the words 'Da Boss' shaved in the back of his hair.

"Da Dummy," I said under my breath as the door slammed shut behind Scott.

Exhausted and all alone again, I sat on the ground and stared helplessly at the door. As seconds stretched into minutes, I began to feel anxious without Nate and Kate by my side. So, using a coping technique my counselor recommended, I closed my eyes and took three deep breaths. I was just about to take in my fifth breath when I heard a popping sound directly behind me, followed by the stench of burning rubber.

"You stuck here?" asked a warm deep voice from behind me.

Spinning around on my backside, I saw a middle-aged man with kind eyes and long black and gray peppered hair, pulled back into a ponytail, standing above me. Stroking his short, speckled beard, the man had a look of bewilderment on his face as he repeatedly looked back and forth from me to the door.

"Yes..." I replied, *"I'm not so sure what I'm supposed to do next."*

"Well, let me assure you that you're not the first person to have experienced something overwhelming at this particular door." The man flashed a quick grin and then continued, *"but it has been quite some time since the last occurrence."*

I stood up slowly and brushed the dust from my backside. *"Well then...I guess I'm just special or unlucky, or maybe especially unlucky,"* I replied.

"My name is Alekzander, and I would say that you, Tate, are especially lucky."

"How do you know my..."

My stomach suddenly tangled in knots as I realized that I was carrying on a conversation with a complete stranger, after more than a year of self-imposed silence.

"Don't worry, your secret is still safe because we're not having, what normal people call, a regular conversation," said Alekzander.

Baffled, I asked, *"What do you mean? Of course, we're having a regular conversation."*

"Are we?" smirked Alekzander.

It was at that precise moment that I realized that neither he nor I were using our actual vocal cords to talk to each other. Somehow, someway, we were speaking to each other in our minds.

Alekzander squatted down in front of me and looked me straight in the eyes. *"It's called telepathic communication,"* he said. *"It's how a telepath, or in this case, how two telepaths talk to each other...by only using our minds."*

"I'm not sure I understand."

"You, my friend, are a telepath."

"Is that bad?" I asked nervously.

"Not at all!" chuckled Alekzander as he stood up and brushed off his pants. *"More will be explained about your special ability, but right now your brother and sister are worried sick about you."*

I turned my head, and squinted, waiting for the intense light to strike me again, but nothing happened as Alekzander reached over and turned the doorknob.

"How can you just turn the doorknob without anything happening? No electricity, no lights, no nothing?"

"That's because it already knows me. Besides, it doesn't seem to be working quite right at the moment because someone just broke it," grinned Alekzander.

"I'm sorry," I said looking down at my feet. *"I didn't mean to."*

"Don't be sorry. It's quite remarkable that it happened again after all of these years," replied Alekzander running his hand along the doorframe and then turning to look back at me, *"but enough talking, we must be off. I'm running a bit behind schedule."*

"So where to?" I asked apprehensively.

"We will teleport directly to your brother and sister at the Gathering Tree, but first, I have one small request before we ship off."

"Okay..."

"I would prefer that you keep your newly discovered power and your issue with the door a secret for the time being if you don't mind."

"I can do that."

"Great," replied Alekzander, extending his hand out for me to grab. I placed my hand in his and felt an instant connection to him.

"How do I teleport?" I asked looking up at Alekzander.

"I'll do all the work. You just make sure you don't let go of my hand, under any circumstances, for the next few seconds," instructed Alekzander.

"Okay," I replied, squeezing his hand even tighter.

"Then, let's go!" Alekzander exclaimed. I watched quietly as Alekzander closed his eyes, took a deep breath, and...

" POOF! "

Suddenly I was here, there, and everywhere, but really nowhere all at once. Within the amount of time it took me to blink, we had teleported to a small gathering of campers standing under an enormous willow tree; its trunk larger and thicker than any ten trees combined.

I quickly located Kate and Nate standing at the back of the crowd. When Nate saw me, he wrapped his arms around my neck and squeezed tight while Kate patted my head.

"We've been looking all over for you," whispered Nate. "We weren't sure if you made it through the door or not."

I smiled and gave Nate and Kate a thumbs-up as the three of us watched Alekzander walk quickly to the front of the crowd.

"Sorry for the delay. We may now begin," said Alekzander, standing shoulder to shoulder next to a plump, gray-haired woman as tall as Kate. The woman waved a quick hello and then went back to examining her clipboard through her small silver-rimmed glasses that were precariously balancing on the tip of her nose.

"My name is Alekzander Fortis and this is Ms. Agatha Grimswood," smiled Alekzander at the small group of new campers fidgeting anxiously in front of him.

"We welcome you to Camp Crusader," said Ms. Agatha, looking up from her clipboard and stepping forward, "Each of you did remarkably well passing through the Gamma-Ray Detection Door, also known as the G.R.D.D. This door has been in use at Camp Crusader since its inception. This remarkable tool was constructed to ensure that only individuals that possess unique abilities are permitted at camp."

"Speaking of the G.R.D.D., I just returned from tending to a small malfunction with it, but I assure you that everyone in this session of camp has passed through the door swimmingly," said Alekzander, meeting my eyes and nodding his head ever so slightly.

Nate leaned over to me and whispered in my ear as Alekzander and Ms. Agatha continued to talk. "You're not going to believe this Tate, but Camp Crusader isn't an ordinary sleepaway camp," he said excitedly. "This camp trains children to be future superheroes. Can you believe that we have special abilities buried deep inside us and…."

I half smiled at Nate, struggling to listen to him, Alekzander, and Ms. Agatha all at the same time.

"Beginning tomorrow, Ms. Agatha will be the star of the show," said Alekzander. "She and her personal assistant, Nicholas Knight, are responsible for all of the wonderful activities you will be participating in over the next two weeks while you're at Crusader."

Alekzander stretched out his arm and pointed to a friendly-looking lanky black-haired boy standing right in front of us. The boy turned around, grinned, and waved his hand. "Welcome to camp. Please come and see me if you have any questions or concerns while at Crusader," said Nicholas.

"...and it's crazy to think that there are people in this world with superpowers and we didn't even know about them," said Nate. "I sure hope flight is my super ability because I've always wanted to fly. One time, I had a dream that I was flying over California, and I was suddenly summoned by a magical wizard because he needed help delivering blended-up bean burritos and fish heads to the Tooth Fairy because an evil dentist pulled out all her teeth and..."

"...and each of you will all be sorted into one of six possible cabins according to the unique ability you possess," stated Ms. Agatha. She reached down and opened a large black velvet sack next to her. "I hope you will find the sorting process quite simple and straightforward."

Reaching inside the bag, Ms. Agatha handed Alekzander six engraved wooden signs. Alekzander held each sign up as he spoke. "The name of each cabin is Latin based. For example, the Animo cabin means mind, Lacertosus means strength, Volant means to soar, Celer in Latin means speed, Elementa means elements, and Mavercius in Latin means the Maverics," he said.

"Every cabin has a rich, long-standing history at Camp Crusader," continued Ms. Agatha, "I'm sure each one of you will find..."

"...I still can't believe that Mom and Dad have superpowers that they never told us about, but I guess it makes sense since they're always so busy, and don't have a lot of time for..."

"...over the course of the next two days, beginning tomorrow morning, each of you will be tested to ensure that you are properly placed into the correct cabin. This will ensure that you will be trained in such a way, that best suits your individual powers."

"...and we get to be here for two whole weeks and do superhero camp things and learn how to harness our powers and..."

"Today, you will be separated into two preliminary cabins, boys in one and girls in the other. These two cabins are simply named The Opperior Cabins, which, in Latin means, to wait for..."

"...Maybe I can morph into a giant stink bug that squirts yellow acid, or turn people into stone by just breathing on them..."

I placed my hand over my left ear to block out Nate because I wanted to focus on what the camp leaders were saying, but he wasn't getting the hint.

"...I mean can you believe that we have superpowers somewhere buried deep inside us? I wonder what powers you have. I wonder what powers Kate has. Maybe we all have the same super..."

"Enough!" I exclaimed, projecting words into Nate's mind. *"I already know what my power is!"*

Nate slowly turned his head, his mouth hanging wide open.

"It's okay, really," I projected. *"I'll explain more, but for now please let me just listen to what Alekzander and Ms. Agatha are saying."*

Like water bursting from a floodgate, Nate's mind exploded in a deluge of never-ending questions and random thoughts that I couldn't block out.

"How did Tate do that?"

"Is this my brother or has he been replaced by an alien?"

"I wonder what we are having for dinner?"

"I wonder if I'm too young to start wearing deodorant?"

"How long has he known that he has superpowers?"

"Maybe my bladder has superpowers because I haven't gone pee in a while."

"Is that a Sasquatch over there?"

"I'm not so sure I want my bladder to have superpowers…"

I laid my hand firmly on Nate's shoulder and gruffly projected, *"Please just stop!"*

Keeping his bulging eyes firmly glued to my face, Nate took two slow steps backward.

"Listen," I projected. *"I've known something strange was going on with me since last year. Alekzander just told me that I'm a telepath, which means I can read minds and can communicate like this. I'll explain more about my power to you later. Right now, I'm just trying to focus on what is being said...and no, I'm not an alien, and no, that's not a Sasquatch, it's a squirrel... and no, I don't think your bladder has superpowers."*

I flashed Nate a quick smile and then went back to focusing on what Alekzander and Ms. Agatha were saying, grateful that he was finally quiet for once.

"...In our midst this year, we have twenty-eight new arrivals from around the globe. I'm quite aware that there are a handful of you that arrived at camp today without any knowledge of your exceptional lineage. No doubt, this has been quite a shock to your systems," said Ms. Agatha glancing down at her clipboard.

"Ya think?" whispered Kate.

Ms. Agatha reached into her back pocket and pulled out a small booklet. She held it up for all of us to see.

"To help guide you on your journey these next few days, we have provided multiple copies of the Camp Crusader Q & A Booklet in both the boy's and girl's Opperior Cabins," said Ms. Agatha. "Please take the time to familiarize yourself with it for this booklet will answer any lingering questions you may have."

Ms. Agatha placed the book back in her pocket and nodded at Alekzander. Alekzander nodded back at Ms. Agatha and then grabbed her right hand.

"Now, if you will please excuse us both, Ms. Agatha and I have some urgent matters to attend to," said Alekzander. "Your first order of business will be to unpack and get settled into your cabin, with the help of Nicholas Knight. We shall see each other again at dinner tonight, but until then, we bid you adieu."

Closing his eyes, Alekzander and Ms. Agatha disappeared, leaving a small puff of gray soot lingering in the air.

Chapter Three

Q & A

"You know, they could have made this thing a little easier to read," said Nate frowning as he turned the Camp Crusader Questions and Answers booklet around and around in his hands.

"How could they have done that?" I asked, plopping myself on Nate's bunk.

"A one-paragraph summary would have been nice. Maybe a dozen bullet points or a graphic novel, but not thirty-seven pages long," frowned Nate as he fanned himself with the book. "It's summer vacation for gosh darn sakes. Who has time to read?"

I snatched the book out of Nate's hand. He looked at me dumfounded and asked, "And by the way when did you all of a sudden start talking? I mean *real* talking, not that weird suck the words out of my brain kind of talking."

I placed the book down next to me on the bunk. I skootched my bottom closer to Nate, so we were only inches apart. "I think I should explain it to you in your mind so no one else can hear," I whispered looking into his eyes. "I promise not to suck the words out of your brain...at least not completely."

Nate stared back at me without blinking, looking a little bit anxious. "Alright then," he sighed, "but be careful in there because my brain is uncharted territory. I can't be held responsible for anything you come across that's mildly inappropriate!"

"Okay, I'll be careful what I step in," I chuckled.

"You do that," giggled Nate.

I reached over and lightly placed my fingertips onto Nate's fingertips. I closed my eyes, slowed my breathing, and concentrated. It didn't take long before I was able to access Nate's mind.

"I'm in," I projected.

"Go ahead…"

"So, I found out that something weird was going on a little more than a year ago. At first, I thought that I was going crazy because I started hearing voices in my head. But after a while, I figured out that I was actually reading people's thoughts. I soon discovered that it was a lot easier to read someone's mind if I was touching them…maybe their arm, shirt sleeve, or whatever. At first, it was fun being able to hear what people were thinking, until one day I went with Dad to Savetime Market and something scary happened. When Dad and I were in line to check out, I accidentally brushed up against someone that had some really disturbing thoughts. I told myself after that experience that I wouldn't pry into people's minds anymore."

"And?"

"And, unfortunately, my powers suddenly started to go haywire. A couple of days after the store incident, I discovered that I no longer had to physically touch someone to read their thoughts. From then on, I only had to talk to someone and whatever was on their mind just popped into my head. This occurred every time I spoke to someone, whether I wanted it to happen or not. I didn't know how to control it, so I just stopped talking. And that's when my anxiety skyrocketed. I guess Mom and Dad didn't like that I stopped talking so they sent me to counseling."

"I'm so sorry," frowned Nate.

"Don't be," I replied. *"I was afraid and confused. I didn't know what was going on, but none of this is your fault."*

"No, not that," smirked Nate, *"I mean, yes, I'm sorry that you were having such a hard time with your powers, but I'm more sorry about something that is about to occur right about...now."*

"What are you sorry about, right now?"

"I just cut the silent cheese and it's gonna smell really bad in here in a couple seconds."

"We better get out of here before they find out it was you stinking up the place!" I said snatching up the Camp Crusader Q & A book.

Both Nate and I hopped off the bed and hurriedly walked towards the cabin door. Just as we pushed the front door open, a tall skinny boy with long blond hair, walked by Nate's bunk and howled, "Dudes, who let one rip?"

Nate and I stifled our laughs as we scurried out the door, hoping the stench wouldn't follow us.

"That was horrible!" I gasped as we walked over to a fallen tree lying between the boy's and girl's Opperior Cabins. Scrambling up onto a log, Nate and I watched campers scurrying from place to place like busy little ants. Looking over at the girl's Opperior Cabin, we saw Kate hanging out by the front door looking down the road towards the dining hall.

Nate howled and waved his arms over his head, "Hey big Sis! Over here!"

Kate saw us, gave us a half-wave, and then headed our direction.

"Don't tell her you're talking yet," whispered Nate under his breath as Kate made her way over to us with a copy of the Camp Crusader Q & A book tucked under her arm, "and don't tell her about your superpower either."

"Okay, but why are we all of a sudden keeping secrets from Kate?" I asked curiously.

"No special reason," said Nate winking at me. "It's just fun to mess with her."

"Okay," I said hesitantly, "But we should probably tell her soon."

"Soon," said Nate out of the corner of his mouth as Kate drew closer. "Just not right now."

"Have you two read this book yet?" asked Kate, waving the Question and Answer book in our faces, "because I just finished it a couple minutes ago and it has a lot of good information in it."

"We just finished reading our copy twenty minutes ago," boasted Nate. "It was fascinating reading."

Kate glared at Nate. "You're such a liar! I'll bet you haven't even read one page," said Kate matter-of-factly, "because I happen to know how much you despise anything that involves thinking over summer vacation."

"That truly hurts right here...but you're right," cried Nate thumping his chest with his fist. "I hate straining my powerful brain cells over the summer. They're still recuperating from a year of fourth-grade torture."

Kate opened up the book and sighed, "Fine, I'll fill you in, but you two really should read it when you get the chance."

"Yeah, yeah, we will," said Nate impatiently, "but in the meantime what does it say?"

"Well, it runs down our daily schedule on the first few pages. For example, we have an early dinner tonight, in about ten minutes."

"My stomach thanks you for that tasty tidbit of information...What else do we need to know?" asked Nate curiously.

"Apparently, Camp Crusader is broken up into two sections. First-year camp, which is where we are now, is about ninety acres, but the rest of the camp covers over ten times that amount. The number of participants for first-year camp is limited to about thirty, but there can be up to two hundred returning campers to the other section of camp on any given year."

"Wow, this is a pretty big camp," said Nate looking around.

"Yeah, it is...and get this," replied Kate. "Crusader II has a bunch of mysterious caves, a frozen black lagoon, and a creepy old well in the middle of the woods that campers aren't allowed to visit."

"Sounds cool," said Nate, "But, why do they keep the first-year campers separated from the rest of the camp?"

"For the safety of the more seasoned campers," replied Kate. "According to the book, new campers can be pretty unpredictable and dangerous. It's going to take some time for us to learn how to handle our new powers."

"Makes sense," agreed Nate.

"This book also says that superpowers usually don't start manifesting themselves in children until they have a deeper understanding between right and wrong, which for most boys and girls is around the age of nine or ten," said Kate. "Which is why Camp Crusader starts accepting campers at the age of nine years old."

"Well, that makes sense for Tate and me since we are nine and a half, but you're fourteen. Why haven't you discovered your powers yet?" asked Nate.

"I haven't a clue," said Kate flipping further into the book. "The book also states that all children born into a family with a hero bloodline, end up having some type of super ability. So, initially, it's the parent's responsibility to begin training their young children until they are old enough to attend camp to further develop their powers."

"Kind of like training puppies," grinned Nate.

"I'm not a dog," spat Kate.

"A puppy," replied Nate. "There's a difference...Puppies are cuter!"

"Anyhow..." said Kate rolling her eyes. "I've been wracking my brain for the past two hours trying to figure out why Mom and Dad didn't tell us before now. It bothers me that I haven't been able to come to Camp

Crusader until today because it seems like I'm about five years too late in developing my super ability."

"Maybe they just forgot to tell us," suggested Nate.

"Doubtful," replied Kate.

I too had a hard time believing that our parents somehow forgot to tell us about our superpower bloodline and Camp Crusader. And the more I thought about them not telling us, the more upset I was becoming. The way I figured it, I could have been spared a lot of pain and anxiety if Mom and Dad would have just been honest with me from the start. I also wouldn't have had to waste a whole year of being absolutely silent.

"I guess we'll just have to ask Mom and Dad when we see them, won't we?" replied Nate, pointing at the Crusader booklet. "What else does that fancy book o' facts of yours say?"

"It goes over the history of Crusader," said Kate opening up to a page towards the front of the manual. "It says that in 1924, a man by the name of Charles Wildenbury discovered his talent for fire breathing, but his kind of fire breathing didn't require a combustible like kerosene or gasoline to work. By the age of eight, while living in New York City with his father, Charles accidentally lit his bedroom on fire when he sneezed. His father, being a power denier, sent Charles away to a boy's boarding school in Chicago. While at the boarding school, Charles did his best to hide his secret. He managed to do fairly well for about a year and a half until, early one morning, while fighting a nasty cold, Charles went into a coughing fit while in class."

"Let me guess," said Nate, "he burned down the whole school."

"Just the science lab," replied Kate.

"I'll bet his teacher was probably fuming when that happened!" exclaimed Nate.

"Har, Har," said Kate sarcastically, "Your jokes are horrible."

"But I thought you lava a good pun," chuckled Nate.

I placed my hands over my mouth so I wouldn't laugh out loud.

Kate looked over at me and then rolled her eyes at Nate, "*Anyway*... before he could be questioned by the authorities, Charles ran away from the boarding school by hitching a ride on a cargo train that was heading toward Philadelphia. As luck would have it, Charles arrived in Philadelphia during the year of the World's Fair where there were lots of vendors and street sideshows. It was down one of those side streets that Charles ran into the Brendenberg Circus and Freak Show. One thing led to another, and he ended up joining up with the traveling circus as a sideshow freak. After ten years of performing as The Man-Dragon, Charles began to wonder if there were more people in the world with powers like him."

"So, he's the one that started Crusader?" asked Nate.

"Yes, because he was very frugal during his circus years, Charles took his life savings, moved to Colorado, bought fifty acres of land, and began his search looking for people with remarkable talents like ours."

"Well, that's an interesting tidbit of history," replied Nate.

I smiled and gave Kate and Nate a thumbs up.

"Well, I also learned something a little sinister that happened at Crusader that wasn't included in the Q and A book," said Kate mysteriously. "Want to hear it?"

"Fire away," said Nate with a wink, "but I sure hope it's interesting in-fire-mation!"

Kate reached up, grabbed our hands, and pulled us in so close that she almost completely yanked us off the log. "Well, get this...just a few moments ago I was speaking to Anne. She's a new girl at camp like us, but she was raised knowing about her family bloodline since birth."

"*And*?" asked Nate.

"*And*, apparently during the thirty-ninth summer camp session, a new camper by the name of Nero, arrived. Nero, who was seventeen years old at the time, had two powers, which for superheroes is extremely rare. In fact, up to that point, only a couple other campers in the history of Camp Crusader had two powers and both those campers and Nero wreaked havoc on the G.R.D.D."

I leaned in closer to Kate, hoping she would talk more about past problems with the G.R.D.D., but she didn't.

"...By the time Nero started camp, he already had well-developed telepathic abilities, but unbeknownst to anyone else at Crusader, he also had the unique ability to extract other people's superpowers and use them for himself."

"So, I assume he ended up taking a camper's power while at camp," replied Nate.

"More than that," frowned Kate. "By the time Charles Wildenbury figured out who the perpetrator was, six students had already become victims. Meanwhile, Nero had amassed a small group of campers who named themselves the Chaos Crew. He led his Crew into battle against Charles and about fifty other campers. After two days of fierce battling, Charles and his group finally defeated Nero and The Crew, but most of the camp was leveled to the ground in the process."

"Well, that's not good," said Nate.

"Not at all," replied Kate. "And get this...Nero wouldn't surrender, even after The Crew was captured. Charles and a group of ten other campers cornered Nero and hit him hard with their combined powers. When the smoke cleared, Nero had disappeared into thin air, leaving behind a giant glowing red ruby lying in the dirt. The ruby, nicknamed The Amulet, is believed to contain Nero's life force and the powers he stole. With Nero gone, the Chaos Crew were forced to disband. Even though years have passed, Nero's followers, including his siblings, have vowed to free him once again."

"Pretty good story," said Nate as Kate looked back at her cabin.

"Yes, but that's not the best part," whispered Kate. "Apparently, the amulet is still stored somewhere at Camp Crusader in room A113. Campers have been trying to locate the room for almost fifty years, but no one's found it yet."

"Sounds like a challenge," grinned Nate.

"I don't think so!" exclaimed Kate, furrowing her eyebrows. "The amulet not only holds the stolen superpowers, but Nero's evil spirit, making it extremely powerful and dangerous."

"Okay, okay," said Nate, "I promise not to use the amulet when I discover its whereabouts...at least not right away."

"Har! Har!" said Kate sarcastically. "Maybe you and Tate should just focus on discovering your super abilities just in case we need to watch each other's backs."

I opened my mouth, ready to spill my guts to Kate when Nate suddenly elbowed me in the ribs. "We'll be sure and tell you when we discover our powers, but for now, I suggest we all take a couple of steps back because today, I seem to be blessed with the power of stinky gas."

"Oh no, you didn't....Ugh!" choked Kate, fanning her hand frantically in front of her face. "You're the most gaseous person I know!"

"Well, gassy or not," said Nate hopping down from the log. "My stomachs says it's about dinner time so let's go eat."

Chapter Four

Evil Mac and Cheese

My stomach growled in protest as I greedily watched the counselors happily tearing into their food from across the dining hall. Following directions from the camp staff to form a line from oldest to youngest, Nate and I waited unhappily at the back of the chow line.

"I wonder what they're serving for dinner because I'm starving," said Nate rubbing his belly.

"Let me take a look-see," I said quickly stepping out of line. "The sign says Tonight's Dinner Choices: bland, boring and completely tasteless vegetarian chili or Frank's Stupendously Scrumptious Macaroni and Cheese Perfection."

"Hmm, I wonder what particular food the cook is trying to persuade us to eat?" asked Nate sarcastically as we slowly and painfully crawled our way forward in line.

"I don't think you should go for the chili because your gas is already bad enough," I said frowning.

"Looks like our sis and her new friend are eating the chili," said Nate pointing over to where Kate was sitting.

"In fact, it looks like everyone in here is eating the vegetarian chili."

Nate was right. As I looked from table to table, I couldn't see a single person in the whole room that was eating Frank's Stupendously Scrumptious Macaroni and Cheese Perfection.

Suddenly, a girl with long straight black hair draped across her eyes and face appeared directly in front of us. "No one's dumb enough to try the macaroni and cheese," said the mysterious girl tipping her tray to reveal she had ordered the chili as well, "and you'd be wise to steer clear of it too unless you have a death wish."

"Who are you?" asked Nate, "And what do you mean death wish?"

"I'm Dolores," she said. She used one hand to brush her hair out of her face and stared at us through pitch-black eyes. "My family has been going to Crusader since the beginning, so I know absolutely everything about this place, including the tainted macaroni and cheese that he's been trying to serve for seventeen years straight."

"Tainted macaroni and cheese?" I asked, trying not to look directly into Dolores' dark and creepy eyes. "It's seventeen years old?"

"Yes, seventeen years old," she replied as she let her long hair fall back in front of her face. "Unless of course, you want to spend the rest of the night sitting on the toilet.

"The mac and cheese is *that* bad?" Nate replied.

"Yes, and the worst part about Frank's Barf-a-roni and cheese is that he does it on purpose," whispered Dolores.

"Isn't it illegal to make people sick on purpose?" I asked suspiciously.

"He doesn't care about consequences because the coward's already been stripped of his power," said Dolores picking up a fork from off of her tray and pointing it at Frank. "Just look at those beady little eyes and that evil twitchy mustache, he's doing it on purpose."

"Seems pretty harsh to have his power taken away because he makes terrible tasting macaroni and cheese and has a weird twitchy mustache," replied Nate.

Dolores smirked, "He was stripped of his power because he was one of the original members of the Chaos Crew. Charles Wildenbury let him back at camp a couple of years after the attack and he's been here since. It's a pity and a disgrace if you ask me."

I scratched my head, "Are you sure he was a member of the Chaos Crew?"

"Just take a look at his hands when you get up close," replied Dolores. "His fingers were melted off in the Battle of Crusader. What more proof do you need?"

"But why would Charles let him back at camp?" Nate asked. "Isn't he still dangerous?"

"Of course, he is," replied Dolores indignantly, "and that's why you want to avoid the macaroni and cheese. It's literally, *to die for.*"

I stood on my tippy toes and peered over the heads of the remaining campers in front of me. I watched as Frank scowled at camper after camper as they ordered dish after dish after dish of the vegetarian chili.

"Be wise like all of the other campers and choose the chili or you'll be sorry," said Dolores turning and walking away, just as abruptly as she arrived.

"That was kind of weird," I projected to Nate.

"For sure," replied Nate, *"But she did have a point. Maybe we should just order the chili, like everyone else."*

"I'm not so sure I am. She was telling the truth about Frank being an ex-member of the Chaos Crew but she's lying about the mac and cheese."

"How do you know that? Were you reading her mind?"

I shook my head, *"I didn't want to though, it just happened. It's very hard to control."*

"Well, honestly, I would rather have the mac and cheese anyway. That way I don't end up with supercharged gas and blow the roof off of our cabin tonight," said Nate, *"But, I just don't know."*

One by one, campers continued to order only the vegetarian chili until Nate and I finally arrived at the front counter. I looked down at the macaroni and cheese and bit my lower lip, feeling Dolores' unnerving presence somewhere nearby.

"What do you want?" asked Frank impatiently. "Boring and utterly tasteless vegetarian chili or homemade macaroni and cheese served in a delicious three cheese sauce?"

"What should we get?" I asked Nate nervously, *"I'd like the mac and cheese, but I don't want to upset anyone at camp, especially on the first day."*

"I think we should order the mac and cheese anyway," replied Nate.

"I'm just not so sure it's a good idea to order the mac and cheese," I replied anxiously.

"If you want it, then order it because I'm going to," encouraged Nate. *"I'm not going to let anyone pressure me into doing something I don't want to do, and neither should you."*

"Okay, but-"

"I got your back, like always."

"Promise?"

"I always have your back, Bro," said Nate patting me on my back.

I wiped the sweat beads from off of my forehead as Frank impatiently glared down at me. Just as I reached out to point at the macaroni and cheese, Dolores slid behind me and whispered, "Remember..." in my ear and then quickly walked away.

Frank cleared his throat, narrowed his eyes, and glared at Dolores as she walked off. "What's he supposed to remember?"

"It's nothing," I said looking up at Frank nervously, "...really."

Ignoring me, Frank pounded on the counter and shrieked, "I said, what is he supposed to remember?"

Everyone in the dining hall grew silent as Dolores turned around and faced Frank. Brushing the hair out of her face, Dolores stared at Frank with her creepy black eyes.

Frank gasped as he looked down at his scarred hands. "Not *another* Diablo at camp!" he complained loudly. "How many of you are there?"

"More," smirked Dolores, "a lot more."

"You and your family need to stop spreading your evil lies about me," hollered Frank. I tried not to stare at Frank's mangled hand clutching the ladle in front of me, but it was difficult not to because it looked really painful.

"Then why don't you leave Crusader and crawl back into the hole you came from?" snapped Dolores. "You're a traitor to this camp and everyone in it."

Frank swung the ladle over his head and then smacked it down on the counter, barely missing Nate, and me. "Why don't you just go back to your swamp, you black-eyed cretin!" bellowed Frank angrily.

I couldn't take the tension between Dolores and Frank, so I quickly reached out and patted the counter near the macaroni and cheese. "I'll have the mac and cheese, please," I whispered apprehensively, getting ready to dodge another swipe of Frank's ladle.

"Wha' did you say?" asked Frank as he slowly lowered the ladle. "Did...you say you want the...macaroni and cheese?" he stammered. "*My* homemade macaroni and cheese?"

Nate sprang up next to me and exclaimed, "I want some too!"

"Two...two," mumbled Frank. "Two campers want my homemade macaroni and cheese?"

"Yes," confirmed Nate, "but please hurry because we're starving."

Dolores cackled, "You'll be sorry," as she walked off and sat down with Scott and two other enormous campers.

Grinning from ear to ear, Frank proudly scooped up two large helpings of gooey macaroni and cheese and slid the plates over to us. "Please enjoy," chortled Frank.

"Thanks," we replied.

Nate and I carefully balanced our mini Everest macaroni and cheese mountains on our trays as we made our way over to the beverage bar to grab something to drink.

"I hope you're right about the mac and cheese because if I end up getting diarrhea and spend all night in the bathroom, I won't be very happy," whispered Nate as he filled his cup up with a mixture of cola, lemonade, and root beer.

"Fine, I'll take the blame," I said, "But I guarantee the mac and cheese won't cause you to end up on the pot, but your drink selection might."

"You really think so?" asked Nate. He took a sip of his concoction and then added an extra squirt of cola into his cup and said, "For good luck."

"It's weird because Dolores's mind is almost unreadable," I said as I filled my cup full of chocolate milk and placed it on my tray.

"That's probably a good thing. Who'd want to read the thoughts of a stenchy swamp creature anyway?" chuckled Nate as he turned towards the dining tables.

"Good point," I replied, grabbing my food tray, and following closely behind. Precariously balancing our trays, we made our way past a dozen curious campers that seemed to be whispering about our daring food choice. Just a few tables away from Kate and Anne, Nate and I turned sideways to let a tall squiggly haired girl squeeze by with her empty tray. Just as we turned back around, Scott stuck his elephant-sized foot directly in front of us.

"Have a nice trip Losers!" bellowed Scott.

Everything happened so quickly.

Like dominoes toppling over on each other, Nate tripped on Scott's foot, I tripped on Nate's foot, and down we went. Hitting the ground hard, Nate's soda cup flew high into the air, tumbling towards a crowd of boys to our left, while his plate soared across the room like a cheese-covered flying saucer. Landing on top of Nate, my food plate smacked him right in the back of his head as my chocolate milk skittered across the floor in front of us.

The whole dining hall broke out in a spontaneous and boisterous round of applause.

My face burned red hot as I reached down and peeled the gooey macaroni and cheese plate from the back of Nate's head.

"That was awesome!" exclaimed a girl from behind us.

"Incredible performance!" yelled another camper.

Struggling to our knees, Nate and I looked up and saw Kate standing in the middle of her dining table, grinning from ear to ear. In one hand, Kate proudly balanced Nate's plate of macaroni and cheese and in the other, she held his soda cup up high above her head, looking like the Statute of Liberty getting ready to enjoy an all-American meal. The roar of the crowd settled down as Kate stepped down from the table and sat back in her seat. Nate and I, covered in sticky orange cheese, stumbled to the two open seats across from Kate and her friend.

Kate slid Nate's food plate and soda in front of us. "Are you guys okay?" she asked sounding concerned.

"Yeah, just feeling a bit cheesy," said Nate, rummaging through the back of his hair and pulling out chunks of gooey cheese globs.

"You are pretty messy," smiled Kate, "but thanks to you two, I discovered my superpower."

"What?" asked Nate wiping his orange sticky fingers on a napkin. "Catching flying food is a superpower?"

"Nope, but super speed is. I caught your food before it hit the ground," Kate said proudly.

"Really? That's awesome!" exclaimed Nate, "but I think you forgot to catch Tate's plate of gouda goo because it smacked me right in the back of my head."

Kate reached over and handed Nate a huge wad of napkins.

I picked up a couple of napkins and wiped a smattering of cheese sauce off my forehead as Kate pointed to the girl sitting next to her. "Oh, by the way, this is Anne. She's the one that told me about room A113."

Anne bashfully placed her hand over her mouth to cover her braces as she spoke. "Nice to meet you," she said shyly, "...cheese and all."

"Hi," muttered Nate, paying more attention to the dripping cheese sauce running down the back of his neck than the smiling girl with the brown ponytail sitting directly across from us.

I reached out and took a swig from Nate's soda concoction while Little Red came over with a fresh plate of macaroni and cheese.

"You two okay?" asked Little Red. "That was quite a spill."

Nate and I looked over at Scott's table. He was laughing and having a good time with two other oversized galoots and Dolores.

Nate pulled out an extra-large chunky bit of goo from his hair as he looked up at Little Red. "I guess I didn't think we'd have to face bullies at a superhero camp," he said sounding frustrated.

"What do you mean?" asked Little Red looking over her shoulder towards Scott's table.

"Snottie Scotty," tripped us.

Little Red turned back to look at us, shook her head, and whispered, "Bullies are everywhere. Unfortunately, having powers doesn't automatically make someone a good person."

"I can see that," replied Nate picking off a piece of smooshed macaroni from the back of his ear lobe and plopping it back onto his plate.

Little Red bent down and wiped up the splotches of macaroni and cheese and chocolate milk from off of the checkered brown and red linoleum floor as I dug into my dinner. As I chewed, I was pleasantly surprised by the taste of Frank's macaroni and cheese. It was a million times better tasting than the stuff that came in the blue and yellow box that we ate almost daily, back at home.

"This is actually really good," I projected to Nate.

Nate scooped up a small spoonful of macaroni and cheese, eyed it suspiciously, and then cautiously placed the fork into his mouth. "It is pretty good...I can't even taste the poison," chuckled Nate.

Kate shook her head back and forth as she looked over at Anne. She was clearly embarrassed that Nate and I were related to her. However, we didn't seem to be bothering Anne too much because she just giggled, grinned, and covered her mouth with her hand.

"Finish up as quick as you can boys," instructed Kate. "You'll need to hit the showers before bedtime."

"Showers on the first night of camp...the agony!" groaned Nate. "What time do we have to get up tomorrow morning anyway?"

"Five thirty in the morning," said Anne, "because we have a whole day of challenges to face to help us discover our individual powers."

Kate looked over at Anne and smiled, "I'm sure you'll discover your power in no time."

Anne covered her mouth again as she smiled.

"Why do you always cover your mouth while you talk?" Nate blurted out between giant bites of mac and cheese.

Kate rolled her eyes and then gave Nate a look that would have turned even Medusa into solid stone. "Nate, that's so rude!" she barked.

"No, it's not," replied Nate.

Kate leaned over and locked eyes with Nate. "Yes, it...is," she said slowly and distinctly.

"No, it's not...because she has a nice smile," said Nate. "Braces and all."

Kate's face quickly softened into a smile, and Anne's cheeks turned a bright shade of red. I thought for sure Kate was going to reach over and give Nate a hug and Anne was going to give him an enormous kiss on the cheek, but thankfully neither of them did that.

"Well, that's nice of you to say that to my friend," chirped Kate.

Nate looked over at me and smiled, apparently pleased with himself that he managed to not offend every single person he met today.

"Well," said Anne looking at Kate, "I can't wait to discover what my power is, although it's probably not as great as super speed."

I took another bite of the macaroni and cheese and looked over at Nate, who was no longer smiling. I crossed my eyes and stuck out my tongue, but Nate suddenly had a worried look on his face.

"What's going on?" I projected.

Nate grabbed my leg under the table. *"Not good…Not good at all,"* moaned Nate. *"I have to let out an enormous gas bomb!"*

"What, again?" I grumbled. *"Right here? Right now?"*

"Yes, and it's not going to be good!"

"But…But…"

"Quick! Cough when I cut the cheese, so no one hears," ordered Nate.

"Can't you just distract yourself? Try and think of something good to eat…candy, donuts, cake, anything!"

"Not working…" groaned Nate, *"Too late…Just cough!"*

Both Nate and I put our hands over our mouths and together we coughed really loud, over and over again. Luckily for Nate, our impromptu coughing fit was just loud enough to cover the sound of his backdoor gas bomb. After a couple of seconds, Nate settled back down in his seat, his face looking more relaxed.

"You both okay?" asked Kate, looking concerned. "That was quite a coughing fit from the two of you."

"For a second there, I thought I'd have to use the Heimlich maneuver," added Anne.

"We're fine," replied Nate. "We just had something stuck in our throats."

"Both of you?" asked Kate suspiciously. "At the same time?"

"Yep," said Nate. "It's a twin thing, you wouldn't understand."

Nate and I looked down at our plates of food. We pushed around the remaining macaroni and cheese with our forks, hoping that the smell that was just released from Nate's nether-region would quickly dissipate under the table.

Unfortunately, it didn't.

Suddenly, Kate and Anne turned and looked at each other with wide eyes.

"What's that smell?" gasped Anne.

"I don't know," said Kate looking over at us, "but...oh..."

Nate plopped his fork down on his plate. "It wasn't me...really, it wasn't!" exclaimed Nate anxiously.

"Well, whatever it is..." said Anne.

"I told you, it wasn't me..." muttered Nate under his breath.

"Of course, it wasn't you," replied Kate tilting her head back and sniffing the air loudly, "but whatever it is, it sure smells heavenly!"

"Oh, my gosh!" chortled Anne. "What is that scrumptious aroma?"

"What?" chuckled Nate. "You think my far-"

I quickly elbowed Nate in the ribs. ***Keep quiet about your stinky gas! Something else is going on...just look around,*** I said, pointing towards the campers and counselors in the dining hall. Everyone around us, including Kate and Anne, had their noses turned up to the ceiling and were wildly sniffing the air.

"Even the counselors over by the fireplace are sniffing away like crazy," said Nate. "Do you smell something Tate because I sure don't."

I tilted my head back and cautiously smelled the air. The smell of fresh-baked cinnamon rolls suddenly tickled my nose. The scent was so strong and intoxicating that I could easily pick out the individual ingredients in the cinnamon rolls: butter, vanilla, flour, eggs, yeast, salt, cinnamon, and cream cheese frosting.

A low moan of pleasure reverberated throughout the room as campers got up from their seats and began wandering around the room, their noses still stuck high in the air as they tried to locate the whereabouts of the fresh-baked cinnamon rolls.

"Oh my gosh," moaned Kate, "those cinnamon rolls smell so good. I have to have one!"

Anne looked over at us with glassy eyes. "Me too! Me too!" she exclaimed.

"I still don't smell a thing," said Nate anxiously. "Why can't I smell anything?"

I sniffed the air again, but this time, my body became warm and tingly all over as my sense of smell began to hijack my brain. I quickly plugged my nose and concentrated hard to keep my thoughts in check so I wouldn't leap up and go cinnamon roll crazy like everyone else around us.

"I have to keep my nose plugged," I projected to Nate, *"because my brain was getting overpowered by the smell of cinnamon rolls."*

Suddenly, the group of boys that were sitting in front of us, leapt up from their seats, overturning their chairs, as they charged up to Frank at the counter.

"Give us cinnamon rolls!" demanded the boys.

"I didn't make cinnamon rolls," replied Frank. "I don't ever bake treats for campers."

Just as Frank finished scolding the boys, a group of girls flipped over their table and chairs in a rush to join the group of boys at the counter.

"We demand that you release the cinnamon rolls!" chanted the girls.

"I said...I didn't make cinnamon rolls," growled Frank. "Now, go sit back down!"

Suddenly, everyone in the room started chanting, "WE WANT THE ROLLS! WE WANT THE ROLLS!" except for Nate and me. We were the only people still sitting in our booth, amazed that a full-blown cinnamon roll riot was breaking out right in front of us.

Frank smacked his ladle on the counter. "STOP THIS RIGHT NOW!" Frank yelled at the top of his lungs just as a plate of food went soaring past his head and shattered on the wall behind him.

All of a sudden, chairs went flying through the air as campers and counselors, including Little Red, shoved their way to the front of the line to insist that Frank hand over his delicious home-baked cinnamon rolls.

"CIN-A-MON! CIN-A-MON!" rang loudly through the air as campers started jumping up and down in unison.

Turning bright red, Frank yelled, "I TOLD YOU, I DIDN'T MAKE ANY CINNAMON RO-" Suddenly, Frank stopped shouting. His eyes glazed over as he reached down and picked up a large bowl of bananas and threw them across the room. Leaping up on the counter, Frank shouted, "I WANT MY CINNAMON ROLLS!"

Nate threw his arms over his head and asked, "What the heck's going on? It's cinnamon roll madness!"

"I've never heard of such a thing," I replied, still plugging my nose.

Nate sniffed the air again. "I still can't smell a thing," he cried, covering his ears as the chanting grew louder and louder.

I reached over and yanked Nate's hands from off of his ears. "He who dealt it, cannot smell it!" I yelled.

"What? I didn't fart out cinnamon rolls!" chuckled Nate, suddenly looking a little nervous. "At least I don't think I did."

"We better double-check," I said pulling on Nate's arm, "because what if laying cinnamon rolls, like some crazy sweet-toothed mother hen, is your super ability?"

"Sounds delicious," chuckled Nate nervously, "but really gross at the same time!"

Standing up, we quickly searched the seat and floor below Nate just to make sure he hadn't actually laid any sweet bread-like products. Lucky for Nate, there wasn't a cinnamon roll, maple bar, or even a raspberry danish to be seen under his backside.

"Whew," said Nate wiping his forehead with the back of his hand. "Glad it wasn't me."

"I'm still not convinced that your fart didn't start this," I replied, "but let's get out of here before things get really out of hand."

Nate and I snuck back to our cabin, showered, and brushed our teeth. By the time we were tucking ourselves into bed, everyone returned to their rightful cabins, looking tired and worn out.

That night, laying my head down on my pillow never felt so good. The day had been long, filled with anxiety and stress, but it also came with some relief because I finally figured out where I truly belonged.

Chapter Five

The Proving Ground

The sun was still below the horizon when we woke up and had a quick uneventful breakfast of pancakes, bacon, and eggs. After the meal, Nate, Kate, Anne, and I joined the rest of the first-year campers in front of the dining hall. Once we were all accounted for, we followed a slow but steady stream of exhausted campers down a windy path behind the dining hall.

"Everyone looks so tired," whispered Nate, looking back at me over his shoulder. "You think it's because of the great cinnamon roll riot last night?"

"Probably so," I projected as we continued winding down the path in the dull morning sunlight.

Arriving at the bottom of the hill, we stepped into an eerie low morning fog that swirled at our feet as we passed the infirmary and an old wooden shed that sat in front of a particularly thick and dark part of the forest.

"That part of the forest gives me the creeps," I projected.

"It should," replied Nate, *"That's the forbidden forest."*

"It is?" I asked nervously.

"Yeah, didn't you hear about what horrible things happened to some first-year campers in the forbidden forest a couple of years ago?" asked Nate.

A chill ran down my spine as I turned my head away from the dark foreboding forest. *"No, what happened?"* I asked, not really wanting to know.

"I don't know…but whatever happened in there must have been tree-mendously scary!" giggled Nate.

I reached out and smacked Nate on the back of his head. *"Your jokes are ten times worse than Dad's!"* I projected.

Leaving the path, we rounded an enormous boulder, walked through a small cluster of tall pine trees, and then stepped out into a vast open field.

"What's that thing up ahead?" asked Kate as we approached a tall wooden structure erected in the middle of the field.

"It's a lookout tower for the Proving Grounds," replied Anne.

Kate added, "It looks like an exact replica of the Eiffel Tower, only a lot smaller."

"Are we in France then?" said Nate pointing at the tower.

"No, why?" asked Kate.

"I wish we were because the cold morning air is making me want to go *wee-wee*!" giggled Nate.

Kate looked over at Anne and rolled her eyes. "An endless supply of potty jokes...I should have known better than to ask," she muttered under her breath.

Anne quietly chuckled, covering her grin. "Does he ever stop?" she asked.

"Nope, never," sighed Kate, "he's inappropriate one hundred and ten percent of the time."

"Unless of course, I freeze to death," complained Nate, "which is currently happening right now."

"Hopefully, his mouth will freeze over," mumbled Kate as she grabbed Anne's hand. Together, Kate and Anne moved forward through the crowd to be near the front of the pack as Nate and I hung a few rows behind. To warm up, I moved in closer to Nate as we waited patiently below the tall structure.

Even though I was freezing, I couldn't help but admire the morning sun as it rose in the east, casting a beautiful raspberry red glow in the sky, just beyond the dusty cow pasture and the lush pond at the edge of the vast open field.

"So that's what the sky looks like super early in the morning," whispered Nate, not sounding very impressed. "Can we go back to bed now?"

I was about to respond to Nate when Ms. Agatha's voice suddenly boomed high above us. "Good morning campers!" she said, precariously standing on a small platform at the top of the tower.

We all mumbled, "Good morning."

"Such a cheery bunch," replied Ms. Agatha. "I suppose you all are a bit weary after last night's inexplicable dinner hullabaloo."

A low groan reverberated throughout the crowd as Ms. Agatha scrutinized us over the rims of her glasses.

"Quite an auspicious start to summer camp, don't you think?" she asked, sounding perturbed.

An uncomfortable silence washed over us as some campers looked down and shuffled their shoes in the dirt. After more than a minute, the awkwardness was finally broken by a woman's loud voice from behind us. "I believe that I may have found the culprit of the aforementioned hullabaloo," announced the voice.

Nate and I turned around just in time to see a tall skinny blonde woman wearing a pink scrub top, blue jeans, and cowgirl boots, round the corner.

"I suspect it was delirium caused by food poisoning, more than likely from the vegetarian chili," replied the woman as she tied her blond hair back into a bun and smiled at us.

"Campers, may I introduce you to Crusader's medical professional, Nurse Carter," said Ms. Agatha, pushing her glasses up the bridge of her nose. "No doubt, many of you will come to know her quite well by the end of camp," said Ms. Agatha, moving closer to the edge of the platform as a gentle breeze lightly tossed her short gray hair high above.

Nurse Carter held up her hand and waved. "Isn't that the truth," she chuckled.

"Whoa! She's got some long pink fingernails," commented Nate, "They got to be at least three inches long."

"Shh," I whispered.

"...and I'm hoping this lot won't be quite as reckless as last year's group," said Ms. Agatha sheepishly, "but I can make no guarantee, especially after last night."

"Let's hope that was an isolated incident," grinned Nurse Carter. "After all, this is my third year volunteering at camp because I enjoy my reprieve from the hospital's daily grind of broken bones."

"Well, I'm glad you'll be joining us today," said Ms. Agatha looking down at her clipboard. "It's always nice having you present during Proving Day."

"I'll just be observing from afar," replied Nurse Carter patting the side of her hair. "Just in case someone decides to break their neck today."

"What an auspicious way to welcome you all out to the Proving Grounds," said Ms. Agatha sarcastically as she raised her arms high above her head with a clipboard in hand. "No doubt you all have enthusiastically read the Questions and Answers booklet, so these next announcements will only come as reminders."

"I wonder how she got up there?" whispered Nate out of the corner of his mouth. "Maybe her super ability is super springy toes."

"Shh," I said, placing my hand over Nate's mouth. "I'm trying to listen."

From high above, Ms. Agatha extended her hand out towards the forest. "Please remember that entering Crusader Forest is off-limits to all first-year campers unless you are being escorted by a counselor. You are also forbidden to enter Camp Crusader II, which houses our more seasoned campers, located through the woods directly behind me." Ms. Agatha adjusted her glasses, and her voice suddenly grew more stern. "If anyone is caught breaking either of these two rules, you shall be permanently expelled from camp. No questions asked."

Nate leaned in close and whispered into my ear, "Maybe she has giant hairy cricket legs under those long black pants?"

I turned and looked Nate right in the eyes. "Maybe she's reading our thoughts right now," I said irritably.

Nate stuck his tongue out at me and pretended to zip his lip as Ms. Agatha glanced down at her clipboard, pushed up her glasses, and announced, "Today you will be sorted into cabins so you may commence your training as a first-year camper. Please note that you will not be fighting each other for cabin placement in a violent game of hungry children nor will I be placing a talking hat on top of your head to sort you."

The campers around me chuckled as Nate replied, "That's a good one!"

"No doubt, some of you have already discovered your unique ability. To these individuals, I say, you will soon have the opportunity to prove your gift to me so that I may properly and speedily sort you into the appropriate cabin," instructed Ms. Agatha as a strong gust of cold wind swept across the field and knocked her forward a few inches so that the tips of her black sandals were now dangling precariously over the edge.

"She's gonna fall," whispered Nate. "I hope she's warmed up her prickly cricket legs because that's a long jump down."

I looked over at Nate and whispered, "She's probably done this a gazillion times. I doubt she's going to fa-"

Suddenly, a powerful blast of cold dawn wind struck the tower. Unable to rebalance herself in time, Ms. Agatha tumbled off her perch and began plummeting to the ground. We didn't even have time to gasp as the tall skinny blond-haired boy from our cabin rocketed up from the ground and caught Ms. Agatha by her waist just moments before she struck the ground.

"Got you," said the boy as he carefully guided Ms. Agatha safely to the ground and then humbly stepped back to rejoin our ranks.

"Well done, young man!" chirped Ms. Agatha as we all broke out into applause. "It appears we have someone that knows his powers," she said calmly clutching her clipboard.

"And not a *single* broken bone...but alas, the day is still young," snickered Nurse Carter.

Ms. Agatha looked down at her clipboard and then beckoned the boy forward. "Well done," said Ms. Agatha tucking her clipboard under her arm. "Calder, is it?"

"Yes, Ma'am...Calder Locke," said the boy as he brushed his long blonde hair out of his eyes.

"Well done, Calder Locke. You just saved me from a very painful death. I'd say you have proven your adeptness at flying," said Ms. Agatha, scribbling on a small white piece of paper and handing it over to Calder. "You may now head back to camp and report to Nicholas Knight. He will assist you in collecting your gear and help you move into the Volant Cabin, in which he too is a member."

A round of applause broke out again as Calder smiled and then threw up a hang loose sign as he headed back up the trail towards camp.

Ms. Agatha flipped through a couple of pages on her clipboard, readjusted her glasses, and asked, "Does anyone else believe that they know what their special ability is?"

Eight campers eagerly raised their hands, including Kate.

"Splendid," replied Ms. Agatha.

Nurse Carter tapped her long fingernails on her chin and said, "This should make for a much shorter day than usual."

Ms. Agatha shook her head as she flipped wildly through her clipboard. "Well then, let's not waste any more time...Shall we start with an easier test to pass?" she asked us.

"Yes!" shouted a short, freckled face boy standing directly in front of me.

Ms. Agatha chuckled, "That Thomas, was what we call a rhetorical question. It doesn't require an answer."

"Oh, sorry," replied Thomas sheepishly.

Ms. Agatha looked down at her clipboard and then up at the eight campers that still had their hands raised, "Do any of you believe you are telepathic? Telepaths have the ability to communicate with people by using their thoughts. Some telepaths may also have the ability to read the thoughts of people around them."

"So how is teleportation different than telepathy?" asked a girl in the back of the group, "or are they the same?"

Ms. Agatha adjusted her glasses and said, "Teleportation is the act of transporting yourself from one place to another instantaneously. Teleporters can transport themselves and one other individual when they travel from location to location."

"And it usually stinks when someone teleports!" exclaimed Thomas, "because when my mom teleports, she always stinks up the whole house."

"Thomas Brine, knowing your mother, I am sure she would be proud that you shared that little tidbit of information about her," chuckled Ms. Agatha. "Now then, since we are on the subject," she said clearing her throat, "If you believe your super ability is teleportation, please raise your hand."

"I'm telepathic," announced a tall tanned faced boy with slicked back, amber-colored hair. "I'm Lance Phillips and I've been studying with Master Burke at the Blackrock Academy for the past seven years," he said proudly as he shoved his way to the front of the crowd.

"So, you must be quite good," replied Ms. Agatha plainly.

"Oh, I am," Lance said puffing out his chest.

"Then you will please step forward and enlighten us," instructed Ms. Agatha.

"Anything to get this ridiculous formality over with," scoffed Lance. "As if you'll be able to teach me anything at this ridiculous camp, anyway."

"And might I say what an absolute joy it is to have you at our little camp this year as well," replied Ms. Agatha sarcastically.

"I wouldn't be here if it wasn't required to progress in my studies at Blackrock," complained Lance under his breath.

"Well then, shall we get this over with?" sighed Ms. Agatha, "Please teleport to the dining hall and fetch me a straw."

"I'm not a dog," said Lance. "I won't be fetching you anything."

I couldn't tell from where I was standing, but I could have sworn Ms. Agatha rolled her eyes as she said, "Will you please *collect* one straw from the dining hall?"

"I can do better than that," replied Lance.

"One straw will do just fine," replied Ms. Agatha flatly.

"Whatever," said Lance rolling his eyes.

" POOF! "

Lance disappeared in a small wisp of gray smoke that smelled horrible. Within seconds, he reappeared with a handful of yellow striped straws, which he held out at arms-length in front of him. Just as Ms. Agatha reached out to collect the straws, Lance dropped them at her feet.

"Oops, my bad," smirked Lance.

Ms. Agatha looked down at her clipboard and hastily scribbled on a white slip of paper, "After you pick up the straws you *accidentally* dropped on the ground, you may proceed to the Celer Cabin."

Lance kicked the straws with his foot and replied smugly, "Was there really any question about where I belong, considering I can easily transport two people at once without even breaking a sweat?"

"Impossible," whispered a voice behind me.

"Impossible *and* dangerous," hissed Thomas.

"Well, then you must be so proud of yourself," said Ms. Agatha raising her pen and pointing toward the dining hall. "Now, you will please pick up the straws before you report to Nicholas back at camp."

Lance grumbled as he leaned over, picked up the straws, and shoved them in his pocket. He then reached over and snatched the white paper out of Ms. Agatha's hand and stormed off towards the dining hall.

Ms. Agatha took a deep breath, then cleared her throat, and said, "Well, that was quite a treat."

"He was quite a jerk!" exclaimed Nate.

The campers around us snickered as Anne looked back over her shoulder and whispered, "Unfortunately, he is both a jerk and a camp donor."

"Figures," muttered Nate.

Ms. Agatha looked down at her notes and asked, "Does anyone else feel that their special ability is teleportation? If so, please take a step forward."

After waiting quietly for a minute, Ms. Agatha scribbled some notes on her clipboard and said, "Very well, if you believe you are telepathic, please step forward."

Suddenly, my stomach felt uneasy as two students raised their hands and stepped forward. I wasn't sure what to do because both Nate and Alekzander asked me not to tell anyone about my telepathic ability and I definitely didn't want to reveal my power in front of the whole camp at that moment, especially to Kate.

My face burned red hot and my forehead suddenly felt sweaty as I tried my best to avoid Ms. Agatha's sweeping gaze.

"Look what you got your me into!" I projected to Nate.

"Sorry, I didn't think keeping power from Kate would end up being such a big deal," replied Nate.

"Well, now I either reveal to Kate that I've been holding out on her, or I stay quiet and pretend that I'm not a telepath."

Ms. Agatha squinted at us over the top of her glasses. "Only two of you this year?" she asked looking over at Nurse Carter. "We usually have quite a few telepaths."

"Must be an off-year," replied Nurse Carter, shaking her head.

After a few uncomfortable moments of silence, Ms. Agatha finally turned her attention to the girl and boy standing in front of her. "Very well," she instructed. "When I point to you, please use your telepathic abilities to introduce yourself. This will be sufficient enough to assign you to the Animo cabin." Ms. Agatha pointed to a tall slender Korean girl with straight black hair that fell past her shoulders. "Let's begin with you, shall we?" asked Ms. Agatha.

The girl took a deep breath and locked eyes with Ms. Agatha. "Okay, here it goes," she said.

After a few seconds passed, Ms. Agatha shook her head up and down, then used her pencil to scribble notes on a small white piece of paper. "I'd like to introduce Ms. Samantha Lee as the newest member of the Animo cabin...Well done young lady, you are dismissed," she said.

Samantha gently took the slip of paper out of Ms. Agatha's hand, gave us all a quick wave, and then headed back towards camp.

"That's three campers down and only twenty-five more to go," said Ms. Agatha taking a step forward and adjusting her glasses. Using her pencil, she then pointed at a short boy with tall spiky black hair. "Please introduce yourself, young man," she instructed.

The spiky-haired boy shuffled his feet nervously and replied, "Uh, my name's Blake-"

"No, no," chided Ms. Agatha. "Introduce yourself using your telepathic powers."

"Oh, sorry," said the boy timidly. He set his feet firmly on the ground and looked up at Ms. Agatha with an intense stare.

After a few moments, Ms. Agatha shook her head, jotted down some notes, and said, "I'd like to introduce you to Blake Silverman. He is also a member of the Animo cabin."

Blake turned around and faced us. "This is awesome!" he said, pumping his fist in the air.

Holding out the white slip of paper in one hand, Ms. Agatha tapped Blake on the back of his shoulder with the other. "You may be dismissed," she said.

"Thanks!" exclaimed Blake spinning around so quickly that he tripped on his own two feet and collapsed in a heap right in front of Ms. Agatha. "I'm okay!" shouted Blake, quickly popping back up to his feet.

"Easy, young Blake! A broken face is not a great way to start your training," chuckled Nurse Carter as Blake snatched the white slip of paper from Ms. Agatha and ran towards the dining hall without looking back.

Scott quietly whispered, "That guy's a goof," to his friend that was standing directly behind me.

I wanted to turn around and smack Scott, but I knew that I was outmatched a hundred times over, so I just remained silent and kept looking forward.

Ms. Agatha took a long deep breath without looking up from her clipboard. "It has been quite an eventful day thus far, we may not survive this summer's group of campers," said Ms. Agatha sarcastically.

"Probably not," chuckled Nurse Carter.

Ms. Agatha looked down at her clipboard again and asked, "Are we sure that there are no more telepaths in the audience?"

Nate leaned over and whispered in my ear. "What are you going to do?" he asked.

I felt my face get red hot again as Ms. Agatha scrutinized us over the rims of her glasses. "Because now is the time to make it known if you feel you may have telepathic abilities," said Ms. Agatha, her eyes finally settling on me.

I hadn't a clue what I should do, so I took a deep breath and projected, *"I'm Tate and I'm telepathic, but please don't make it known in front of all these people. It's a complicated situation and Alekzander told me not to say anything."*

"I understand," replied Ms. Agatha, *"Alekzander told me that your situation may be a bit usual, but I would like to know the extent of your telepathy either way."*

Ms. Agatha cleared her throat and then smiled up from her clipboard. "Just a moment campers, I need a few moments of silence to jot down some pertinent information before we move on if that is okay."

Ms. Agatha looked down at her clipboard again and pretended to scribble down some notes while everyone stood in silence.

"What exactly can you do with your telepathy?" asked Ms. Agatha still looking down at her clipboard.

"Well," I projected, *"I can hear people's thoughts."*

"And what else?" asked Ms. Agatha. *"Alekzander implied that there may be more to you than meets the eye."*

"I can talk to people in their minds," I replied. *"Kind of like I'm doing now."*

"Anything else?"

"And...a couple of times I could actually feel what my brother was feeling, and I could even see through his eyes."

"You could see what your brother was seeing?" asked Ms. Agatha. *"...He wouldn't happen to be your twin, would he?"*

"Yes."

"Telepaths call that type of connection, a deep link. It is a rare ability that only occurs between a telepath and their twin if they have one."

"Then, I guess I've deep linked with Nate without him or I understanding what was going on. I thought it was just a weird twin thing."

"Well, now you know," replied Ms. Agatha. *"How about you stick around for the day and let us see what else we can discover about your unique ability before I assign you to the Amino cabin?"*

"Thank you."

"You are quite welcome."

"Oh, and one more thing...Can I use the bathroom?" I asked.

"You mean, may I use the bathroom," corrected Ms. Agatha. *"Yes, you may. It is directly to your right at the edge of the forest."*

Ms. Agatha stopped pretending to jot down notes on her clipboard and adjusted her glasses. "Well then, I've got my notes sorted out," she said. "Let us move on to the next trials, shall we?"

I felt an instant sense of relief, but my stomach ached a little and my face still felt hot and sweaty. I didn't really have to use the bathroom, but following the advice of my counselor, I felt like I had to get away for a couple of minutes to take some slow deep breaths without calling attention to myself.

"I'm going to the bathroom," I projected to Nate, *"by myself."*

"Okay," replied Nate. *"Are you sure you don't want me to come al-"*

"No, I need some time to myself," I projected.

Leaving the group, I followed a dirt path that led me down a small embankment to an old outhouse that was barely visible at the edge of the woods.

The outhouse, about the size of my tiny closet back at home, leaned to the right at an odd angle, as if it shouldn't be standing up at all. Mottled brown crumbly slats hung from the rickety frame, held together by thick vines, growing up the sides. I took a deep breath, unsure whether I was going to actually go in or not. It wasn't until I heard a branch snap somewhere within the forest, that I made up my mind to go in.

As I reached out and opened the old wooden door, a foul smell smacked me right in the nose. I held the door open to help things air out a bit, but the bad-tempered smell hung around like two skunks on a long honeymoon, so I just held my breath and went in. Closing and locking the door behind me, I sat on the faded pink toilet seat, tucked my nose in my shirt collar, and read some of the many messages scrawled the outhouse walls.

Welcome to Outhouse A –
The Queen of the Outhouses!

Help...I fell in....Blub, Blub, Blub 2009

Blondie + Clint 1954

Little Red Wuz Here!   Live, Laugh, Poop! 1985

ARVID WAS HERE 1945

I Read the Book by Willie Makeit –
It was published by Betty Didn't.

Chaos Crew = Chaos Poo! *J Luv Kim-2003*

To get Outhouse "A" cleaned, dial 718-0113
(phone number permanently disconnected)

"Some of these are just plain weird," I whispered to myself as I took in a shallow breath, got up from the toilet seat, and pushed open the outhouse door, "but hilarious."

Luckily for me, no one was waiting in line outside to use the outhouse which wasn't a surprise because it could barely be seen from the proving grounds. Making my way across the field, I felt a lot better as I re-entered the group of campers. Only Nate noticed me arrive because everyone else was busy looking up, watching a boy fly around the mini Eifel Tower.

"Sorry again," whispered Nate, looking over at me with a pouty face. "I only asked you to keep your powers a secret because Alekzander told me to make sure you didn't tell anyone."

"You spoke to Alekzander?" I projected.

"Yes, but only briefly."

"Well, what did he say?"

"Just that he knew you'd tell me about your power because we're twins and all, but to hold off on telling anyone else," Nate said still looking up at the sky. *"Kate was just kind of a bonus."*

"I guess I can forgive you then," I said smirking at Nate. I wanted to ask him more questions about

Alekzander, but I got sidetracked when a boy zoomed directly over our heads at an amazing speed.

"This is the flying test," said Nate pointing up at the top of the tower. "I think this kid's the third one to go. He's supposed to fly to the top of the tower as quickly as possible and retrieve Ms. Agatha's teacup."

"He's pretty darned fast," I whispered, watching him zip to the top of the tower, grab a small white teacup, and zoom back down for a bumpy landing.

"Not bad," said Ms. Agatha looking down into her teacup. "Very speedy, but you did manage to spill a good portion of my tea in the process. I hope you'll learn some flying finesse over the next two weeks because it's not all about speed, Bruce."

Looking a little miffed, Bruce ran his fingers through his wavy brown hair before he turned his back on Ms. Agatha and walked off towards camp with his white slip in hand.

"Well, that concludes our Volant campers," said Ms. Agatha tucking her clipboard under her arm. "Please remember that it is our goal to place all campers in their rightful cabins by the end of the day. If for some reason we are unsuccessful in teasing out your special ability today, we will place you in the Maveric cabin for the time being. After all, the Maveric cabin is specifically reserved for campers whose powers do not necessarily fit into any one of our more traditional cabins."

"Sounds like the loser cabin to me!" blurted Scott as two enormous campers standing on either side of him burst out laughing.

"That will be quite enough from you, young man. No cabin is better than the other," snapped Ms. Agatha.

Suddenly, a boy with sandy blond hair and oversized glasses stepped forward. "In that case, I believe I fit in with the Maverics because I can be super stretchy," he said bravely.

"Is that so?" asked Ms. Agatha. "Then please step forward and demonstrate."

"Sure, my name is Logan Adams and I'm ten by the way," said the boy looking across the field. "Shall I pick you a flower?" he asked, brushing his hair out of the front of his glasses.

"His special powers are picking flowers!" chuckled Scott loudly. "Wonderful power," he said sarcastically. "What's he gonna do, give the bad guy allergies?"

Nate and I spun halfway around, locking eyes with Scott as some of the campers around us giggled. Sneering, Scott flexed his bicep and then pounded his enormous fist into his palm.

"Every power is important," replied Ms. Agatha firmly, "and you will please keep your opinions to yourself young man or I shall assign you to the latrine cabin."

Scott looked around at his bulging buddies and asked, "Is that a good cabin to be in? Maybe I deserve to be in the latrine cabin."

Nate looked back over his shoulder and giggled, "That's exactly where you belong."

Scott gave Nate a dirty look as Ms. Agatha continued to talk with Logan.

"Mr. Adams, I would like you to pick me that dandelion about ten yards away," instructed Ms. Agatha, pointing to a tiny yellow flower in the distance. "Yes...that one will do nicely."

Logan squinted, pushed his enormous glasses up the bridge of his nose, and said, "I'd like a little more of a challenge if that's alright with you."

"Very well," said Ms. Agatha nudging Logan forward. "Have at it."

Logan readjusted his glasses, scanned the field in front of us, and rolled his shoulders to loosen up.

"Hurry up flower child!" grumbled Scott. "We haven't got all day."

Ms. Agatha glared at Scott. "Again...That will be quite enough," she said.

Nate turned back around and stuck his tongue out at Scott and yelled, "You can do it, ten-year-old Logan!"

Looking more confident, Logan squared his shoulders, raised his arms, and turned his body towards the dining hall. Without warning, an enormous gust of wind rushed past us as Logan's arms shot out like bullets, stretching almost a hundred yards across the field. It was difficult to tell what was going on because his arms were stretched so far out.

"All done," announced Logan as his arms rocketed back with a small bouquet of red and orange wildflowers for Ms. Agatha.

"I saw these on the way in and thought you'd like them a bit more than a dandelion," smiled Logan.

"Why thank you," said Ms. Agatha. She attached the stems of the flowers onto her clipboard and handed him a white slip of paper, "...and you are correct in your earlier assumption about belonging to the Maveric cabin."

"Thank you," said Logan as he took his slip of paper and headed back to camp.

"Kiss up," hissed Scott under his breath.

Ms. Agatha scribbled a few notes on her clipboard and said, "Now, let us head on down to Frog Pond for our next test."

"This is going to be toad-ally awesome," croaked Nate as we marched off across the open field.

The warm sun felt good as we walked north across the field towards a lush green pond filled with hundreds of yellow-flowered lily pads. I couldn't help but smile as we all watched hundreds of energetic frogs jump from lily pad to lily pad.

"Welcome to Frog Pond," said Ms. Agatha looking at the pond with her back turned towards us. "We will be testing super speed at this location."

Nate chuckled, "Speed on water?" just a little too loudly. "Why not test on land?"

Ms. Agatha turned around, noisily cleared her throat, and stared right at Nate. "Some of our more inquisitive campers may be wondering why we don't test for speed ability on land. To them I say...because we don't," grinned Ms. Agatha.

I elbowed Nate in the ribs the moment Ms. Agatha stopped staring at him, and he elbowed me back.

"In this test of speed, campers are asked to run across the water or lily pads and collect just one of Frog Pond's many excitable frogs. Return with a frog in a reasonable amount of time and I will be assured that Celer is the correct cabin placement for you."

"And try not to drown," added Nurse Carter. "I'd rather not get my boots wet this morning."

"Yes, and try not to drown," repeated Ms. Agatha looking over at Nurse Carter. She then added, "Shall we begin?"

"Yes!" said Thomas Brine excitedly.

"That was another rhetorical question, my dear," replied Ms. Agatha, "but thank you for your permission *and* enthusiasm, Thomas."

"What's prehistorical mean?" whispered Nate. "Does she like dinosaurs or something because she keeps using that word?"

"Rhetorical means that she's not expecting an answer," I replied.

"Oh," replied Nate. "That makes a lot more sense when you put it that way."

Ms. Agatha looked down at her clipboard and said, "We have quite a few campers remaining. Is there anyone that would like to try their hand at catching a frog, first?"

Kate's hand quickly shot up along with five other campers. Ms. Agatha looked up from her clipboard and pointed at Kate. "Let's have you go first, young lady. What is your name?"

"Kate Larson, Ma'am," Kate replied confidently.

"Well then, Miss Kate Larson. Please run across the pond and collect one frog as quick as possible."

"Okay," said Kate stretching out her legs. "One second, please."

"Please begin when you are ready," said Ms. Agatha, "but the sooner, the better since we have quite a few campers awaiting this challenge."

"Okay," said Kate looking over at Ms. Agatha.

"Hurry up!" groaned Scott. "We haven't got all day!"

After waiting a few more seconds for Kate to begin, Ms. Agatha looked up from her clipboard and asked, "Does *okay* mean that you are ready to begin now?"

"No, *okay* means that I've already gone and come back," replied Kate.

"You have?" asked Ms. Agatha squinching up her face, "but you haven't even left yet."

"But I did leave, and I brought you back the cutest little guy in the pond," Kate said, carefully opening her hand to reveal a tiny green frog, with beady little eyes, resting comfortably in her palm. "I hope this one is okay?"

Ms. Agatha cocked her head to the side as she examined Kate over the rims of her glasses. "You mean to tell me…You just now retrieved that frog…from the pond?" she asked, stepping forward to examine the frog.

"Yep, he was a little difficult to catch at first because he's quite the little jumper," chuckled Kate. "Can I go ahead and put him back now?"

"Remarkable," whispered Ms. Agatha. "Yes, you may return the frog from whence you found him."

"Okay," said Kate, gently holding the wide-eyed frog in her hand. "I'll be right back."

I watched closely as Kate gently closed her hand around the frog. I wanted to witness Kate's super-speed firsthand so I stared intently at her; However, I must have blinked because before I knew it, she was back.

"Done," said Kate opening up her hands to reveal that the frog had been returned.

Ms. Agatha looked at Kate's empty hands and quickly scribbled something on her notepad. "Quite remarkable," Ms. Agatha whispered as Kate took the small slip of paper from her.

"Thank you," said Kate beaming.

"You have adequately proven yourself to be the newest member of the Celer cabin. Please head back to camp while I test the others."

Kate walked over to us, wished us good luck, and then headed off towards the dining hall as Ms. Agatha continued testing the remaining four campers. Once the speed tests were complete, Ms. Agatha looked up from her clipboard and said, "Right, let us walk over to the next testing area...the cow pasture."

As we followed behind Ms. Agatha, Nurse Carter added, "And campers, I'd rather not get dirty today either, so please try not to get stomped to death by an angry bovine."

Nate plugged his nose as we moseyed on over to a pasture full of fat brown and black and white speckled cows. "I hope my power doesn't have anything to do with cows because that would stink...literally!" said Nate plugging his nose.

"They are a bit smelly," I replied as we came to a stop behind a rusty metal gate where a dozen content cows grazed on the green grass in an otherwise muddy field.

"Here we are," said Ms. Agatha. "Who here feels that their super ability is strength?" asked Ms. Agatha. Five hands quickly shot up, including Snottie Scotty's.

One by one, Ms. Agatha called up students to enter the pasture and gently pick a cow up from off of the ground. The first four campers did as they were instructed without any issues, so they were handed their passes and promptly dismissed to gather up their gear and join the Lacertosus cabin.

"You saved the best for last!" shouted Scott, strutting around in front of us like a proud peacock.

"Okay, young man, please tell me your name," said Ms. Agatha looking over the top of her glasses at Scott, seemingly unimpressed.

"I'm Scott Stoutman," said Scott proudly, smacking his chest with his colossal hand.

"You may now enter the pasture and pick up a cow of your choosing, but be please gentle," warned Ms. Agatha.

"No problem, I'll find the biggest one here, but even that won't be a challenge for Scott Stoutman!" exclaimed Scott confidently as he unlatched the gate and swaggered to the middle of the pasture.

"If it's bulk that you want, then you can't get any larger than Big Bertha to your right," replied Ms. Agatha. "She's a holstein and weighs almost two thousand pounds."

"Ladies and gentlemen," said Scott talking in a loud voice as if he were narrating some bizarre reality show. "Twelve-year-old Scott Stoutman is about to prove his awesome strength by picking up Big Bertha," he announced, "but before he does that, his muscles need a little breathing room." We all looked on as Scott reached his hand up, grabbed his shirt collar, and completely tore off his tee-shirt. Standing bare-chested in the pasture, Scott flexed his muscles like he was competing in a Mister Universe competition.

"Oh brother, I hope two thousand pound Bertha falls on top of that showoff," whispered Nate.

"Wouldn't it be funny if Bertha reached out with her two front hooves and picked up Scott? He'd have to live in the pasture eating grass and she would get assigned to the Lactose-Milkus cabin and train to be a super cow," I said chuckling.

I turned to look at Ms. Agatha and by the look on her face, she didn't seem to be very happy with Scott's antics either. "Please get on with it," said Ms. Agatha. "This is a test, not a performance."

"This young man is definitely going to end up in my infirmary before the end of camp," smirked Nurse Carter.

"Unfortunately, you are probably correct," replied Ms. Agatha as Scott spit on his enormous hands and rubbed them together.

"Here, I go...everybody, watch what I can do!" said Scott easily hefting Big Bertha up and over his head.

"Well done," said Ms. Agatha flatly. "You may put her down and join the Lacertosus Cabin."

"Okay," said Scott still hefting Big Bertha over his head, "but first, I think this little lady wants to go for a ride."

Ms. Agatha took off her glasses and glared at Scott, but he was too busy showing off to even notice.

"Big Mama, keep your arms, legs, and tail inside the ride at all times!" chuckled Scott as he raised Bertha up and down over his head like he was doing curls with his new cow weight set. "That's one...that's two...that's three...I could go all day....that's four..." Scott announced proudly.

"Oh brother," grumbled Nate out of the corner of his mouth. "I'm liking this guy less and less every second."

Agatha angrily stepped forward and placed her hands on the metal pasture fence. "Scott Strongman, put Bertha down this instant before you injure her!" barked Ms. Agatha.

"Oh, she's fine," said Scott, grinning ear to ear. "This big fat cow likes it!" exclaimed Scott as he adjusted his grip and began to swing her over his head like she was a black and white cow helicopter.

"This is making me really angry!" I projected to Nate, *"I can't stand by and watch him mistreat that poor cow!"*

"I know," replied Nate. *"He's going to hurt Bertha and he's making a complete fool of himself at the same time."*

"Place...the cow...down...now!" commanded Ms. Agatha as she walked over and began to unlock the gate.

"Hold on because I'm not quite finished just yet," replied Scott as he readjusted his handhold and threw Bertha ten feet up in the air, and then caught her.

I couldn't take it anymore. With balled-up fists, I stormed past Ms. Agatha and ripped open the gate. "STOP IT RIGHT NOW!" I yelled, stomping into the pasture.

Scott caught Big Bertha midair and placed her back on her feet. "What are you, an animal lover?" he snickered.

"As a matter of fact, I am!" I snarled, "so leave her alone."

Scott lumbered up to me like an enormous shirtless troll. "I was just shaking her up because I wanted a milk shake," he chortled.

Ms. Agatha opened the pasture gate and hollered, "That will be quite enough! You two will come out of the pasture before I am forced to take further action."

Ignoring Ms. Agatha, Scott growled, "I'm Da Boss, so get out of my way cow lover!"

"You're Da Doofus!" I roared, stepping into Scott's personal space.

"Get outta my face!" exclaimed Scott, reaching out and poking me hard in the chest with his two enormous fingers.

Stumbling backward, I came crashing down on my backside right under a brown cow that didn't seem particularly interested in what was going on.

Nate angrily stomped his way toward the pasture gate as I got to my feet. "Get your hands off my brother, you big oaf!" he roared.

"Why don't you come in here and teach me a lesson, little baby?" chuckled Scott flexing his muscles.

Ms. Agatha stepped into the pasture. "That will be quite enough, boys!" she exclaimed.

"But I have so much more to show you," complained Scott, "and these two pipsqueaks are throwing off my groove. Let me just show you how much...how much..." All of a sudden, Scott started walking around in circles, sniffing the air.

"What in the world are you doing now?" asked Ms. Agatha sounding exasperated.

"Let me show you how much...I LOVE PIE!" shrieked Scott as he leaned over and began collecting piles of dried cow poop near his feet.

"Young man, I've had just about enough of your antics," grumbled Ms. Agatha. "I need you to exit the pasture this very instant!"

"Not until I've gathered up all these yummy homemade chocolate pies," replied Scott greedily. "There are so many of them just lying around on the ground...and they're all for me!"

I looked over my shoulder towards Ms. Agatha, Nurse Carter, and the remaining campers. Each person behind me had horrified expressions on their faces, except for Nate, who was doubled over, laughing his head off.

With his arms full of dried cow pies, Scott sniffed his stenchy bouquet and hollered, "Ahh, heavenly chocolate pies!"

"OH, DON'T DO IT!" cried a camper.

"I CAN'T WATCH!" cried another camper.

But it was too late.

Without hesitation, Scott plunged his head into a thick juicy cow patty. "This is such a delicious chocolate pie. It's even cream-filled!" he exclaimed, taking an enormous bite.

Everyone looked like they wanted to throw up right then and there as Scott greedily feasted on the fly-infested cow patty in the middle of the pasture.

"Mmm...so good!" moaned Scott between swallows. "Compliments to the chef!"

Looking confused, a small black calf walked up next to Scott, titled his head to one side, and mooed.

Scott glared down selfishly at the calf when it mooed again. "Mine...all mine!" he shrieked, lowering his shoulder, and angrily pushing the cow away.

"Stop trying to hurt the cows!" I bellowed. "That's enough!"

"Not enough!" roared Scott. He lowered his shoulder again and rammed the calf. "I'm not sharing!" he squawked.

The black cow tumbled helplessly to the ground.

I threw my arms up in the air and yelled as the cow tumbled to the ground. "Get him! Get that bully!" I thundered.

Suddenly, all of the cows in the pasture abruptly stopped eating to look over at me as if they understood what I was saying.

"I'm taking some of these chocolatey treats with me!" exclaimed Scott as he collected cow pies on the way to the pasture gate. "Does anyone have a doggie bag?"

"A barf bag's more like it!" chuckled Nate loudly.

Scott reached out to unlatch the gate as Ms. Agatha took a half dozen steps backward, looking disgusted.

I looked over at the cows and then pointed at Scott. "That bozo hurt Bertha and your baby and now he's getting away!" I shrieked. "Get him!"

The cows mooed simultaneously as they rushed past me with Bertha taking the lead. As Scott reached down to open the gate, Bertha struck his massive rump with such force that she launched him up and over the fence.

Landing in a heap at the feet of Ms. Agatha and Nurse Carter, Scott looked up dazed and confused as cow pies rained down on them. After a long awkward silence, Scott finally got to his knees, shook his head, and asked enthusiastically, "So how'd I do because I think I proved that I'm, by far, the strongest one here."

Ms. Agatha cleared her throat as she pushed up her glasses. "Yes, you indeed proved you were strong, but why on Earth did you..."

"Why did I do what?" asked Scott, still on his knees. "Why did I do such an amazing job impressing everyone with my skill-z?"

"No," replied Ms. Agatha, "Why would some like you..."

"She wants to know why you decided to eat cow pies?" finished Nurse Carter.

Scott slowly smacked his lips. "I....ate...dried...cow...poop?" he asked slowly.

"Not all of them were dry!" yelled Nate standing near the pasture fence. "Some of the cow patties were warm, fresh, and mushy!"

Lined up at the pasture fence with all twelve angry cows and one calf, I hollered, "And that's what you get for being a bully!"

Scott struggled to his feet. "I really did eat dried cow poop?" he asked Nurse Carter. "Really?"

Nurse Carter slowly shook her head and grimaced, "Yes, and you seemed to be enjoying yourself."

Grabbing his stomach, Scott bent over and groaned, spitting repeatedly on the ground.

"Young man come with me to the infirmary so I can look you over," instructed Nurse Carter. "I believe that I may even have an extra toothbrush and some mint toothpaste you can have...and perhaps some mouthwash."

"I also suggest you get some lunch after your clean-up," said Ms. Agatha, "because a little human food may do you some good."

"He definitely won't be hungry for lunch now," chuckled Nate loudly. "He's ruined his appetite with all those tasty cow treats."

"Maybe I should just beat the living tar out of you and your brother!" snarled Scott as he stood straight up and glared at Nate and me.

Ms. Agatha quickly stepped in front of Scott and pointed her finger in his face. "You touch these boys and you will be expelled from camp...forever," she replied menacingly.

Scott grumbled something under his breath, pointed at me, and then said, "But that brat fed me cow pies, I'm sure of it."

"Correction," said Ms. Agatha plainly. "You freely partook of the cow pies. He just spoke to the cows and convinced them to stand up to your aggressive tactics."

"But it was them, I know it was because I don't eat animal poop!" bawled Scott, "...normally."

A roar of laughter filled the pasture as Scott wiped his tongue on his hairy bare arm.

"That will quite enough," smirked Ms. Agatha, "Let us not make fun of others just because they have different tastes in food."

"If you call that food," giggled Nate.

Nurse Carter reached into her pocket and handed Scott a tissue. "Time to go," she said.

Ms. Agatha replied, "And after your stop at the infirmary, you may join the Lacertosus cabin. Let us hope they teach you some humility."

"Whatever," said Scott huffing off towards the infirmary with Nurse Carter following a safe distance behind.

"As for you, young man," said Ms. Agatha, walking over to talk to me at the pasture fence. "I must confess, in all my years at Crusader, I've never met a camper that can control animals and..." Ms. Agatha suddenly stopped talking and hurriedly scribbled down some notes on her clipboard. "Tate Larson, please join the Maveric Camp," she said handing me a white paper pass.

"Thank you," I said walking over to the gate and unlatching it. "May I say goodbye to my brother first?"

"You may," replied Ms. Agatha.

I walked up to Nate and gave him a big hug. "I'll see you back at camp in a little bit," I said happily.

"Good job Bro," replied Nate, squeezing me tightly. "I'll be joining you soon, once I discover what my power is."

As I walked off with my Maveric pass in hand, I heard Ms. Agatha informing the remaining campers that they would be breaking for lunch shortly and to not resort to eating the leftover cow pies in the pasture.

Chapter Six

The Maverics

Logan and Little Red helped me carry my gear from the boy's O.P. cabin to the Maveric cabin. I claimed a bottom bunk directly across from Logan, unpacked a few things, and then slid the rest of my gear underneath. While we waited for other campers to join us, Logan sat with me on my bunk and explained how his parents were persistent in helping him harness his unique ability once he turned eight and a half years old.

After about ten minutes of getting to know each other, Little Red came to check in on us to make sure we were doing okay since our male counselor was off running errands. Overhearing that Logan lived in Kentucky, Little Red explained how she had many fond memories of his home state, and it wasn't just because they had good fried chicken. Little Red explained how, at the age of five, her parents left her on the doorstep of the local Kentucky fire department because they were unable to take care of her anymore. After two years of moving from foster home to foster home, Little Red was finally relocated to Georgia.

"Georgia is a good state as well," replied Logan. "A little warm and humid in the summer, but a good state, nonetheless."

"It was a good state, but unfortunately it was a difficult time in my life. By the time I turned ten years old, I lived in six different homes," she said frowning.

"Just how tall *are* you?" I asked trying to quickly change the subject because I was starting to feel uncomfortable.

"It depends on the day," chuckled Little Red. "My height is more of a range rather than a consistent measurement."

"What do you mean? I asked, grateful that I was successful in changing the subject.

Little Red walked over and sat on a bunk across from us, her knees almost touching her chin. "Well, by the age of eight I started to realize that my body was changing," she said.

"We know..." moaned Logan. "It's called puberty and I'm kind of hoping it doesn't happen to me."

"It wasn't exactly puberty," snickered Little Red. "It was more of my super ability beginning to develop early."

"So, you grew super tall all of a sudden?" I asked.

"That's the thing," replied Little Red. "Some days I would wake up eight feet tall and the next day I would be five and a half feet tall and no one around me could explain what was going on. Not only did it freak me out, but it creeped out my foster families too since we didn't have a clue that superpowers were a real thing."

"How'd you fit in your clothes?" asked Logan.

"Lots and lots of stretchy pants," chuckled Little Red.

"So, how'd you end up at Camp Crusader?" I asked.

"On my twelfth birthday, I was sent to see a hormone specialist called an endocrinologist in New York City," said Little Red, "and the next thing I knew, I was on a plane to Crusader."

"I'll bet the N.H.B, was involved in helping locate you," replied Logan.

"They were," said Little Red, "Unbeknownst to me, the specialist was on the board of the N.H.B.."

"What's the N.H.B.?" I asked.

Logan moved to the edge of my bunk and dangled his legs. "N.H.B. stands for the National Hero Bureau. It's a secret government agency that has connections in every state. They're looking for people with special abilities like us," replied Logan. "I hear they even have a couple of branches in Europe now."

"Thousands of individuals looking for people like us," grinned Little Red, "and it all started with Charles Wildenbury."

"So, what exactly is your super ability?" I asked, "and can you control it?"

"I can now," replied Little Red. "Want to see it in action?"

"Heck yeah!" I exclaimed.

"Well then," said Little Red getting up and walking to the door. "Get off your rear ends and follow me!"

We hopped off the bed and followed Little Red outside. "Is the N.H.B. different than the Blackrock Academy?" I asked.

Little Red scanned the top of the pine trees as we walked behind the cabin. "Where'd you hear about that place?" she frowned.

"A mouthy boy named Lance," I replied.

Little Red scowled, "It wasn't Lance Phillips, was it?"

"It was," replied Logan indignantly. "He treated Ms. Agatha like she was his servant girl."

"He's used to bossing people around because his parents are rich," said Little Red stopping under a particularly tall pine tree. "The Blackrock Academy is a prestigious boarding school for kids with super abilities. It was founded by Michael Blackrock in Maine about fifteen years ago after Alekzander got complaints from some of the wealthier parents. I guess the richies felt their kids weren't being treated special enough at Crusader, so they started their own elite training school."

"So why do kids like Lance even bother to come to camp if they don't like it here?" I asked. "Can't they just stay at Blackrock over the summer?"

"I can answer that one," replied Logan adjusting his glasses. "Blackrock students are required to attend at least one summer session of Crusader before their senior year if they want to be considered for a job with the N.H.B. after they graduate."

"And because working for the N.H.B. is prestigious," continued Little Red, "all the Blackrock kids want to work for them."

"Which means that we have to put up with him for two whole weeks?" I asked disappointedly.

"Yep, but be grateful it's only for two weeks," said Little Red pointing up at a cluster of pinecones growing high above us. "So, let's forget about Lance for now, and let me show you what my ability is."

"Go for it," I replied excitedly.

"See those pinecones about twenty feet above our heads?" asked Little Red pointing upward.

I looked up into the blinding sunlight filtering through the tall pine tree and located the clump of prickly pinecones she was talking about.

"Yes," I replied. "I see them."

Little Red cracked her knuckles and stretched both arms skyward. "Well, watch this," she said winking.

Logan and I watched as Little Red stretched upward like a rubber band. "You're stretchy like Logan," I replied.

"Kind of," replied Little Red coming back down with two large pinecones in her hands. "You see, there are different variants among the same abilities. For example, I'm pretty sure Logan can stretch super far, but the maximum I can stretch is only about twenty-five feet."

"The max I've been able to stretch is about one hundred feet," replied Logan.

Little Red said, "My ability works a little different than yours...take a look." Logan and I watched eagerly as Little Red suddenly shrunk down to the height of a milk jug. "I can also get tiny when I need to," she squeaked happily.

"You can stretch and shrink," smiled Logan. "That's something I definitely cannot do."

"And now we know why they call you Little Red," I said looking down at her.

"Nah, right now, my nickname's Big Red because I'm incy wincy," chuckled Red in a tiny voice. "But now..." she said, springing back to her full-sized self, "you can call me Little Red."

"That's pretty funny," I replied. "How'd you get those reverse nicknames?"

"From a former camper named Margaret Lynne," replied Little Red with a grin. "She found humor in the unusual. That's why she named her dog, Cat, and her cat, Dog, and she always said ice cream tasted way better on cold, snowy days."

"Hilariously confusing!" I chuckled.

"Yes," replied Little Red dreamily, looking up at the cloudless sky. "She was a great friend."

"Speaking of confusing, what about that weird power of yours?" asked Logan as he reached over and nudged me with his elbow. "The ability to talk to animals and convince people to eat their droppings!"

"I had nothing to do with Scott eating cow pies!" I exclaimed, "but you're right about the animals. I did convince those poor creatures to stand up to him."

"That's why you're a Maveric," said Logan reaching out and patting me on the back. "An unusual power that doesn't fit into a neat little package."

Little Red grinned, "And that's why Crusader was established, to help kids like us to discover and then develop our unique abilities in a safe and secure environment."

"That is, *if* we ever discover it!" hollered Nate as he and Anne trudged up the dirt pathway towards us.

"Does that mean you haven't figured out your power yet, Bro?"

"Nope, I still don't have a clue," replied Nate, "but Anne sure discovered hers and it's pretty amazing!"

"I'm a Maveric as well," said Anne, looking satisfied with her cabin assignment. "Today, I discovered that I can change my body into different materials."

"Like a rock or a cheese puff?" I asked.

"Pretty much," replied Anne.

"I think you should show them," said Nate excitedly.

Anne stepped forward and rolled up her sleeves just past her elbows. "Okay, somebody name something that is not alive," she said.

"How about a steel beam?" suggested Logan. "Like the kind that construction workers use to build tall skyscrapers."

"Give it a shot Anne!" encouraged Nate.

"Okay, I just have to focus hard on the object," she said scrunching up her face as she concentrated. "My skin should turn a different color while my clothes stay their regular hues and textures."

"It appears to be working," replied Logan, leaning forward to examine Anne's rusty red skin.

Nate balled up his fists and held them up menacingly in front of his face. "Can I punch you?" he asked Anne.

"Nate!" I exclaimed. "You know Dad taught us to never hit girls. "

"For demonstration purposes only," replied Nate sheepishly.

"I don't mind," replied Anne. "Go crazy Nate, but don't sock me in the face just in case my power doesn't hold up as expected."

Nate tightened up his right fist, reached back behind his head, and threw a solid punch into Anne's belly. "YIPES!" cried Nate flapping his hand wildly about. "That hurt a lot!"

"What'd you think was going to happen?" bellowed Little Red laughing hysterically.

Anne covered the braces on her dull gray teeth with her red metal hand as she grinned. "I think I'm gonna love this superpower!" she exclaimed.

Logan reached down and picked up a large broken tree branch as thick as my arm and asked, "Can I smack you with this tree branch, Anne?"

"Logan!" I screeched.

Anne squealed with delight, "DO IT!"

"Awesome," replied Logan.

"But let's try it out on my back," said Anne spinning around excitedly.

Logan said, "You got it!" as he rubbed his hands together and brushed his sandy blond hair out of the way of his oversized glasses. "But I got to warn you, I used to play baseball."

With her back still turned to us, Anne replied enthusiastically, "Then don't hold anything back!"

Logan took a deep breath and swung the branch with all his might.

"CRACK!"

Anne didn't budge an inch as the tree branch shattered into a thousand pieces around her.

Little Red grinned as Anne turned back around. "That's a very cool power," said Little Red.

"Ms. Agatha helped Anne figure out that her skin can turn into anything that's not living or breathing," said Nate.

"So, she can turn into a shoelace, but not a cat?" I asked, "or a ham sandwich, but not an aardvark?"

"Exactly," confirmed Anne, "but as cool as my power is, I'm really interested in finding out what Nate's ability is because it appears to be very elusive."

"I was one of the last campers left," complained Nate. "We tried and tried, but still nothing."

"I wouldn't necessarily say...nothing," I replied sliding up next to him. "I think I have a pretty good idea about what your ability is, but we should probably all huddle up first because it's a little, shall I say, *controversial*."

"I'm intrigued," replied Little Red, looking Nate over from head to toe. "Let's all huddle up so we can hear what Tate has to say."

Moving into a tight huddle, we placed our arms around each other's shoulders like football players getting ready to run a pivotal, fourth downplay.

"So, what's the play coach?" asked Nate.

I turned my head and asked Nate, "Do you remember the two times you became angry at camp over the last day and a half?"

"Kind of," replied Nate.

"Well, they both had to do with Scott," I said helping him out. "The first time you got ticked off was when he tripped us in the dining hall."

"Yes, I was pretty mad, but I was trying to keep it bottled up. I knew if I attacked him in the dining hall, he would just pound me flat and then we'd probably end up getting kicked out of camp on the first day."

"And then earlier today, you got angry when Scott was messing with me in the cow pasture."

"Yes, I was furious then, as well," confirmed Nate. "So, what are you getting at?"

"Well, do you remember what weird things happened both times you got angry?"

Nate looked at me, cocked his head to the side, and slowly replied, "...People started getting...really hungry?"

"And?" I asked.

"And...and...what?"

From across the huddle, Anne looked me directly in the eyes and asked, "You think it was Nate that drove us cinnamon roll crazy last night at dinner and not food poisoning?"

"I believe so," I replied. "Partially because I had to stop myself from going cuckoo along with the rest of you and I ate the mac and cheese. I also think it was Nate that caused Scott to imagine he was eating chocolate pies when he was actually eating cow poo-pies."

"So, my superpower is that I make people want to eat weird things. What kind of lame power is that?" scowled Nate.

"It's more than that," replied Little Red confidently. "It sounds like you have a different variant of telepathic power, something I was explaining to Logan and Tate earlier. I think you can get into people's heads and mess with their senses."

Logan's eyes narrowed behind his oversized glasses. "OH! OH!" he exclaimed. "Last night, I couldn't think straight because I truly wanted a cinnamon roll. I vaguely recall that I drank a whole bottle of spicy yellow mustard because I imagined it was cinnamon roll juice...and the thing is, I despise mustard."

"And I saw other campers leap over the counter and raid the kitchen's fridge. Calder and Amber were eating shredded cheese by the handful and Jake and Zavian were chowing down on raw eggs...shells and all," chuckled Little Red, "but I couldn't stop them because I was too busy gnawing on my tennis shoe!"

"So...we know you were mad at Scott," I said patting Nate's shoulder, "but were you thinking about, perhaps, having something sweet during dinner last night?"

"I wasn't thinking about cinnamon rolls if that's what you're asking," responded Nate.

"No, but I did suggest you distract yourself by thinking of something good to eat when you were about to...you know," I said nudging Nate with my hip.

"...Oh yeah," uttered Nate finally. "I wasn't thinking about cinnamon rolls, but I did momentarily think about how much I missed the Glacier Mountain Jellybeans Amanda would give us."

"And what flavor did you think about?"

"My favorite of course," replied Nate, "Cinnamon-"

"Cinnamon roll flavor," I interrupted. "Which happens to be both of our favorite Glacier Mountain jellybean flavor."

"Yes...so," replied Nate, still sounding disappointed. "I guess my power is to make people *really hungry* and *really unhealthy* when I get angry or anxious...It's still a lame power."

"Not so much," replied Little Red. "If that truly was you last night and today, your power is so strong that you can cause people to not think straight. It's actually a great power."

"How so?" asked Nate.

"Just imagine if the five of us were in a battle with a bad guy and all he could think about is eating cheesy broccoli or some spicy gumbo. We'd win without even throwing a punch!"

"Game over!" chirped Anne excitedly.

"Well, I guess when you put it that way," replied Nate. "It does sound a little cool, all except for the cheesy broccoli part."

"We'll have to test your powers out again sometime soon to see what you're truly capable of," I said patting Nate on the back, "but in the meantime, let's keep this on the down-low because if Scott finds out you were the one that influenced him to eat creamy cow pies-"

"We'd be dead meat," finished Nate.

"That's for sure," replied Logan. "It's a good idea to-"

"What's a good idea?" snarled an angry familiar voice from behind us. "It's a good idea that all you losers go home?"

Breaking from our huddle, we turned around and saw Dolores standing impatiently behind us, clutching a gray and black backpack. Standing next to Dolores, with a sleeping bag and pillow tucked under his arm, was a tall skinny counselor with shaggy brown hair and intense green eyes.

"Oh, hey Griffin," said Little Red awkwardly. "You're back with Dolores already."

Griffin rolled his eyes and replied, "Yep, just picked up her stuff from the infirmary."

"Well," said Little Red cheerfully to Dolores. "We're glad you can join us for tonight."

Dolores huffed, frowned, and was probably rolling her eyes under her long black bangs, but it was difficult to tell.

Little Red shrugged her shoulders and then pointed at Griffin. "If you didn't catch it, this is Griffin, he's the Maveric's boy counselor," she said warmly.

Logan looked up at Griffin and asked, "So what's your special ability, Griffin?"

"I have super senses," replied Griffin. "My eyesight, hearing, sense of taste, and smell are all heightened."

"Can see you at night like an owl?" Nate asked.

"Yep, like it's daytime," replied Griffin, "and I can hear sounds miles away, so my abilities come in handy for things like reconnaissance missions."

"So, you'll be a huge advantage when we play capture the flag?" I asked hopefully.

"We've won every year since I've been attending Crusader."

"Cool," replied Logan pushing up his glasses, "because I love winning."

"And I love having a clean toothbrush," replied Nate earnestly.

Dolores pushed her black bangs out of her eyes and glared at Logan and Griffin. "And I just adore listening to all this masculine gloating," muttered Dolores sarcastically.

Anne cleared her throat and then asked, "How about you Dolores. What's your super ability?"

"I haven't discovered mine yet. I've been in the infirmary since last night. That's why I couldn't join you at the grounds, not that I wanted to be near any of you anyway," grumbled Dolores.

"Well, we hope you feel welcome for the time being until you discover your powers," replied Little Red.

"Whatever, Sunshine," hissed Dolores. "The sooner I get away from the Maverics, the better."

Griffin rolled his eyes behind Dolores' back again and said, "Let's go get the rest of your gear from the girl's O.P. cabin so we can get you settled in."

Dolores, Griffin, and Little Red lead the way as the rest of us kept a good distance away from them.

"Aren't we lucky to have Dolores hanging out with us?" chuckled Nate sarcastically. "She's going to be loads of fun."

"Life of the party!" chuckled Logan

Anne frowned, "And I get to have her all to myself in the cabin until she discovers her power."

"She'll probably only be with us for another day or two," I said hopefully.

Anne looked up the road towards the girl's Maveric cabin and said, "Either way, I better hurry up and grab my gear before the black-haired demon girl claims the whole room," she muttered as she walked off towards the girls O.P. cabin.

"I'll give you a hand, Anne," replied Logan, scampering after her.

I grinned as Logan followed behind Anne like a yippy puppy dog. "I think Logan's in love," I chuckled.

Nate laughed, "With Dolores?"

"With Anne."

"I think you're probably right," Nate agreed shaking his head.

"But what I'm trying to figure out is how Dolores ended up in the infirmary in the first place," I asked.

Nate grinned, "Oh, that's an easy one. I heard that last night during the Great Crusader Cinnamon Roll Riot, Dolores leapt over the counter and ate the rest of the macaroni and cheese, thinking she was devouring delicious cinnamon roll pudding."

"You mean she ate the whole batch of macaroni and cheese?" I asked. "That was about five pounds of food!"

"Yep, I heard she was barfing all night," grinned Nate.

"Serves her right," I chuckled.

We practiced our best barfing noises while we moved Nate's gear into the Maveric's cabin. Once we were finally situated, we had an hour to kill before dinner. However, instead of doing anything productive, we sat down on the floor of our cabin and played card games. It was during the third round of gin rummy that Kate unexpectedly barged into our cabin looking all hot, red, and sweaty.

"What are you doing in our room and why are you out of breath?" I asked Kate without thinking. "Is someone chasing you?"

Nate looked over at me and shook his head as Kate's eyes grew wide. "When did...you....start talking again?"

I bit my lower lip and shrugged my shoulders, acting as if I hadn't a clue about what she was talking about.

"He just started recently," replied Nate.

Kate narrowed her eyes, cocked her head to the side, and asked, "Just how recently?"

"Newishly, recently," I responded.

Placing her arms across her chest, Kate gave Nate and me a cold stare. "I don't think that any of this is funny! You two should have told me that Tate was-"

Nate suddenly popped up from the floor like a jack in the box. "Enough already Sis!" he exclaimed. "Why'd you barge in on us anyway? We could have been naked or somethin'."

"Playing cards naked," replied Kate. "What a laugh! You'd never do something as ridiculous as playing cards nake..."

Nate placed his arms across his chest and grinned ear to ear.

"Never mind," Kate said. "I'll be sure to knock next time."

"So why *are* you here?" I asked.

"I heard a rumor that I thought you should know about," Kate said sitting down on a bunk next to us.

"What rumor? Did Scott run away from camp?" I asked hopefully.

"Nope," replied Kate. "I heard something else."

Logan brushed his sandy blond hair out of the way of his glasses and asked, "What'd you hear? Is it serious?"

Kate scooted off the bed, knelt on the floor, and whispered, "So get this...Braeden and Alaena, from my cabin, said they were taking an afternoon stroll by the infirmary about fifteen minutes ago. As they walked past an open window, they heard some voices talking, so they went over to investigate."

"So, they're creepy stalkers...so what?" asked Nate.

"Well, they just so happened to overhear Nurse Carter and Alekzander talking about one of the new campers suddenly losing his powers," she said. "They weren't exactly sure how it happened, but an emergency camp meeting is going to be called tonight right after dinner."

"That's in like thirty minutes," replied Nate looking up at the clock in the cabin. "Which means that we still have time to play a couple more rounds of gin rummy."

Kate scrunched up her face. "Nate, this is serious. How can you think about playing cards at a time like this?"

"Easy," replied Nate holding up his cards for Kate to see, *"because*...I'm winning!"

I looked over at Kate and said, "We'll see you at dinner and then we'll walk over to the meeting together."

"Okay," said Kate, "but be careful in the meantime."

"We will," replied Nate looking down at his cards, "but until then, let us get back to our game, please."

"Okay," scowled Kate, "but I think maybe you should consider being more careful because-"

"Here goes!" exclaimed Nate. He placed his cards face down on the floor, stood up, grabbed the bottom of his tee-shirt, and pulled it up over his head. "You better get out of here because it's stripping time!"

"Fine," griped Kate, rolling her eyes, "but don't coming crying to me when you lose *your* powers!"

"Okay, we won't," Nate replied, pulling his shirt completely off.

"Boys," grumbled Kate as she turned around and stomped out the door.

Nate sat down, put his shirt back on, and went back to playing cards. "I thought she'd never leave," he muttered.

By the time the three of us finished playing a couple more hands of gin rummy, it was time for dinner. Luckily for us, chow time was quiet and uneventful, with no one having a craving for cinnamon rolls, cow pies, or cinnamon roll-cow pies. Placing our dirty dishes in the tray, Nate,

Kate, Anne, Logan, and I joined the crowd that had gathered in front of the mess hall.

Somberly, we followed a line of campers down a well-worn path until we arrived at a large outdoor amphitheater at the edge of the forest. Sitting down on one of the well-worn benches carved from a dead fallen tree, we stared dreamily at the roaring bonfire.

"Here come the older kids," whispered Logan, as more than a hundred campers from Crusader II entered the far end of the amphitheater and either filled in the remaining seats or quietly stood behind them.

Looking from Kate to Logan to me, Nate whispered out of the corner of his mouth, "What's with all this waiting around business? When's something good gonna hap-"

" POOF! "

A whisp of gray smoke and the smell of burning rubber filled the air as Alekzander and Ms. Agatha appeared in front of us. Everyone's eyes silently followed Alekzander and Ms. Agatha as they stepped in front of the roaring fire.

"Campers, we welcome all one hundred fifty-three of you here tonight. We wish our first Crusader bonfire of the summer would have been under better circumstances, but sadly this is not the case," said Alekzander as he reached down, placed a log on the fire, and then continued. "I believe some of you already know that a first-year camper from Volant cabin, Calder Locke, is currently being treated by Nurse Carter...Having visited Calder just a few moments ago, I can assure you that even though he is currently unresponsive, his vitals are stable."

Alekzander looked over at Ms. Agatha and nodded his head. Ms. Agatha nodded her head in return, tucked her clipboard under her arm, took a step forward, and said, "After some deliberation, both Alekzander and I have concluded that Calder has been stricken with a similar malady that struck our campers more than three decades ago. Unfortunately, these same campers lost their super abilities in the process. Which is to say, we strongly believe that Calder no longer has his ability to fly."

A nervous whisper echoed throughout the amphitheater as Alekzander looked around and then held up his hand to silence us. "I have contacted Calder's parents along with your parents and the N.H.B. I will be escorting Calder home the moment Nurse Carter has him stabilized enough to teleport," said Alekzander, "and because I will be gone for a few days, I will be leaving Ms. Agatha in charge. In the meantime, please make sure you move about camp with at least one other person as your companion. You are not to be alone, at any time, under any circumstances until we find out who or what is behind this unfortunate predicament."

I looked around nervously. Kate, Anne, Logan, and even Nate were silently leaning forward in their seats, hanging on to every word Alekzander was saying.

"You will be in good hands while I am away," Alekzander assured us. "If I had any concerns about your safety, then you would be packing to go home at this very moment. However, at this point in time, camp is the safest place for you as long as you look out for each other and stick together. So please, carry on with your training and we will get to the bottom of this as quickly as possible."

Alekzander picked up one more log and threw it into the fire. "Ms. Agatha will now address any concerns you might have," he said, "but for now, I bid you all adieu."

"POOF! "

And just like that, Alekzander was gone again.

Walking to the center of the amphitheater, Ms. Agatha adjusted her glasses, looked down at her clipboard, and said, "As Alekzander just mentioned, your safety is our top priority. He and I have been talking a great deal these past few hours about how to best address the issue at hand. Make no mistake, this is quite a serious matter insomuch that I must reiterate that-"

"Tate...Can you hear me?" hummed a voice in the back of my head.

"I can...Who is this?"

"Alekzander."

"Where are you?"

"I'm standing out front of the infirmary. I'm going to check on Calder's wellbeing."

"What's going on?"

"I don't know but I intend to find out. In the meantime, I need to talk to you about something important."

Feeling uneasy inside, I nervously replied, *"Okay."*

"Ms. Agatha and I have been diligent in making sure no one finds out that you have two distinct super abilities."

"Okay, but I don't understand why that's such a big deal."

"I can't go into great detail about that right now, but I must inform you that there are very few people, both past and present, that have been granted more than one special ability."

"Okay…"

"And those individuals with more than one power usually are connected through their bloodlines."

"You mean, they are related somehow?"

"Precisely."

"So, who else has had two powers that you know of?"

"You and a former camper named Nero, to name a few."

"I know about him and the amulet," I said, beginning to feel even sicker to my stomach, *"but are you saying that I am related to...to Nero?"*

"Yes, but there's more."

"More?"

"Yes, I also believe that individuals such as yourself may have the capability to hold infinite powers within themselves."

"You mean I can have more than two powers?"

"Exactly...and that is what puts you in grave danger."

"How?"

"When we finally caught Nero, he was in the possession of seven abilities."

"I thought there were six victims. Which means that with his two powers, he should have had eight super abilities altogether."

"Which means not only did he have the ability to take powers, but he was also able to pass them along to others."

"So, what does that have to do with me?"

"You may have the same ability to take away and give powers. This means if someone finds out that you possess two powers, they may-"

"Try to get me to release the powers from the amulet," I concluded. *"If they find it."*

"Unfortunately, that may be the case. However, it also appears that someone on campus may be able to steal powers just like Nero did so many years ago."

"So, what do you want me to do?"

"Your best bet is to make sure you don't tell anyone, except those you completely trust, that you have more than one power."

"Ok, but-"

"That's all I can tell you right now. I have to get back to Calder. Ms. Agatha and Nurse Carter will look after you for the time being...stay safe."

The words *stay safe* rang through my head over and over again. I distinctly remembered mom's closing remarks in her letter saying the same thing. I tried not to think too hard about the danger I was in, as my mind drifted back to the meeting at the bonfire.

"...and the nine o'clock curfew will be in effect until further notice. You risk expulsion from camp if you break any of the rules I have just discussed," said Ms. Agatha tapping her clipboard with a pen. "That is all. Please walk back to your cabins with a partner and try and get a good night's sleep. Training, as usual, will continue tomorrow morning bright and early...good night." Ms. Agatha pushed up her glasses, tucked her clipboard under her arm, and smiled as we filed past her.

It felt like we were taking part in a funeral procession as we silently sulked our way back to our cabins. Once we arrived, Nate, Logan, Griffin, and I, laid down on our bunks, leaving one light on in the far corner of the room, just in case. Feeling an enormous sense of uneasiness, I tossed and turned the whole night. It wasn't until the morning sun peeked through the cabin window that I finally felt safe enough to fall asleep.

Chapter Seven

Surviving the Hike

After breakfast and once our water bottles were filled, Nate, Logan, Anne, Dolores, and I met up with Little Red and Griffin in front of the dining hall. With large tan backpacks thrown over their shoulders and walkie-talkies clipped to their belt loops, Little Red and Griffin led us across camp, through the proving grounds, and to the edge of the forest. Walking past the outhouse, we left the boundaries of camp following a thin dusty trail, marked by faded yellow signs.

Logan read a sign aloud as we hiked deeper into the forest. "Crusader Cave, four miles," he said dabbing his forehead with a red and black hanky.

"I've never walked four miles before," replied Nate, looking back at Anne nervously.

"You'll be fine, city boy," replied Anne. "Just one foot in front of the other."

"It'd be a shame if you die of exhaustion," murmured Dolores sarcastically behind Anne.

"You'll all be fine," replied Little Red. "Just keep moving forward."

The pathway wandered this way and that way through the forest, weaving in and around trees, shrubs, and lichen-covered boulders, seeming to be in no rush to go anywhere in particular. After about an hour of hiking, we came to an enormous fallen pine tree blocking our path.

"Ok, quick water break," said Little Red as she and Griffin hefted their packs off of their shoulders and laid them on the ground, "and while we're waiting, take a couple of minutes to brainstorm how we're going to get over that humongous log."

Nate and I took big swigs of water and then joined Anne and Logan at the enormous tree blocking our way.

Logan reached up and patted the tree. "This baby is close to eight feet tall laying on its side," he remarked. "I don't think we can go around it because there's thick brush just off of the path at either end."

"Do you think we can climb over it?" I asked.

"Let me give it a try," said Nate. He placed his water bottle on the ground, rubbed his hands together, and tried to pull himself up the tree. However, only making it about five feet up, Nate tumbled down on his backside when a clump of bark came loose in his hand.

"Slightly dangerous," said Logan, peeling off a piece of bark.

"You could have told me that earlier," replied Nate dusting off the back of his pants. "It would have saved me from falling on my butt."

"And then we'd have missed a good laugh," chuckled Logan. "Besides, I think you would have tried it anyway."

"Both true," grinned Nate.

"Well, it looks like we'll need to use our powers to get us up and over," I said.

Anne looked over at Logan and asked, "Can you stretch us over?"

"I could easily stretch myself and our gear over this monstrosity, but I wouldn't be able to carry any of you over because I don't have super strength," replied Logan.

"What about you Anne?" I asked. "Can you turn into something to fly us over?"

"Like what?" giggled Nate. "Like an airplane, blimp, or a rocket ship?"

Anne looked up at the sky and shook her head. "Tate, I can't actually turn into things, and I don't fly."

"What I mean is, can you turn your skin into one thing and then your insides into something else?" I asked.

"And why would I want to do that?" asked Anne. "It sounds a bit gross and possibly very painful."

"Maybe you can't turn into an actual blimp but maybe you can turn into a balloon."

"And how would I do that?" asked Anne.

"You could turn your skin into rubber latex and your insides into helium," I suggested.

"Brilliant idea," said Logan.

"It's only brilliant if it works," I replied. "Want to try it, Anne?"

Anne thought for a moment and then abruptly nodded her head. "Oh, heck yeah! Let's do it!" she cried.

Nate turned towards Dolores, Little Red, and Griffin. "Hey everyone, gather around. Anne's going to try and float us over this huge tree," said Nate.

Little Red and Griffin threw their backpacks over their shoulders and joined us as Dolores sluggishly slumped over.

"Okay, here goes nothing," said Anne, in front of the tree not looking very confident.

"Literally nothing," muttered Dolores, standing in the back of our group.

We all ignored Dolores as Anne's skin suddenly began to change a light shade of pink.

"It's working!" exclaimed Anne, looking down at her arm.

Logan reached over and poked Anne's springy pink neck with his index finger. "She's rubbery and she's beginning to fill up with gas," he said happily.

"That's my problem, too...I'm usually full of gas," chuckled Nate as Anne's body began to swell to three times its normal size.

"Grab onto a leg!" blubbered Anne, beginning to float in the air like a Thanksgiving Day parade balloon.

Leaping up and each grabbing a leg, Nate and Logan pulled Anne back down to Earth.

"Increasing power," squeaked Anne as her enormous skin expanded under her ultra-tight clothing. Doubling in size, Anne hefted Nate and Logan up and over the enormous tree.

"We made it!" bellowed Nate from the other side of the tree as Anne came floating back over to pick the rest of us up.

Once everyone was safe and sound on the far side of the tree, Anne deflated and then returned to her normal size, shape, and color.

"Well done," chirped Little Red, patting Anne on her back. "You discovered something new about your ability today."

"And you managed to figure out a way to solve our predicament," grinned Griffin.

Anne smiled between her fingers, pointed at me, and said, "Thanks to Tate. It was his idea."

"Well done, both of you," replied Little Red as she reached down and ruffled my hair.

I felt my cheeks get hot and flushed as I looked up at Little Red and smiled. "Thanks," I mumbled.

Griffin threw this backpack over his shoulder, looked up at the brilliant blue sky filled with white billowy clouds, and said, "Well, time's-a-wastin' and I'm getting hungry."

"Our training ground is about another thirty minutes further, so let's move out," said Little Red, throwing her oversized tan backpack over her shoulders.

We followed the dirt path for another half a mile, rustling our way between patches of thick razor-sharp raspberry bushes that spilled over on the pathway until we finally arrived at a set of rocky stairs that lead down to an enormous canyon below.

"Sixty-seven steps down to the bottom," said Little Red as we stopped a moment to admire the striped orange and red canyon walls far below.

"Take the stairs slowly," ordered Griffin from the front of the line, as he took the first step to descend into the canyon. Forming a single file line, we cautiously followed Griffin, being careful not to trip on the uneven, rocky stairs.

Finally reaching the bottom, Nate chuckled, "Well, nobody fell down the stairs and plummeted to a violent death, so I'd say it's been a pretty successful trip thus far."

"Not so much," murmured Dolores still hanging at the back of the pack.

"Welcome to the Black Hole," replied Griffin pointing to a jagged four-foot cave opening to our right.

"This cave entrance is the only way in and out of Crusader Cave," said Little Red as she opened the top of her backpack and retrieved a tattered yellow rope, "and there's an interesting story around these parts that tells of a boy named Benjamin that got lost in this cave in 1955."

"What'd he do?" asked Nate.

"He wandered away from his group and was never found," replied Little Red.

"And legend has it," continued Griffin, "he's still wandering around in the dark looking for his way out." Griffin grabbed one end of the rope from Little Red and tied it around his waist. "It's tricky going in the dark, I'll lead us through by enhancing my senses," he said. "It's your job just to hang on to the rope and don't wander off like poor Benjamin."

"Why not just use flashlights?" asked Nate.

"That's a good question," grinned Griffin as he finished tying the rope around his waist. "Okay, let's get everyone hooked up so we get to our training ground ASAP because I'm starving," he said rubbing his hands together.

"Okay, everyone fall in," said Little Red. "I'd like Anne to follow behind Griffin, then Logan next, then Tate, then Nate, then Dolores, and I will pull up the rear."

I looked back at Nate. He didn't look so thrilled about being in front of Dolores.

Everyone grabbed the rope in single file order. "Just hold on tight and Griffin will lead us safely through," instructed Little Red.

"You'll be fine, it's only about eight minutes in pitch black. Just stay quiet so the vampire bats won't hear us," said Griffin turning his head back with a sly smile.

"What?" yelped Logan. His eyes grew wide behind his glasses. "Nobody said anything about vampire bats?"

"Oh, don't worry Logan," said Griffin. "The bats only like the taste of dirty flesh."

"Great, I haven't showered since I got here!" yelped Nate, "and don't even ask me if I'm wearing clean socks and underwear."

"Then you'll be the first to go," chuckled Little Red.

"And good riddance," sneered Dolores. "I can't wait to see them suck out every last ounce of blood from your body."

"Lucky for you they're vampire bats," replied Nate, "because you don't have any blood left in your veins to suck, creepy zombie girl."

"You better watch your back Nate," hissed Dolores.

"That'll be quite enough nonsense from the both of you," said Little Red. "No one's going to get sucked dry by vampire bats, but I would advise all of you, especially the boys, to have better hygiene from here on out."

"Alright, alright, let's go," ordered Griffin impatiently as he ducked under the mouth of the cave and looked back at us, "but seriously, don't let go of the rope or you could end up like poor Benjamin...and I'm not kidding about that."

Nate, Logan, and I barely had to duck to get under the mouth of the cave. Once inside, we stood up with ease, admiring the tall shadowy ceilings of solid rock all around us.

"What are the red arrows for?" asked Anne pointing at the granite walls. "Do they lead the way to your training ground?"

"That they do," replied Little Red.

Holding tightly onto the rope, I kept a close eye on my feet as we walked along the jagged rocky path that led us deeper into the mountain. After we walked for a couple of minutes, I could no longer see the red-painted arrows or my feet as the cold blackness completely swallowed us.

"Step carefully here," instructed Griffin in the darkness. "The path slopes down a bit and then goes back up."

"Steady as she goes," said Little Red from behind us.

"Steady as she goes," repeated Griffin from the front.

Seeing absolutely nothing, I tried to take slow cautious steps, but I was forced to move faster than I wanted because the rope was pulling me forward.

"We'll be heading up an incline in about ten feet," Griffin echoed. "Then we'll make a sharp right and then a quick left turn. Just keep holding on to the rope and you'll be fine."

"You're all doing great," encouraged Little Red from behind us.

I did my best to try and memorize the path we were taking but I quickly became disoriented in the cold blackness as we pushed farther and farther into the mountainside.

"It's pretty dark back here," said Little Red after we made a sharp left turn.

"It's about right," replied Griffin from the front of the line.

"About right, what?" asked Nate, his voice echoing into the darkness as we suddenly stopped moving forward.

"Um, why'd the rope just drop in front of me?" yelped Anne, "and where'd Griffin go?"

"What do you mean, where did Griffin go?" asked Logan sounding anxious. "He's *supposed to be* in front of you."

"I know *he's supposed to be* in front of me," cried Anne, "but he's not here anymore and the rope is lying at my feet."

From the back of the line, Dolores replied plainly, "Red is gone too, maybe they died."

"Great!" yowled Nate. "Both of em' sucked dry by Dolores!"

"Very funny," replied Dolores. "So funny that I forgot to laugh."

"None of this is very funny!" growled Anne, her voice echoing off the walls around us. "How are we supposed to find our way out of here in the pitch black?"

"I knew we should have brought flashlights," muttered Nate, "but Griffin was acting all weird when I asked him why we didn't bring any."

"Well, what do we do now?" asked Logan.

"I guess we're all doomed," replied Nate. "We'll be wandering around this cave with that little ghost boy...but at least we'll have a new friend!"

"Not funny, Nate!" yelped Anne again.

"Don't worry Anne," I quickly replied, "We'll be able to find a way out if we put our heads together."

"It's probably just another test," replied Nate.

"Good point," said Logan, "I think if we take a breath and think rationally about this, we should be able to easily solve this pr-"

"Oh, man!" Nate suddenly yelped from the back of the line. "Who farted because all of a sudden it stinks really bad in here. Was that you Logan?!"

"It wasn't me!" said Logan. "You're the one with all the gas issues!"

"It wasn't me either," I said, "but it sure was a stinky one!"

"Boys, enough with the gas jokes," snapped Anne. "We have a serious problem here that we have to solve or else we'll end up like that creepy Benjamin kid."

"I might be able to get us some help from the resident vampire bats if we need to," I said.

"Last resort!" yelped Logan. "Very, very last resort!"

"I don' think turning my skin into something else would help in this situation either," replied Anne.

"Maybe Logan can stretch his way out of here," I suggested.

"It's worth a shot," answered Logan, "but, I may be stretching pretty far so someone will need to hang on to my feet because if I expand too far, then my lower body will just shoot off after my top half, like a rubber band being flung."

"And then you'll be lost by yourself in the darkness which'll make matters worse," concluded Nate.

"I'll hold down your feet since I'm already standing behind you," I said squatting down and grabbing Logan's ankles.

"Okay, hold them tight," instructed Logan.

"I got them."

I held tightly onto Logan's ankles as he stretched his upper body forward to feel around in the cave. After a couple of minutes of fumbling around in the dark, Logan returned.

"No luck," said Logan. "I can feel the edges of the wall and possibly the pathway forward, but I'm not one hundred percent sure and I wouldn't want to lead us off in the wrong direction."

"Can anyone else think of how we could use our abilities to get us out of this situation?" asked Anne.

"What about you Dolores?" asked Logan near the front of the line.

"Yeah, now would be a good time to discover your power," said Nate curtly. "Maybe you'll actually be useful for once."

But Dolores didn't bother to answer.

"Good, the silent treatment," said Nate sounding agitated. "I prefer it that way anyway."

"What about you Nate?" asked Anne.

"Right now, I wish I could dull my senses because I can still smell someone's stenchy gas bomb!" exclaimed Nate.

"Hey, wait a minute," replied Logan. "That gives me an idea."

"It does?" asked Nate.

"It sure does," Logan replied. "Remember how we were discussing that you may have the ability to manipulate senses?"

"I don't think we are going to eat our way out of here," replied Nate sounding doubtful.

"Wait a second, Nate, I see where Logan's going with this," replied Anne. "You've already proven you can influence people's senses to make them believe they see and smell something they don't. It may be possible that you can manipulate people's other senses like hearing or vision."

"That was exactly what I was thinking," Logan said. "I'm curious if Nate can magnify the rod cells in the back of our eyes to aid our ability to see in the dark."

"That might work," replied Anne hopefully.

"I say give it a shot," I replied. "After all, what can it hurt?"

"Don't even ask that question," responded Nate nervously, "because I don't completely understand my abilities."

"Just take it slow and concentrate," I replied.

We all stood quietly anticipating what would happen next when the horrific smell filled the cave again.

"That wasn't me," yelped Nate loudly sniffing the air. "At least I don't think it was."

"Well, whoever it was, really let one go," choked Logan, "...again!"

"I'm sure it was Nate," replied Dolores. "He hasn't showered for a couple of da-"

"Oh, now you decide to speak!" interrupted Nate, "Well, how about you and everyone else stay quiet for a few minutes so I don't accidentally end up exploding your eyeballs out of your head."

As we stood quietly in the still cold blackness, I nervously wondered if Logan's idea was going to work or if our eyeballs really were going to end up exploding out of our heads. I tried pushing the dreadful thought out of my mind, but waiting in the choking darkness kept sweeping it back in. It wasn't until I heard Nate finally utter, "Okay, I think I got it," that I realized I had been holding my breath the whole time.

"Hold on to your peepers!" exclaimed Nate as the cavern suddenly flooded with brilliant light.

"It worked," whimpered Logan, "but do you think you could lower the lights a little? It's pretty intense."

"Sorry," replied Nate. "Let me see if I can dial it back a couple hundred notches."

Just as our eyes adjusted to a more manageable brightness, Griffin stepped out from behind a rocky outcropping in front of us.

"Well done," remarked Little Red with a grin as she stepped out from around the corner behind us. "You all passed two big tests today."

"And pretty quickly, too," commented Griffin. "You beat last year's group by about fifteen minutes."

Anne hid her smile behind her hand and proudly said, "It was all because of Nate."

"Actually, it was all because someone passed some serious gas," chuckled Nate. "Otherwise, Logan may not have thought up the idea of upgrading our senses."

"Well then, you can thank the cave gas," replied Griffin. "It happens quite regularly around here."

"I'll remember that excuse next time I need one...Sorry, everyone, it was just cave gas!" chuckled Nate.

"Either way, it doesn't matter who pulled it off," said Little Red. "You all did a fine job putting your heads together and working as a team to figure out a solution to your predicament. This group is quickly discovering that our cabin has a distinct advantage over all the other cabins. As Maverics, we are forced to learn how to work together with each other's different abilities to solve some pretty difficult problems."

"I'm just glad that you didn't ditch us," I replied.

"I would've been okay with that," muttered Dolores under her breath.

"Well, how about you lead us the rest of the way to the training ground?" asked Little Red, looking over Dolores' head, towards Griffin.

Griffin picked up the rope from off the ground, looped it, and stuck it in his backpack. Sure," he said. "It's right behind me."

We took a dozen more steps, rounded a corner, and came to an abrupt stop in front of a tall wooden door with a large ornate $\mathcal{M}$ carved into it.

"Not another doorway," I complained. "I hope it's not like the G.R.D.D. because that kind of door doesn't like me."

"Then it's a good thing this is just a regular door," replied Griffin fishing through his pocket and pulling out an old black key that looked more like it unlocked a pirate treasure chest than a door.

"Mind your head when you enter because the corridor leading to our training room is pretty low and tends to be quite damp," said Little Red as Griffin inserted the key into the lock.

"That's because we are right under an underground river called an aquifer," continued Griffin as he opened the door.

"Luckily for us though, our training ground has been updated with a few modern-day conveniences," said Little Red.

Sticking his hand through the doorway and into the darkness, Griffin instructed Nate to turn off our upgraded night vision abilities.

"Will do," replied Nate. "The deed is done."

Just as my eyes began to adjust to the darkness, Griffin flipped a light switch on the wall. A string of what looked like old miner's lanterns, hanging from the ceiling, lit up the long damp narrow corridor.

"You can thank Michael Lee for the lighting. He was a Maveric that used his ability to help bring electricity to our training grounds about twenty years ago," said Griffin.

"Well, thank you, Michael," replied Anne as we walked single file through the doorway and into the long drippy, moss-covered passage.

"It's like I'm walking through a sprinkler with my shoes on," complained Logan as we splashed through hundreds of puddles along our path.

"Are we going to eat soon?" asked Nate running his hand along the cavern wall, "because these little green plants are making me so hungry that I'd even eat a salad."

"I'll take mine with ranch dressing and croutons please!" chuckled Logan.

"Bottom feeders," hissed Dolores under her breath.

"Nate, your stomach has impeccable timing," snorted Little Red from the back of the line, "because from back here, it looks as if we have arrived."

Griffin stopped our line and pointed towards an enormous pitch-black cavern directly in front of us. "Red and I would like to officially welcome you to Maveric training camp and our unofficially official headquarters!" he said.

"Got any light in there?" asked Anne.

"Have we got lights? Have we got lights?" asked Griffin enthusiastically, "...I don't know Red, have we got lights?"

"Oh, yes we do!" exclaimed Little Red reaching over and flipping a light switch hidden in a small crevice to our right.

Suddenly, the enormous cavern, ten times as tall and wide as my school gym back at home, lit up like a beautiful Christmas tree. Hundreds of strings of both colored and white Christmas lights strung up along the high ceiling splashed color around the room from high above. An enormous rock, chiseled with the words **Maverics,**

sat in the middle of a lush green lawn that looked more like carpet than grass. The perfectly manicured lawn stretched to every corner of the cavern, ending at another outhouse in the far right corner of the cavern.

"This is beautiful," cooed Anne.

"Like Christmas in the summertime," agreed Logan.

"I've seen better," complained Dolores.

We followed Griffin and Red over to Maveric Rock. Laying her backpack down on the grass, Little Red fetched a white and red checkered picnic blanket out of her backpack while Griffin handed out small hand towels so we could dry off our sopping wet heads.

"The Elementa cabin helped us grow the grass in here," said Little Red. She sat down on the blanket and ran her hand over the soft green blades. "It's pretty remarkable because the grass stays lush all year long and doesn't ever require mowing or watering."

"It is pretty amazing," said Nate. "Is it edible?"

"Of course not," grinned Little Red reaching back into her backpack. "That's why I brought some real food along."

"Well, what are we waiting for? Let's chow down!" chirped Nate eagerly.

Little Red took out clear plastic containers filled with salami, cheese, crackers, apple slices, grapes, and cookies. Relaxing on the tarp, we stuffed our faces, until all our bellies were bulging.

Soon after, Griffin yawned, laid his head on his backpack, and covered his face with a Colorado Rockies Baseball cap that he fetched from his front pocket. "Time for a little nap before we get down to business," yawned Griffin from under his baseball cap as the rest of us polished off the last of the chocolate chip cookies.

"Griffin doesn't appear to be much of a morning person?" I said looking at Red.

"He's not a day *kind of person* either," chuckled Little Red.

"That's about right," muttered Griffin from under his cap.

"Well," said Nate wiping his hands on the front of his jeans and standing up, "I'm a have-to-go-to-the-bathroom-right-now, *kind of person.*"

"I'll go with you," I replied, brushing the cookie crumbs from off my lap.

Logan shoved the last bit of cookie into his mouth and said, "I think I'll join you as well."

After Nate went to the bathroom, I climbed into the outhouse and conducted some very important business of my own, grateful that this particular outhouse wasn't as smelly as the other one. As I went about my business, I read the outhouse walls under a string of white Christmas lights, laughing quietly to myself.

This outhouse is the property of ACME Co.
(Meep – Meep!)

Little Red Wuz Here, Too!

Help! I fell in many "moons" ago! – 2001

~~The Crew 1972~~

~~N+J+L+A+F+B+S+R~~ (Losers! 2013)

Maverics Rule!!! (The other cabins drool!)

I wuv M.N.B.A. – 1971

To get Outhouse "B" cleaned, dial 718-0114
(phone number permanently disconnected)

Try the gray stuff, it's delicious-1991

Lucky loves Lucy and her beautiful yellow hair – 2020

Just as I barely finished reading the walls and completing some personal business, a loud knock rattled the door behind me. "Hang on, Logan," I muttered under my breath as I zipped up my pants. Two seconds later, another thundering knock shook the outhouse door as I reached for the door handle.

"Hold your pants on would ya' baboon butt!" I bellowed as I shoved the outhouse door open and suddenly came face to face with Ms. Agatha.

"Well then...," smirked Ms. Agatha from behind her glasses. "I'm quite pleased that I chose to wear my leopard print belt today, otherwise it would be rather embarrassing if my trousers fell down and revealed my hairy baboon backside."

"I'm...I'm...so...sorry," I sputtered, glaring at Nate and Logan, who were bent over in hysterics behind Ms. Agatha. "I really don't think you have a hairy monkey butt..."

Stepping aside, Ms. Agatha said, "Never mind young man, I need to have a private conversation with you."

With her clipboard tucked securely under her arm and

one of Griffin's towels draped over her shoulder, Ms. Agatha led me to a far corner in the cavern. "Sit here, if you please," said Ms. Agatha, patting a large flat boulder to her left. Hurriedly scrambling up the smooth boulder, I sat down and dangled my legs out in front of me.

From a hundred yards away, Ms. Agatha and I watched Logan and Nate sprint across the grass and then somersault onto the picnic blanket.

"I have some news that you may find upsetting," said Ms. Agatha, laying her clipboard upside down next to me.

"Okay," I replied apprehensively.

"Alekzander has gone missing," said Ms. Agatha uneasily. "He cannot be reached. Even our most advanced telepaths have not been able to reach him since last night."

"That's not good," I replied trying not to giggle as I watched Nate do a crazy jig for Anne on the picnic blanket.

"No, it is not good at all," said Ms. Agatha seriously. "We have been trying desperately to track his location for the last twenty-four hours..."

"Well, how can I help?" I asked, quickly glancing up at Ms. Agatha.

"I am glad you asked because I need to know everything Alekzander discussed with you before he left," replied Ms. Agatha. "Every single detail."

I looked up at Ms. Agatha and asked, "But I thought Alekzander and you already discussed what happened at the G.R.D.D. and what's been going on since then."

"Humor me," smirked Ms. Agatha smoothly.

I sat up straight, looked over at Nate, and then back at Ms. Agatha, beginning to feel a little bit uncomfortable.

"I...I'm not so sure that-"

"It may help us locate Alekzander," said Ms. Agatha quickly. "You do want to help us find Alekzander, don't you?" she asked, placing her hand firmly on my shoulder.

"I do, but-" I said apprehensively, looking down at my lap.

"Are you aware that you are a prime suspect in Alekzander's disappearance?" chided Ms. Agatha as she reached down, grabbed my chin, and brought my face up to meet hers.

"I didn't have anything to do with Alekzander's disappearance!" I exclaimed anxiously.

Ms. Agatha grimaced as she shook her head. "I believe you my dear, but I daresay that others don't see it that way," she said puckering her lips and furrowing her brow, "but I can protect you if you tell me all you know."

I took a deep breath, rubbed my still damp hair, and whispered. "Okay...Alekzander told me that I needed to be careful because if someone found out I had two powers, they might try and use me to release the powers in the amulet."

"Interesting," replied Ms. Agatha. "Did he also tell you about a former camper by the name of Nero?"

"Yes, he said that I'm related to him," I replied, "but he didn't explain how."

Ms. Agatha looked eagerly into my eyes and asked, "Did he divulge the location of the amulet to you?"

"No, of course not," I replied. "He never would have told me that."

Lowering her head, Ms. Agatha looked deeper into my eyes as she probed further. "What else...what else did he tell you?" she asked, her green irises quickly flashing to a brilliant blue and then back to green. "I must know all that you talked about."

"No more," I whispered. "I have to get back to my training now."

"Well, that's a start," said Ms. Agatha as she gave me a quick smile and haphazardly flung her clipboard under her arm. "I will be calling on you again very soon."

"Okay," I replied, nervously sliding down off of the rock as Ms. Agatha turned her back on me and marched off. I suddenly felt a tight knot in my stomach as I watched Ms. Agatha walk past the Maverics and exit the passageway without saying a word to anyone else. Taking in a slow deep breath, I wondered whether I had made a mistake by telling her about my discussion with Alekzander.

"Tate! Tate!" yelled Nate waving his arms over his head from across the grassy field, "We need you!"

"Coming!" I shouted as I jogged to the picnic blanket.

"We've got to get back to camp," said Little Red packing up her backpack.

"By why?" I asked. "We just got here...We haven't even started our training yet."

"We know," replied Griffin, anxious snatching up the picnic blanket from off of the ground and stuffing it into his backpack. "We just got word, over our talkies, that someone else has been attacked on campus."

"What?... When?"

"Not sure how long ago," replied Little Red, "but some campers from Crusader II are on their way to teleport us out of here. Now please go stand over by the rest of the campers."

I walked over to Nate, Anne, Logan, and Dolores who were standing in a semicircle, clutching their gear tightly and not saying a word.

With backpacks haphazardly stuffed and thrown over their shoulders, Little Red and Griffin joined us. "Remember," said Little Red, "Each of you will have your own guide to teleport you back to camp. Please be sure to keep a tight grip on your tele-guide's hand until you complete the teleportation process."

"What happens if I let go?" asked Nate.

"You'll be lost."

"Lost where?"

"To the darkness. Stuck eternally between one location and the next," replied Little Red seriously.

"Trust us, it is not a good place to be," frowned Griffin.

"That'd be one rough game of hid-n-go-seek," replied Nate. "I'd better hold on tightly then."

"Or let go," sneered Dolores. "I wouldn't mind, and you wouldn't be missed."

Nate stuck his tongue at Dolores just as the teleporter's appeared in the cavern.

" POOF! "

All at once, five students from Crusader II and Lance Phillips from the Celer cabin appeared before us in an enormous cloud of stenchy gray smoke.

Nate waved his hand past his nose. "Whew!" he moaned, "There's that farty smell again."

I sniffed the air. Nate was right. It was the same horrible stench we smelled in the cave about an hour before.

"Why are there only six tele-guides?" asked Little Red looking at the new arrivals. "There are seven of us."

Lance stepped forward and puffed up his chest. "Because I convinced Nicholas that I'm more than capable of taking two transportees," he said confidently.

"You can't take two, that's extremely unstable," replied Little Red.

"Not for someone who's been properly trained at the academy," sneered Lance, "but I guess a *seasoned camper* like yourself wouldn't have a clue about being *properly trained,* now, would you?"

By the look on her face, I could tell Little Red was furious, but she just bit her lip and turned away as Lance pushed past her.

Lance flung his hands out towards Logan and me. "Grab my hands and be quick about it because I have more important things to do than to be a little baby boy taxi service," he said impatiently.

Logan and I grabbed hold of Lance's hands as the rest of our cabin met their transportation partners. Nate gave me a weird look as he grabbed the right hand of a tall girl with shoulder-length black hair tied back with a yellow ribbon.

"What?" I projected.

"Good luck with that jerk, Lance Phillips!"

"He's trying to be a show-off."

I only had a couple of seconds to take one last look around our training grounds before Lance, Logan, and I disappeared into the unknown.

" POOF! "

Seconds later, Nate, Logan, Anne, and I were standing shoulder to shoulder in front of the dining hall with the rest of the first-year campers. Winding her way through the crowd, Kate joined us. "Have you heard what's going on?" she asked.

"We did, but only minutes ago," Anne replied nervously. "Do you know who the victim was?"

"Rumor is that it's one of the telepaths from the Animo cabin. I'm just glad it's not any of you because when I heard, I just assumed it might have been...," said Kate, her voice trailing off as she looked over at Nate and me.

Anne reached over and patted Kate on her shoulder. "We're all okay," she said gently. "We've been sticking together."

Kate sighed and then whispered, "That's good."

Ms. Agatha suddenly appeared in a puff of gray smoke, holding hands with the same telepath that transported Nate. "Thank you," said Ms. Agatha before she stepped forward and stood next to Nicholas Knight.

Nicholas nodded his head towards Ms. Agatha, then turned to us and announced, "Campers, Ms. Agatha now has the floor."

"Thank you, Nicholas," replied Ms. Agatha as she reached up and shakily adjusted her glasses. "I apologize for summoning you back in the middle of your first training day, but unfortunately, we've had another mishap at camp."

I looked over at Nate and mouthed the words, 'Mishap?'

"It appears that another one of our campers has lost her powers, akin to the predicament yesterday with Calder Locke. Currently, Miss Samantha Lee is not conscious, but like Calder, she is being expertly attended to by Nurse Carter in the infirmary."

I inched in closer to Nate as a nervous whisper resonated through the crowd.

"Please, do not fret," said Ms. Agatha, holding her hand up to silence the crowd. "Like Calder, Miss Lee is in stable condition. I have been in contact with Alekzander. He will be returning tomorrow after he ties up a few loose ends at the N.H.B. He will collect Samantha and return her safely to her parents. From there, we will decide on our next best steps. Until then, he and I have agreed that it is in your best interest to remain locked down in your cabins until his return. Once you are dismissed from here, you will have thirty minutes to get your affairs in order, but you will need to remain locked down thereafter, only leaving for meals, and always with at least one other companion."

"What...What did she just say?" I projected to Nate, suddenly feeling like I wanted to throw up.

"We're locked down to our cabins."

"No, No! Who did she say she just spoke to?"

"Alekzander, I think, but I wasn't really listenin-"

"She couldn't have!"

"She's a big girl, I'm pretty sure she can talk to whomever she wants."

"That's not what I mean. She just told me five minutes ago, back in Maveric Cave, that Alekzander had gone missing and that no one could find him."

"Well...maybe she just found him."

"I don't think so...something's not right."

Ms. Agatha was still discussing the parameters of the lockdown when I asked Kate to bend down so I could whisper something in her ear.

"I need you to sneak a peek at Ms. Agatha's clipboard," I said cupping my hands around her ear as I spoke.

Kate stood up and looked me directly in the eyes as said, "Those papers are strictly confidential. She'd kick me out of camp for sure if she knew I'd peeked at her clipboard," hissed Kate.

Kate looked around at the crowd and then up at Ms. Agatha.

"Listen...I need you to do this! It's life or death...seriously," I pleaded.

"I can't."

"You don't have to read her private papers. Just tell me if she has a lot of notes scribbled on her clipboard, that's all."

Kate took a deep breath. "Fine," she said, finally relenting, "but you owe me."

"Fine," I said, "but please make sure-"

"Done," said Kate.

"Well?"

"I didn't read the papers if that's what you want to know," replied Kate irritably.

"I only need to know what the sheet of paper on her clipboard looked like?" I asked desperately.

"Which one?" asked Kate. "She has a dozen sheets attached to her clipboard with tons of notes scribbled on them...Why?"

My whole body suddenly felt hot like it was on fire. I could feel my forehead getting sweaty as I stood on my tippy toes and placed my lips right into Kate's ear. "Listen,

Kate," I whispered. "I've been keeping a secret from you but please don't hold it against me right now."

"What are you talking about?" asked Kate sounding even more irritated.

"Not only can I talk to animals, but...*I'm telepathic too and I think I'm about to become the next victim.*"

Chapter Eight

Room A113

Kate sat with us in a small tight circle in the far corner of the Maveric cabin. I looked out the cabin window to make sure the coast was clear. Satisfied that no one else was around to overhear our conversation, except for Griffin who was snoring loudly on his bunk, his baseball cap pulled over his eyes, I began to talk.

"Thanks for coming…I have some things to tell you even though Alekzander asked me not to," I whispered, leaning in close, "but because we all may be in serious trouble, I think it's okay now."

"Go on," said Logan, looking anxious as he brushed his hair out of his face and pushed his glasses up the bridge of his nose. "You can trust us."

"Okay here goes," I said taking a deep breath and looking everybody briefly in the eyes. "As you already know, most superheroes have one special ability."

"Yes, except for that scoundrel, Nero," said Anne. "He had two."

"Well, actually there have been a couple other campers at Crusader in the past, besides Nero, that have had two powers."

"How'd you come by that information?" asked suspiciously Kate. "It didn't say that in the camp Q & A Booklet."

"Alekzander told me," I replied cautiously.

"Alekzander as in *The* Alexzander?" asked Kate. "Why would he tell you that information?"

"And more importantly, did he give you specific names?" asked Anne.

"Yeah, spill the beans, Bro," added Nate.

"He didn't give me any specific names," I replied, "but each of the individuals with multiple powers were related to Nero in some way."

"Must be some power anomaly that runs in that family genes," replied Logan.

Anne scowled, "Well, that doesn't seem fair. I mean why should people in that disgraceful bloodline have two powers when the rest of us-"

"I have two," I blurted out, quickly looking down at my feet.

"Inconceivable!" yelped Logan.

Sitting up taller, I looked across the room to make sure Griffin was still sound asleep and then I continued. "And... apparently, the three of us are related to Nero..." I said looking at Nate and Kate.

"Double inconceivable!" yelped Logan again.

Nate shifted uneasily on his bottom. "But how can that be? We didn't even know we had superpowers until a few days ago."

"And now we find out we're related to an evil madman..." finished Kate. "Maybe that's why Mom and Dad didn't allow us to attend Crusader for all these years."

"That's not all," I whispered.

"Hold the phone," growled Kate. "There's more?"

"Unfortunately..." I said feeling sick to my stomach again. "...Alekzander believes that I may even have a third power, the ability to extract and grant powers just like Nero did when he was alive."

"Whoa, whoa, whoa!" grumbled Nate. "What you're saying is, you get three powers and I have one lousy power? That doesn't seem fair that the youngest child in the family gets to have-"

"I didn't choose to have extra powers!" I exclaimed irritably. "Just like you and Kate, I didn't choose to be related to Nero."

"Tate's right, he can't be blamed for any of this...None of us can," replied Kate.

Logan leaned in closer and asked, "Did Alekzander say how you three are related to Nero? I mean maybe you're like Nero's second cousin's roommate's uncle or something obscure like that."

"I don't think we are. We must be pretty closely related for Alekzander to bring it up," I replied. "Both he and Ms. Agatha have been trying to keep my second power a secret because Nero's siblings have been trying to find the amulet for a long time now. Alekzander was afraid if word got out, Nero's family, our relatives, would force me to extract the powers from the amulet and release Nero in the process."

"Well, we just have to make sure no one finds out you have two or more powers," said Anne pretending to zip her lip. "You can trust me and Logan, we won't say a word."

"That's not the problem," I muttered. "I know you two won't rat me out but someone else at camp just found out my secret."

"But how?" asked Kate. "You've been with Nate the whole time. I mean, I can see Nate making a mess of things...but you?"

"Hey!" barked Nate.

"I accidentally told someone," I said looking away from Kate.

"What?" barked Kate. "How do you *accidentally* tell someone that you have multiple powers and that you're related to Nero?"

"I'm afraid that I may have mucked things up," I said cautiously looking back at Kate, "because back in the cave, I thought that I was talking to Ms. Agatha."

"But that *was* Ms. Agatha back in Crusader Cave an hour or two ago," replied Nate.

"I don't think it was," I replied. "Just someone made up to look like her."

"You mean like, someone used Hollywood special effects or something?" asked Kate.

"More like a shape shifter," interrupted Logan.

"Sure, a shoplifter," replied Nate. "I'm sure the imposter was trying to steal a loaf of bread and bottle of root beer from our pic-i-nic basket, Boo-Boo."

"Not a shoplifter, dork," snapped Kate. "A shapeshifter."

Logan smirked as he sat up straighter and adjusted his glasses. "Shape shifting is an extremely rare power that allows individuals to take the form of another living thing."

"But Tate, what makes you think that wasn't the real Agatha we saw earlier today?" asked Anne.

"Because the fake Ms. Agatha asked me things that I know Alekzander already told her," I replied, "and she was also carrying around a clipboard."

"Which Ms. Agatha does," replied Kate skeptically. "She carries that thing around constantly."

"That's why I had you take a closer look at her clipboard a few minutes ago because I caught a glimpse of her clipboard right before she tried to hide it from me when we were back in the cave."

"What'd you see on it?" asked Nate.

"The fake Ms. Agatha had only one blank sheet of paper on her clipboard with a couple scribbles on it, but mysteriously a few minutes later, during our emergency camp meeting, her clipboard was filled with tons of papers with notes scrawled all over them."

"Tate's right," confirmed Kate. "I checked the real Ms. Agatha's clipboard for him, and she had pages and pages of notes."

"And get this," I said, "just for a moment when I was talking to her in the Crusader Cave, her eyes flashed from green to blue and then to green again...I thought I was seeing things."

"And that, my wise Sherlockian Holmes, is the one and only way to tell a shapeshifter apart from a real person," confirmed Logan.

"Their eyes change colors?" asked Kate.

"Not only that," replied Logan, "because one of the drawbacks to being a shapeshifter is that they sometimes glitch. Which means if you're super observant you might see a freckle appear on their chin or their fingernails suddenly grow longer for a brief second, but most of the time it happens too quickly to spot. And the funny thing is, generally the shape shifter doesn't even know they glitched."

"How do you know all these facts?" asked Nate.

"From the Encyclopedia of Super Abilities," responded Logan.

"You just made that up!" giggled Nate. "There's no such thing as an en-clo-peed-i-a."

"It's called an encyclopedia," chuckled Logan. "It's a resource book with information in it, similar to the internet but only a lot slower.

"Oh, it's one of those things," Nate replied, shaking his head. "Kind of like the olden days when my dad walked to school in the snow with holes in his shoes, uphill both ways."

Anne covered her mouth and giggled behind her fingers.

"I just happen to know a lot about superpowers because I've been researching every possible super ability since I was six...in my old-fashioned *en...clo...pee...di...a*," smirked Logan.

Kate shook her head as she looked from Logan to Nate. "But we can't just accuse someone of being a shape shifter unless you specifically catch them in the act."

"And an empty clipboard isn't enough to prove that someone's been impersonating Ms. Agatha," concluded Anne. "Do you have any more proof than that?"

"I got nothing else," I replied, "but I think Dolores Diablo may be involved in all of this as well."

"I knew the Double D was a baddie!" exclaimed Nate. "She's a grouch and her breath smells worse than an onion eating hippopotamus with harry-toes-us."

Logan reached over and shoved Nate's shoulder playfully. "The scientific name for bad breath is halitosis," he chuckled.

"But be that as it may," scowled Kate, "You can't just go around accusing someone of being evil because they have bad breath."

Nate crossed his arms in front of his chest. "I can and I will," he griped.

"Anyway," said Logan looking over at me, "I do have a little more information on shapeshifters that you may find interesting."

"Do tell," replied Kate.

Logan pushed his glasses up the bridge of his nose and continued. "A shape shifter only has enough energy to shape shift two or three times a day, maximum. Also, something else important to note...A shape shifter not only takes the physical appearance of someone or something, but they also take on the corresponding energy level of their victim."

"Meaning what?" asked Nate.

Logan sat up straighter. "Okay let me explain it this way. If a shapeshifter takes the place of a grizzly bear then they become big, strong, fast, and powerful. However, if a shapeshifter takes the place of the bear during winter, then the shapeshifter becomes big and powerful, but also tired, sleepy, and lethargic."

"So, if a shapeshifter changes into something dying, say like a fish out of water, then the shapeshifter will die also?" I asked.

"Precisely," replied Logan. "Unless of course, the shapeshifter can quickly transform again, before that happens, and *if* the shapeshifter has enough remaining energy to do so."

"Sounds like a weakness to me," said Nate.

"Which can be exploited," finished Anne. "Under the right circumstances."

"I may have a little more proof that Dolores could be the shapeshifter," I replied hesitantly, "besides her bad breath of course."

"Continue," said Logan looking at me inquisitively.

"Well, do you remember when Little Red and Griffin ditched us in the cave today and Nate thought somebody farted...twice?"

"Nate!" frowned Kate. "I can't leave you alone for one minute without you embarrassing our family."

"What?" asked Nate. "I didn't let a stinky one go in the cave."

"No, it wasn't you...at least not that time it wasn't," I replied.

Nate grinned at me and asked, "So, are you claiming Dolores cut the cheese?"

"Enough about farting you too," moaned Kate. "It's disgusting!"

Ignoring Kate's plea, I continued. "No, but I think Dolores teleported out of the cave and then back into the cave, while we were in the dark. That nasty odor we smelled had a similar stink that teleporters make when they travel from place to place."

"And guess who wasn't saying a thing when we were trapped in the dark," added Anne, tapping her fingertips together as she contemplated. "That does make a lot of sense."

"...and it just so happens that thirty minutes later we find out that Samantha's powers were stolen," I whispered. "I think Dolores can either teleport or had someone teleport her in and out of the cave so she could steal Samantha's powers."

"Curse Double D!" barked Nate as he slammed his fist into his hand.

"It sounds like we have some investigating to do to find out if Dolores is really involved in this," said Kate.

"And we probably should try to obtain the amulet," added Logan.

Anne looked at Logan as if he'd completely gone mad. "Are you crazy?" she asked, "Why in the world would we want to find the amulet? We need to keep that thing away far away from these three, so no one gets hurt!"

"I respectfully disagree because it seems someone is determined to locate the amulet," said Logan confidently, "So, I say we find it first and then hide it where no one will ever find it."

"But people have been looking for the amulet for years and so far, no one has found it," replied Kate.

"Yet," responded Logan, "but that shouldn't stop us from trying to find it because we're pretty smart when we put our heads together."

"And whoever is looking for the amulet will be *really* motivated to find it now that they know Tate may be able to unlock it," finished Nate.

"I think it's a good plan," I replied, "but maybe we should go and see if we can find the real Ms. Agatha or another adult to help first."

Nate shook his head back and forth vigorously, "Are you kidding? Adults can't be trusted...I don't think they know what they are doing half the time anyway."

"What about finding a trustworthy camper that has been at Crusader long enough to know where we should start looking for room A113," suggested Anne. "Maybe a staff member or counselor?"

Nate grinned from ear to ear, "I know just the right person for the job, she'll be super excited to help!"

"Are you insane?" asked Little Red, scratching the dirt with the toes of her shoes outside the Maveric cabin. "After all you just told me, and you still want to go looking for the amulet? You're just asking for trouble."

"I know, but think of it this way, we can re-hide the amulet, so someone won't be able to surprise attack us with it," Nate said, looking up at Little Red.

"We'll have more control over the situation because we can hide it well and check on it regularly," I added.

"But it's already hidden well," replied Little Red not looking very impressed.

"But ninety-nine percent of this camp has probably been picked over the past forty-something years," said Logan. "Which leaves very few places left for the baddie to search. He or she will find it sooner than later."

Kate stepped forward and stood next to Little Red. "Maybe Red's right," said Kate, "Why don't we just hang tight and let the real Agatha handle this because she's more than cap-."

"But I thought we agreed that Agatha's been compromised," interrupted Nate.

"And that is a legitimate reason to keep her out of all of this," agreed Logan.

Little Red ran her fingers through her hair and looked at all of us without saying a word.

"Come on, do it for your father," I added. "Alekzander may be in some serious trouble for all we know."

"I'm responsible for you all so I just can't let you go traipsing around Crusader looking for the amulet-"

"But we need your help," I replied.

"You didn't let me finish," said Little Red looking me straight in the eyes. "...As I was saying, I am responsible for you all and I won't let you go around traipsing through Crusader...without me."

I reached over and gave Nate a high five, he gave Logan a high five, and then Logan gave Anne a high five.

"It's good to have someone older than fourteen on our side," grinned Logan. "You're practically an adult."

"Not quite," replied Little Red looking like she was about to blush.

"So where do we start looking?" I interrupted.

Anne turned and looked at Little Red and asked, "Do you have any idea where room A113 could be?"

"Possibly...Like Logan said earlier, campers have been all over this place looking for Room A113 for a long time, and some places have been searched a dozen times over."

"So how can we expect to be successful if thousands of campers have already failed in locating the amulet?" asked Kate.

"It does appear hopeless," sighed Anne.

"Not completely," replied Little Red. "You see, you have something that all those other campers didn't have."

"What's that?" asked Nate. "A winning smile and sparkling attitude?"

"Nope," replied Little Red, patting her chest and grinning. "You've got me."

"No offense," replied Nate, "but how are you any different than all the other campers or staff members here?"

"None of them have spent day after day on this campus. I live here full-time, year-round because Alekzander homeschools me. This is my home and because it's my home, I think I may have figured out the location of the amulet."

"You have?" asked Logan, "But after all this time, why haven't you retrieved it?"

"It's in a horrible place," replied Little Red.

"Is it locked in a haunted room full of ghosts?" asked Logan.

"No haunted room or ghosts."

"Has it been swallowed by an acid-spitting dragon and the only way to get it out is to have an alien burst out of its chest with the amulet in its mouth, showering everyone with sticky guts and squishy intestines?" asked Nate.

I laughed as Logan reached over, patted Nate on the shoulder, and chuckled, "Man, you've got a lot of weird stuff bouncing around inside your head."

"Thanks," chuckled Nate.

Little Red shortened her legs and then beckoned us to form a circle around her. "The amulet is in a place so revolting that no one would ever contemplate going there," she whispered.

"I knew it!" yelped Nate. "It's in Dolores's underwear drawer."

"Hush!" giggled Anne.

"Nope, worse than that," said Little Red lowering her voice to a whisper. "It's in a toilet."

"The amulet is in a toilet?" asked Anne.

"No, the room that's storing the amulet is in a toilet."

"What?" chuckled Nate, "and Logan thought I had some weird ideas!"

"No, listen," whispered Little Red seriously. "There are six outhouses spread throughout Crusader Camp I and II. Three of them are in our camp, which we lovingly call Baby Camp, and three outhouses are in Crusader II. Outhouse A is located at the Proving Ground, Outhouse B is located in Crusader Cave, and Outhouse C is located at the edge of the woods near the entrance of camp. I believe they are all connected underneath by a series of caverns, passageways, and vaults."

"But what makes you think that one of the outhouses is a portal to room A113?" asked Kate.

"*Hello*! Because it's a portal-potty!" giggled Nate hysterically.

Logan and I chuckled while Kate and Anne rolled their eyes as Little Red continued. "Each outhouse, or portal-potty as Nate lovingly calls them, have been holding clues to the whereabouts of the amulet for years."

"Clues in outhouses," said Anne looking a little queasy. "That's pretty revolting."

"And brilliant!" exclaimed Logan. "I mean, who'd ever suspect?"

"So then, how'd you discover it?" asked Kate.

"Last summer, it all just clicked while I was adding another year to my outhouse graffiti at the proving ground," explained Little Red. "That was when I suddenly realized that there are similar messages on all of the outhouses."

"I've been in two of them," I replied.

"Then you probably remember the message written on the wall in the Crusader Cave outhouse that says, 'To get Outhouse "B" cleaned, dial 718-0114."

"Yes," I replied, "but the outhouse at the proving ground says the same thing."

"Not quite," grinned Little Red. "The message in that outhouse says, 'To get Outhouse "A" cleaned, dial 718-0113."

"And there's your A and 113," replied Kate clicking her fingers. "Outstanding detective work, Red."

"Thanks, I thought so too, but I needed to dig a little deeper," said Little Red. "That's why I've spent over a hundred hours examining the proving grounds outhouse for secret buttons, levers, or anything unusual, but I have yet to come up with anything. Which leads me to believe that room A113 is actually down in the toilet muck, but I'm still not one hundred percent sure."

"Well, it appears we've hit a dead-end because no one would be foolish enough to dive down into a toilet that's been collecting human waste since gosh knows when," said Kate frowning at Anne.

"Don't look at me," groaned Anne. "I'm trying my hardest to not throw up right now."

"What about him?" asked Logan pointing at Nate. "He's downright crazy enough."

"What?" yelped Nate. "You want me to go swimming in a stinky old toilet full of who knows what to find a magical ruby that contains the soul of a madman?"

"Sounds like a very strange plot to a twisted book," I snickered.

"It does," chuckled Little Red.

Nate scowled, scratched his head, and then asked, "Have any of you heard the joke about the guy that accidentally dropped a dollar bill down an outhouse toilet?"

"This is not really a time for a joke," Kate said looking at Nate disapprovingly.

Nate ignored Kate and continued, "So, this man's friend came in just as the man opened his wallet, took out a twenty-dollar bill, and purposely threw it into the outhouse toilet, right next to the dollar bill. Confused, his friend asked, 'Why would you throw a perfectly good twenty-dollar bill down the outhouse toilet?' The man replied, 'Well you didn't think I'd go down in that muck for just a dollar, did you?"

Kate and Anne stared at Logan and me as we laughed until we were out of breath. Once we stopped to inhale, Kate folded her arms across her chest and asked, "So, what is that joke supposed to mean?"

Scrunching up his face like he was thinking really hard, Nate finally replied, "That means... I guess I'm going swimming an outhouse toilet since there's a valuable ruby down at the bottom."

"Well then, we have ourselves a brave volunteer," said Little Red looking pleased. "We can slip out in the middle of dinner tonight, one at a time. If you get caught, just tell whoever that I'll be personally escorting you back to your cabins."

"But I'm not convinced Nate should be swimming in a toilet full of... full of..." sputtered Kate, "I just don't think Mom would approve."

"I don't think Mom would approve of the bad guys hurting Tate, or any one of us for that matter," replied Nate, patting Kate on her shoulder. "Just let me do my thing, Sis."

"Fine," said Kate finally relenting, "but just make sure you take a long hot shower afterward."

"You got it," grinned Nate. "Now let's get some chow before I go swimming in an enormous warm tank of poo!"

Sneaking out of the mess hall during dinner was easier than any one of us could have imagined. Most of the counselors were busy running around trying to make last-minute preparations for the lockdown so we didn't end up seeing most of them, including Griffin. Standing behind the outhouse in the fading daylight, we anxiously watched as Nate stripped down into the swim trunks that he had on under his blue jeans and tee-shirt.

"Well, I guess I'm ready to deep-sea dive down the toilet," he said concealing his clothes in the knee-high grass behind the outhouse.

"I don't believe I'll hear anyone make a statement like that ever again," chuckled Logan.

"I think you're right," giggled Anne, covered her smile with her hand.

Little Red looked around the corner of the outhouse towards the twinkling lights of the dining hall. "Looks like the coast is clear," she said nudging us onward.

One at a time, we carefully tiptoed out from behind the outhouse and slipped through the rickety doorway. Because the space inside the outhouse was so cramped, Nate had to balance precariously on top of the faded pink toilet seat so we could all squeeze in, everyone that was, except for Anne, who happily volunteered to stand outside and be the lookout for the time being. Once Little Red closed the door behind her, she turned on her flashlight and shined the beam on Nate's feet.

"Whatever you do," whispered Little Red, "you've got to be quick about it because we only have about forty-five minutes until camp goes on complete lock down for the night."

"Got it," replied Nate. "I'm going to use my own powers to trick my senses into thinking that I'm diving down into a pool of chunky chocolate pudding."

"Did you have to go there?" moaned Logan, completely covering his mouth and nose with his hand.

"He always goes there," replied Kate shaking her head. "You should see him when he's not on his medication."

"Yep, I'm what they call a hot mess, but I'm about to get a whole lot messier, " said Nate proudly as he stepped down off the toilet seat and onto the floor, forcing our backs up against the outhouse walls. Reaching down, Nate grabbed hold of the toilet seat and lifted it up. We half looked down into the dark muck, trying not to gag at the horrible smell that engulfed the outhouse.

"Maybe we should come up with a different plan," said Logan plugging his nose. "We can't expect Nate to dive down in that stenchy sludge."

"I disagree," replied Little Red. "With his ability to manipulate his sense, Nate's our best shot at locating the amulet."

Nate pounded on his bare chest and said, "Don't worry everybody. Me got this!"

"I'm glad somebody does," moaned Logan, turning his head away from the toilet.

Taking two deep breaths and rubbing his hands together, Nate confidently climbed back up onto the open toilet and looked down into the putrid pit of sewage. "Forget it, I'm not going to imagine this is chocolate pudding..." scowled Nate.

"Thank goodness because that's a horrible, horrible...image," sputtered Logan.

"It looks more like a giant root beer float with lots of gooey swirls of vanilla soft serve ice cream anyway," snorted Nate.

"I think I'm gonna' be sick," moaned Logan, looking a little green in the face. "Please hurry up..."

"Fine...Here goes nothing," whispered Nate as he closed his eyes and slowly counted down, "7...6...5...4..."

Anne peeked her head through the outhouse door while Kate and Logan covered their eyes.

Even though the smell was making me sick to my stomach, I couldn't look away because this was a once-in-a-lifetime opportunity to watch someone take a dip in an outhouse toilet.

"3...2...1..." whispered Nate, his foot dangling just inches above the chunky muck.

I held my breath as Nate began to slowly lower his foot into the thick filth below. "Root beer float...root beer float..." he repeated over and over again.

I looked over at Little Red just as she took a deep breath and held it, her cheeks bulging out like a fully inflated puffer fish.

"Root beer float...Root beer float!" chanted Nate as his toes touched the thick sludge, "ROOTBEER FLOAT! ROOTBEER FLOAT!"

Starting to get queasy, I wondered if I was about to throw up, just as I saw the contents of the toilet turn from dark brown to a brilliant blue. While everyone else was looking away, including Nate, I watched my twin lower his whole foot into what appeared to be a beautiful, glowing tropical, outhouse ocean.

"Stop!" I cried, rubbing my eyes to make sure I was seeing what I was seeing.

"What?" yelped Little Red, shining the flashlight directly into my face.

"Down there!" I exclaimed, pointing at Nate, who was now half-submerged in the toilet. "Point the flashlight down there!"

Little Red lowered the flashlight, shining it directly on Nate, who was now submerged up to this neck in crystal clear water.

"Amazing!" cooed Logan. "It's almost as blue as the ocean in Waikiki. I'm kind of expecting to spot a sea turtle swimming down there with you."

"Probably won't see a turtle down here. More like a big brown trout!" laughed Nate looking down at his feet.

"Again, with the inappropriate comments," scowled Kate.

"But how can this be?" I asked. "It changed right before our eyes."

"Maybe it's the horrible fumes in here," replied Logan nervously. "It's driven us all mad!"

Kate turned and looked at Anne who was still peering in from the doorway, "But Anne can see this from the doorway, and she hasn't inhaled nearly as many fumes as we have. Right Anne?"

"I can see clear water, too," responded Anne.

"I think it's real, fresh water because it's warm," said Nate.

"It's a pot full of poo that's been stewing down there for more than eighty years, it's going to be warm either way!" snickered Logan.

"It does look like clean, fresh water though," replied Little Red.

"Either Nate has manipulated our sense or Alekzander has," replied Logan. "A great trick too, because no one in their right mind would ever think about searching down there for the amulet."

"Good thing I'm not in my right mind," said Nate sucking some water into his mouth and spitting it out at us like a sprinkler.

"I still probably wouldn't have done that," moaned Kate.

"Why not? It's delicious!" beamed Nate as he happily bobbed up and down, "...I just love my portal-potty!"

"Can you dive below the surface and see how deep this goes?" asked Little Red shining her flashlight down at Nate's feet. "It looks like there's something just underneath you, perhaps the amulet or a door?"

"Sure, just a sec," said Nate quickly disappearing under the water. We watched as Nate swam down and disappeared just out of the sight of the flashlight beam.

"I'm not going down there to rescue him if he gets stuck, even if that water *does* come straight from Hawaii," muttered Logan.

As if right on cue, Nate popped up out of the water and said, "I'd say this water is about ten feet deep. There's a large pipe just at the bottom and a bit to the left. If you swim into the pipe, it shoots straight up for about four feet and then, *dumps*, pun intended, you into a small underground room."

"Sounds like some of us will need to take the plunge with you because I can't have you exploring a potentially dangerous underground room all by yourself," replied Little Red.

"I volunteer," I blurted out. "I've never been to Hawaii before, especially Toilet Hawaii!"

"I guess I'm in as well," replied Kate. "It won't hurt to have an extra set of eyes on Nate."

"Yippee, Mommies coming along!" scowled Nate sarcastically.

"Count me in too," replied Anne from the doorway. "It'll be fun."

"I'll guess I'll go, too," said Logan looking down at the toilet suspiciously, "but I can't help thinking that my mom would've sent along a snorkel, or at least some hand sanitizer if she knew one of our summer camp activities was going to be competitive outhouse swimming."

"Oh, so now all of you want to take a dip in my secret swim spot...funny how that happened. Just a few moments ago, no one wanted to take a dip, when you all thought I was swimming in warm poo," chuckled Nate.

"That appears to be the case," replied Little Red, as she climbed onto the toilet seat and looked down from high-atop her pink throne. "Well, time's a waist'n," she said, "so let's get crack'n!"

Chapter Nine

The Amulet

One by one, each of us leapt into the toilet with Anne being the last to take the plunge. It was an easy swim straight down through the crystal clear waters and into a large pipe at the bottom left of the toilet. After a quick three strokes straight up, we pulled ourselves out of the pool of water into a small solid gray granite room lit only by the sparkling blue water below us.

Squeezing the excess water out of her hair, Kate looked over at Little Red and said, "We should probably get moving so we don't run out of time."

"Agreed," replied Little Red, pulling out a damp green scrunchie from her pocket and tying her damp hair back. "Looks like the only way out of this room is down this very dark and creepy staircase," she said pointing to a black spiral staircase that disappeared into a dark unnerving abyss below.

"I'm not going first," blurted Nate. "I've already volunteered once tonight already!"

"I'll go first," replied Little Red. "Nate and Tate will follow behind me, followed by Anne, and Logan, with Kate pulling up the rear. Each of you put one hand on the railing and the other hand on the person's shoulder in front of you."

"Glad I'm not going to be the one to get eaten first," I nervously whispered as I placed my left hand on Nate's shoulder and grasped the cold metal railing with my right hand.

"So spooky," mumbled Nate as we descended into the quiet darkness.

Unable to see, I counted each stair in my head, feeling certain that the next step I was about to take was going to be my last. After nervously counting one hundred creaky stairs, we finally stepped onto solid ground.

"It's still so dark in here," whispered Anne.

"Nate, do you think you could use your powers to help us out?" asked Logan.

A faint glow of light suddenly lit up the small rocky room, casting eerie shadows upon the walls around us.

"Wow, Nate!" exclaimed Kate, sounding impressed. "That sure was fast."

"It wasn't me," chuckled Nate. "I'm good, but not that good!"

"It was me," snorted Little Red. "I kind of forgot that I stuck a waterproof flashlight in my back pocket when we were back at camp."

I sighed loudly and then muttered, "We could have used that flashlight five minutes ago when we were walking down that creepy staircase."

"Yes, we could have," replied Little Red, moving the flashlight directly under her chin so her face glowed eerily, "but wasn't it fun creeping down the dark stairs, wondering if something sinister was about to devour us at any moment?"

"Not really," I replied. "I'd much rather have had the flashlight on."

"Me, too," replied Logan.

"Doesn't really matter much now because there's probably something evil waiting behind that door anyway," said Nate, pointing to an old wooden door just to our left.

"For an outdoor camp, this place is full of doors in all kinds of weird places," I whispered.

"You should see some of the doors in Crusader II," replied Little Red as she reached out and eagerly tugged on the black iron door handle with both hands.

"What's behind the door? Is it bad news?" asked Logan as Little Red cracked the door open and looked inside.

Little Red grabbed the door with two hands and dramatically flung it wide open. "On the contrary, it's magnificent!" she exclaimed.

I couldn't believe my eyes as we walked into a cavern twice the size of Maveric Cave. Countless veins of glowing milky quartz and gleaming gold flecks covered the granite ceiling, walls, and floors all around us, lighting up the enormous room. Stepping further into the cave, I felt as if I was floating among a million golden stars, intermingled with powerful crackly veins of shimmering quartz lightning bolts.

"Amazing," I whispered, as my eyes followed an enormous pulsating vein that branched off into smaller crackling streaks, which ended at four massive vault doors, constructed into the solid rock.

"The amulet has to be behind one of these," said Little Red, stepping up to the first silver door and placing her ear on it.

"Or it could be down either of those two passageways," said Kate pointing to the far end of the cavern where two shadowy corridors branched off into opposite directions.

"It's more than likely behind this first vault door," said Logan walking up next to Little Red. "Being that the amulet is so important."

Anne walked over and carefully spun the silver and black combination lock on the vault door. "We are so close," she said smiling back at us. "This is so exciting."

Nate stepped forward and placed his ear on the cold vault door between Little Red and Anne. "What's that spooky noise coming from the vault?" he asked, his eyes growing wider. "It's whispering...the vault is whispering something."

"What are you going on about?" breathed Kate nervously as each of us cautiously stepped up and placed our ears against the vault door and held our breaths.

"Can you hear it?" asked Nate. "It's very unnerving."

"I can't hear anything," whispered Logan.

"I think I hear something," muttered Anne.

"It's saying beware..."

"Beware of what?" I whispered anxiously as a cold chill ran up the back of my spine.

"Beware of..."

"Beware of what?" I mouthed, "Beware of what?"

"Beware of the alphabet grenade because if you throw it, it could spell disaster!" snorted Nate.

"Ugh!" moaned Kate taking her ear off of the door and smacking Nate on the back of his head.

"Okay, enough bad dad jokes," chuckled Little Red. She reached out and placed her hand on the silver and black combination lock and slowly began to spin it. "We're running out of time. We need to hurry up and try to figure out the combination."

"Maybe it's Alekzander's three favorite numbers," suggested Logan.

"Out of one hundred," replied Kate. "That's an awful lot of numbers to choose from."

"It'll probably take all night to figure that one out," grumbled Anne. "Maybe we should come back tomorrow because someone's bound to discover that we're missing from our cabins."

"I disagree," countered Kate. "We came all this way. I think we should at least try some numbers while we're here. It'll only take a few more minutes and who knows, maybe we'll get lucky."

"I agree. Let's try a few different three number sets...but where to start?" asked Little Red tapping her chin.

"Maybe it's part of a phone number or zip code or something like that," suggested Logan.

"I guess I can try Alekzander's birthday, April 26, 1961," said Little Red spinning the combination to…04…26…61.

"That's a good start," I replied, as Little Red grabbed hold of the door handle and tugged.

"Nope, not his birthday," said Little Red. "The door didn't budge."

"What about the date the camp opened, something important like that?" suggested Kate.

"July 2, 1937…So maybe 07, 02, 37?" she said quickly spinning the dial and trying out the handle. "…Nope, not that one either."

"I think maybe we should head back if the next one doesn't work," said Anne sounding anxious. "I'd hate to get caught and kicked out of camp."

"A couple more," said Nate. "Who knows when we'll get another chance to get back here."

"Besides that, I think we're on the right track," I continued, "it's got to be a date that is important to him, but probably something no one else knows very well."

"I can't think of anything else, except maybe the address of this camp or the birthdates of his parents that live in Denver," said Little Red.

"What about the date he bought his first car?" suggested Logan.

"I don't know that," responded Little Red.

"What about you?" I asked looking up at Little Red.

"What about me?" asked Little Red. "You think it could be my birthday or something?"

"Of course," said Kate. "It's got to be something like that."

"Let me try my birthday…08…24…03," said Little Red as she spun the combination lock and pulled on the handle.

"No such luck," said Kate clicking her tongue.

"Well, it's time to go," said Anne looking more and more anxious.

"Just a couple more," I suggested.

"At this rate, it'll just be a couple more, then a couple more, then a couple more," rumbled Anne grumpily.

"Maybe the amulet is safer in there because no one else even knows about this cave's existence except for us."

The enormous room grew quiet as we all looked at the door in silence.

"How about just one more?" whispered Kate, "and then we go."

"But I really can't think of any other numbers that would be important to Alekzander," frowned Little Red.

"What about the date your adoption was finalized?" asked Logan.

"That's a good one," I replied. "There can't be a more important date to Alekzander than that."

Little Red smiled weakly. "It's an important date to me but I'm not sure about him," sighed Little Red. "I haven't been the nicest, kindest daughter lately..."

I gently reached up and grabbed hold of Little Red's hand. "We all have our good days and bad days," I whispered as I placed her hand on the combination lock. "Just give it a try."

"Last one," muttered Little Red as she carefully dialed 10...05...16.

"Come on, come on," whispered Nate under his breath.

Little Red let out a long slow breath as she tightened her grip on the handle and pulled. The door, as large and heavy as it looked, swung open easily.

"It worked," smiled Kate, patting Little Red on the back. "You did it!"

I looked up at Little Red and winked, "Looks like you are one of the most important dates in Alekzander's life."

Grinning from ear to ear, Little Red pulled the enormous door completely open. "Well, here we go," she declared. "Now, let's find the amulet."

We followed behind Little Red into the long, cold vault; our breaths sending little smoke signals up from our mouths to the high ceiling above.

"It's like a frozen museum in here," said Logan pointing at the countless white wooden tables meticulously lined in long rows inside the vault.

Leading us past a long white table piled high with gold, silver, and copper coins, Little Red firmly said, "Don't touch anything in here, not even the amulet if you find it."

"Let's split up," suggested Anne flashing a quick smile.

"I'm not so sure that's a good idea," replied Little Red. "I think we should-"

"Great!" chirped Anne, suddenly darting off towards the far back left corner of the vault by herself.

"What's gotten into her?" asked Kate as she watched Anne scamper off.

"I'll go with her," said Logan, winking at Nate behind his oversized glasses.

"Good idea," replied Nate, winking back at Logan.

"Uh, okay...I guess we're splitting up," muttered Little Red as Logan scurried after Anne like a lost puppy.

Nate grabbed my hand and said, "I'll go with Tate and you two girls stick together. Let us know if you find something."

Little Red chuckled as she gave Nate a half salute. "10-4, bossy britches," she said before she and Kate headed off down the long center aisle.

Carefully moving from table to table, Nate and I examined what appeared to be random garage sale items carefully organized on each table.

"What the heck is this?" I asked pointing at a raggedy multicolored, one-eyed, stuffed teddy bear that looked like it had been won as a prize at the county fair.

"Very random," Nate whispered as we moved to the next table filled with countless piles of keys, laid out and organized by color, shape, and size.

I pointed at a rusty keyring that had three skeleton-faced keys attached to it. "Creepy and random things," I said as I walked over to another table and examined an old brown leather glove with the knuckles cut out of it and a pair of round spectacles with bright silver frames.

"These aren't creepy," whispered Nate as he lightly ran his fingertips across the blade of a long silver broad sword and shield, carefully propped upright on a table.

"I'm pretty sure Little Red warned us not to touch anything," I said, frowning at Nate.

"I can't help if I'm a tactile learner," replied Nate, "besides, this shield has an awesome picture of an eagle's head and lion's body engraved on it, so I can't help but touch it."

"I think that's a manticore," I said, turning my attention to a tall clear vase filled with strange blue orbs that were bobbing up and down in what looked like thick white milk.

"I don't think it's a manticore," replied Nate, lightly tapping on the shield.

"Well, it's not the amulet," I replied reaching out and gently touching my fingertips on the clear vase. "This vase is freezing," I whispered to myself as I watched ice crystals form around my fingertips.

"Who's Mr. Touchy Pants, now?" asked Nate, glaring over at me, "...and just so you know...You may want to take your hand off that incredibly large boba drink before all your fingers freeze to it."

I gasped when I looked down at my fingers because three of them were almost completely encased in ice.

Without thinking, I quickly broke my ice-encrusted fingers away from the jar. "Kind of like dry ice," I whispered as the ice quickly dissipated into whisps of blue smoke right before my eyes.

Nate and I continued to move from table to table, examining dozens of fuzzy old white wigs, a globe and a map with unrecognizable lands and oceans printed on them, a dismantled golden cuckoo clock, and a dried-up bag of Moo-Moo Marshmallows.

"Keep moving," I said pushing Nate's hand away from the bag of shriveled marshmallows.

We examined table after table until we reached the last one in the far right corner of the room full of carefully lined up gems.

"Look at all these diamonds, shiny green emeralds, and sparkly red rubies," said Nate, practically drooling on the glittery jewels.

"I think we found something!" I exclaimed, my voice echoing through the vault.

Logan, Anne, Little Red, and Kate quickly jogged over to our table.

"Whoa! The amulet's got to be one of those," said Logan pointing to the row of pulsating rubies.

"I'm sure you're right, but I haven't the foggiest idea which of these is the amulet because all three are glowing," I replied as I carefully examined three of the largest red rubies, each the size of my hand.

Little Red bent over and closely examined each of the rubies as well, lowering her face right next to mine. "They all basically...look...the same," she muttered to herself.

"Let's just take all three of them and maybe a couple of diamonds just to be on the safe side," suggested Nate.

"That's thievery," chided Kate. "We can't just snatch up a handful of jewels. As it is, we're already going to be in big trouble for taking the amulet."

"Well, I call it payment," chuckled Nate. "It's just a little somethin' somethin' for being forced to swim in a poopy toilet."

"Your payment will be that you get to keep your super ability," retorted Kate, "and that should be good enough."

"And who knows what powers these other gems possess," continued Little Red. "They may be even more dangerous than the amulet."

"Fine," sighed Nate folding his arms across his chest, "but don't ask me to swim in stinky poo water again, unless of course, you're gonna' pay me in diamonds."

The six of us stood silent, each wondering which of the three rubies we should take until Anne finally suggested, "Maybe Tate can use his ability to figure out which one is the real amulet?"

I shrugged my shoulders and said, "I'm not so sure I can."

"It'd be worth a try," replied Logan. "Give it a go, Tate."

Everyone squeezed in, with Nate sliding directly behind me, breathing his hot breath down the back of my neck.

"Which one should I try first?" I asked.

"Try the first one on the left and go in order," suggested Anne.

I reached out and carefully placed my fingertips on each of the rubies, not sure what I was hoping to feel.

"...ttm..." whispered Nate, his hot breath, puffing in my ear, "...ttm..."

"I'm trying to focus here, and your hot dragon breath is roasting my ear," I projected. *"What do you want?"*

"TTM means, talk to me."

"What's so important all of a sudden? I'm about to tell everyone that ruby three is most likely the amulet because there's a lot of energy coming from-"

"Tell them it's ruby one," interrupted Nate.

"What?"

"Trust me, tell them it's ruby one. I'll take care of the rest."

"Okay, but that's a lie..."

"Just do it."

Glancing over at Kate and Anne, I slowly moved my hand back over the first ruby. "The power from this ruby is really strong and I don't feel anything from the other two," I whispered nervously, feeling like Kate was going to see through my lie. "This one has to be the amulet."

Nate reached out and snatched the ruby from under my nose. "Behold, the AMULET OF POWER...DUM, DUM, DUM!" he announced dramatically, holding the giant ruby triumphantly over his head.

Kate fumbled around in her back pocket until she located a small plastic baggie stuffed with a wad of carefully folded napkins. "I snitched some extra napkins at dinner because I thought Nate could use them to clean up after taking a dip in the outhouse toilet," she said.

"Probably would have needed a bit more than a tiny wad of napkins to clean myself off after diving into a deep steamy pot of poo," grinned Nate, "but...it was very thoughtful of you."

Kate held out the small pile of ruffled napkins. "Well, now you can wrap the amulet in them and put it in the baggie," Kate suggested. "For a little added protection."

I grabbed the napkins, carefully wrapped the ruby in them, placed everything in the plastic baggie, and carefully handed it over to Kate. Kate reached out and carefully clutched the bag, cradling it like a newborn baby.

"Um...I think maybe I should hold on to the amulet for the time being...just in case," grinned Anne nervously. "I mean, seeing as you three are related to Nero and all...no offense."

"No offense taken," replied Kate, carefully handing the ruby over to Anne.

"You can hold it for the time being Anne," replied Little Red as we headed towards the vault door, "but you'll need to hand it over to me once we reach topside."

Nate glanced back at Logan, over his shoulder, and winked as we exited the vault. "Yes, Anne, make sure to keep the amulet safe so the baddies don't get it," he said loudly.

"What is going on?" I projected to Nate, *"and what's up with all the winking?"*

"Better that you not know...."

"Better that I not know, what?"

"Oh, I'm not going to fall for that trick. Just trust me. Logan and I have things covered," replied Nate.

Nate and I helped Little Red close the giant vault door. She then reached up, spun the dial, and said, "That should about do it. No one will ever know we've been here."

"Except for me," boomed a deep voice that echoed throughout the cavern. "I know exactly where you've been and what you've been up to."

Little Red shone her flashlight across the cavern towards the door that would lead us back to our exit.

"Try and find me…" echoed the voice as Little Red bravely stepped in front of us.

"What are you, five years old?" hollered Little Red, "Just show yourself!"

"Alright, here I am," replied Griffin, stepping out of the darkness and into the light. "You all surprised to see me?" he asked.

"Griff…Griffin?" stammered Little Red. "What are you doing here?"

"Tailing you," smirked Griffin as he stepped further into the cavern.

Little Red put her left hand behind her back and directed us to step backward as Griffin continued to slowly advance towards us.

"But *how* did you find us? I mean, we dove down an outhouse toilet to get down here for goodness sakes," said Nate. "This has got to be the all-time best hiding spot in camp!"

"I have my ways," hissed Griffin.

"Well congratulations, you found us. So, what do you want?" asked Kate, courageously stepping next to Little Red as the rest of us remained three feet behind the two of them.

"Griffin!" exclaimed Nate loudly.

"Yes, that's already been established," I replied, looking over at Nate. "That's Griffin standing in front of us."

"No...that creature on the shield in the vault. It was a Griffin," declared Nate.

"Griffins are powerful creatures entrusted to guard treasure and priceless possessions," replied Griffin, "which means it's my duty and destiny to take the amulet off your hands."

"But why?" asked Logan peering around Little Red. "What do you want to do with it?"

"I'm going to persuade Tate to release Nero."

"You want to release Nero so he can finish stealing everyone's powers?" asked Logan, "including ours?"

"Great plan...Let the psycho out so he can cause more mayhem!" roared Nate leaning out from behind Kate. "Am I the only one who can see where this is heading?"

Griffin sneered, "Apparently, you've all been fed a sanitized version of Nero and his downfall, but I know the messier version....the true story of Nero and the Chaos Crew."

"There's a messy version?" asked Logan.

"A messy, true version that you should all hear," replied Griffin before Little Red could respond. "That way you can figure out for yourselves whether or not you're fighting on the right side."

"They don't need to hear the other version to know that," replied Little Red, her cheeks looking a little more rosy than usual.

"Of course, they need to hear it. After all, it involves Kate, Nate, and Tate's mother," jeered Griffin. "They should hear the horrible truth about her."

"Leave our mother out of this!" barked Kate angrily. "She had nothing to do with Nero and those horrible people that followed him!"

Griffin tilted his head back and laughed eerily, his voice echoing off the cold rocky walls.

"Your mother had everything to do with it. She was the whole reason the crew was formed in the first place!" exclaimed Griffin furiously.

Nate balled up his fist and bellowed, "That's a lie! Mom would never get herself involved in something like that."

"Not true," replied Griffin, "because of her, people died."

"People...died?" muttered Logan anxiously. "That's not the version of the story I heard."

"Yes," whispered Little Red, looking down at her feet. "Some campers and staff died in the battle for Crusader."

Nate pushed his way between Kate and Little Red. "Then tell us *your* version so we can finally be rid of you!" he roared.

Griffin adjusted the baseball cap on top of his head. "Now Nate-y, that's not a nice way to talk," smirked Griffin, "especially to your cousin."

"We're not related," I said squeezing in next to Nate. "Mom never told us about you or this camp."

"That's because if she told you," responded Griffin, "then she'd have to explain how she was instrumental in everything that happened that year at camp."

Nate sputtered, "I...I don't believe a word you're saying."

"You don't need to know," replied Little Red, gently patting Nate on his shoulder. "It was a long time ago."

Kate looked up at Little Red and said, "I'd still like to hear what he has to say anyway, so I can decide for myself."

Little Red smiled weakly at Kate and then nodded her head at Griffin. Griffin took two steps forward, moving directly in front of Kate, Nate, Little Red, and me. Taking off his baseball cap, Griffin tucked it under his arm and ran his fingers through his hair. "What Alekzander conveniently failed to mention is that Nero had three siblings. One sibling was Nero's twin, my mother Julianna. His other siblings were his younger sister, your mother Lilliana, and her twin, Alekzander," Griffin said.

"Is this true?" asked Kate turning to look at Little Red, "Nero and Alekzander are our uncles?"

Little Red's shoulders slumped. "Yes, that part is accurate," she said, sounding hesitant.

Griffin took two more steps forward and continued, "Our grandparents, didn't allow their children to attend camp for the longest time because they had difficulty accepting their own powers, let alone the powers of their children. Year after year, your mother, aunt, and uncles, begged to attend camp. It wasn't until Charles Wildenbury insisted that the children attend Crusader, that our grandparents finally relented. That's why Nero and my mother attended camp for the first time when they were much older than typical campers."

"Go on," said Kate. "I'm sure there's more."

"Initially, on the first day of camp, Nero had no intention of revealing his second power but the G.R.D.D. exposed the truth, just like it did with Tate. The G.R.D.D. also revealed that Alekzander had two powers, which he wasn't already aware of."

"Did our mom and your mom have two powers as well?" asked Kate.

"No, they only had one."

"So how come the boys got two powers and the girls didn't?" asked Kate.

"Some people would call it DNA," replied Griffin, "but others would call it fate."

"But why?" asked Kate.

"Your mother was the reason for the whole disaster at camp that year because she was the perfect target for camp bullies. She was small, thin, awkward, wore thick glasses, and appeared to have one pathetic super ability...light manipulation. On the second night of camp, following the evening campfire, three campers grabbed your mother while she was walking alone back to her cabin. Laughing and mocking, they challenged your mother to a fight, but she was no match for them, so the three girls beat her senseless. It was right after that incident, while cleaning up her bloodied fat lip, that Lilliana swore to get revenge on anyone she thought didn't deserve special abilities."

"Maybe she was right," said Nate. "I don't think some bullies deserve superpowers either."

"I'm not quite finished telling the tale," replied Griffin sharply, "because the best is yet to com-"

"I think they've heard enough to make up their minds," interrupted Little Red.

Griffin placed his baseball cap back on top of his head and continued. "It was your mother who convinced Nero to strip the powers from those three bullies," he said.

"Again...what's wrong with that?" asked Logan. "I tend to agree with Nate, some bad people don't deserve to have super abilities."

"I'm not finished with the story yet because it didn't stop there," replied Griffin. "After the initial three victims, Alekzander and your mother Lilliana convinced Nero to begin a campaign to rid the camp of *everyone* they thought were undeserving of their powers. To form the Chaos Crew, your mother and Alekzander found seven more like-minded campers to join the cause. Secret tribunal meetings were held nightly in Crusader Cave where they discussed the behaviors of every camp participant. And it was your mother that had the final say on who became the next victim, thus she became judge, jury, and executioner for the whole camp."

"Wasn't your mom in the crew, too?" asked Kate defiantly. "So don't go blaming just our mother."

Griffin glared at Kate momentarily and then continued. "It got to the point that *your mother* and Alekzander were convincing Nero to extract powers from campers for even the smallest infractions…and once Nero started taking powers, he could no longer stop himself. The more abilities he extracted, the more intoxicated he became, and the more intoxicated he became, the more irrational his behavior. My mother was finally able to convince Nero to rid himself of the excess powers that were driving him mad...Minutes before the Crusader battle broke out; he granted your mother a second power. Just as he was about to pass on a second power to my mother, the Crew was attacked by Charles and his goons."

"I think that's quite enough," said Little Red folding her arms across her chest. "You've said your peace."

Griffin glared at Little Red but did not say another word.

I shrugged my shoulders when Kate looked back at me with a confused expression.

"I'm not so sure I'm buying your story about our mom," said Nate finally breaking the silence. "I think you're spreading rumors because your mom was jealous since she never received a second power."

"And I think you're making excuses, so you'll feel better about your trouble-making mama," replied Griffin heatedly. "After the battle, Lilliana should have had her powers stripped by the N.H.B. as a consequence for her actions but instead the tribunal took pity on her. It doesn't quite seem fair that Nero ended up in a rock for eternity and your mother and Alekzander got off with a slap on the wrist."

"Stop talking about my mother like that," spat Nate. "For all we know, you're lying about our mom to cover up for your mom!"

Griffin's face suddenly turned red and the veins on his neck bulged angrily as he balled up his fists. "How about you just give me the amulet now before I beat the living tar out of all of you?" Griffin snarled through clenched teeth.

Little Red held both of her hands out in front of her. "Slow down tiger," she said. "I'm sure we can find a compromise."

"We can...as long as the compromise guarantees that I leave with the amulet," rumbled Griffin.

"The Bureau ruled that Nero was ultimately responsible for his own actions because he was practically an adult. Every member of the Chaos Crew accepted their consequences, including Lilliana, and they have since been trying to rebuild their lives," replied Little Red, "so no, you can't have the amulet to free Nero."

"I'm with Red. I say that we keep the amulet for the time being," agreed Kate. "Alekzander can decide what the next steps are going to be when he returns to camp."

"Alekzander was always jealous of Nero, which means he can't be trusted to do the right thing...even now," argued Griffin looked directly at Anne. "How about you hand over the amulet and let's set things right."

I looked over at Anne. She had a death grip on the amulet. "You're not getting the amulet because as you implied earlier, no one has the right to be the judge, jury, and executioner," rumbled Little Red as she stepped forward and poked Griffin in the chest with her pointer finger. "Including you."

Griffin adjusted his cap and took a step back. "Well, in that case, I guess I'll just have to leave empty-handed," he said grinning.

"You just do that," replied Kate.

"But Dolores doesn't have to," chuckled Griffin.

Suddenly, the smell of burning rubber filled the air as a dark cloaked figure teleported behind Anne, grabbed her and the amulet, and quickly vanished in a whisp of black smoke.

Griffin pointed at Kate and chuckled, "You should have used your super-speed Cousin because it appears that your friend and that little glowing rock just went bye-bye."

"You won't get away with this," yelled Kate furiously.

"I already have, but I'm not quite done yet," said Griffin glaring at me, "because Tate's next on my list."

"Grab my hand, quickly!" I hollered to Logan and Nate. Logan and Nate quickly stepped next to me and grabbed my hands. "Dolores can't take all three of us at the same time."

"Clever," smirked Griffin, "but I have a feeling that you'll be joining me soon enough."

"I'll never join you!" I howled.

"You will, whether you want to or not because you three can't hold hands forever," laughed Griffin as another puff of black smoke filled the air directly behind him. "I wonder if Nate can see where this is headed now?" sneered Griffin as Dolores reappeared, wrapped her arms around Griffin, and then disappeared in a puff of black smoke, leaving us empty-handed and feeling defeated.

"What are we going to do now?" cried Kate. "Griffin and Dolores have Anne and the amulet."

Little Red turned and gently patted Kate's shoulder. "It's my fault. I should have suspected something was up with Griffin," she said sounding disappointed in herself.

"Just let them go," said Nate, "I didn't like that Anne in the first place."

"I didn't like that Anne either. She was kind of bossy," chuckled Logan reaching over and giving Nate a high five.

"How could you two be so cruel?" snapped Kate. "She was our friend!"

"That Anne wasn't," replied Nate.

"Of course, she was!" shrieked Kate. "How could you two be so cavalier about what just happened here?"

"That wasn't the real Anne," interrupted Logan. "It was the shape shifter."

"How do you know that?" asked Kate, irritably crossing her arms in front of her chest. "How can you be so sure? I didn't see her glitch."

"She didn't have to," said Logan, "because I could tell it wasn't the real Anne."

"But how?"

"She always covered her mouth when she grinned or laughed," responded Nate. "She did it to hide her braces."

"How'd you...When did you?"

"Notice?" asked Nate.

"Yes."

"C'mon...Logan's in love with Anne," chuckled Nate. "He notices every little detail about her."

Logan's face turned bright red. "Well, you have to admit that she is nice," he muttered, shuffling his feet.

Kate turned, put her hands on her hips, and looked down at Logan. "Just when did you notice the shape shifter take Anne's place if you don't mind me asking?"

"Since we pulled ourselves out of the toilet a bit ago," replied Logan, half looking up at Kate through his glasses. "She was last to take the plunge so the shape shifter must have taken her place then."

"But that means she could still be in danger," replied Kate.

"She'll be fine for now," I replied, "besides, we may be able to find out who the shape shifter is if we play along."

"And if she does get in trouble, we'll save her," replied Nate. "Logan won't let anything happen to his true love."

"Okay, okay," muttered Logan looking red in the face. "I think everyone here gets your point."

"So, we don't have to worry about Anne for the time being, but what I don't understand is why you let me hand over the amulet to her if you knew she was the shape shifter?" asked Kate. "What were you two thinking?"

"Don't worry about that Mini Mama," smirked Nate. "We've got that covered, too."

Kate quickly looked from Nate, to Logan, to me, and then back to Nate again. "So, the success of this whole operation is dependent on three smelly boys?" she asked.

"Well, it sounds absurd when you put it that way," grinned Logan through his glasses.

"We are absurd!" chuckled Nate as he reached out and wrapped his arms around Logan's neck.

Kate smacked her face with her hand and muttered, "This mission is doomed."

"Probably," chuckled Little Red, "probably."

Chapter Ten

Up, Up and Away

"Can't you give Red and I a small hint as to what exactly is going on?" asked Kate, leading us towards the doorway to exit the cavern. "I'm a little nervous having you boys in charge...no offense."

"Offense taken...but even with all your amazing compliments, you still won't get any hints from me," chuckled Nate sarcastically as we reached the door.

Placing her hand on the black iron door handle, Little Red pulled, but the door wouldn't budge. "This thing won't open," said Little Red, leaning back and tugging repeatedly on the handle. "I think Griffin may have jammed it from the other side."

Logan pointed down at our feet and yelped, "I think he did more than that!"

"Is that water coming from under the door?" asked Kate.

Nate took a step back. "That's not fresh water," he said, pointing at the steady stream of thick brown muck creeping its way across the milky quartz floor.

"Griffin's trying to flood us out!" yelped Logan running back into the cavern. "We're all going to drown down here in this putrid sludge!"

"Relax, there's not enough water in the outhouse toilet to flood us out, but he did manage to make getting out a bit more inconvenient and foul," grunted Little Red as she tugged one last time on the black iron door handle, "because this bad boy is shut incredibly tight!"

"Guess we're just going to have to find another way out," said Kate, avoiding the filthy brown water.

"Everyone, head back to the other side of the cavern towards those two passageways," ordered Little Red.

Carefully tiptoeing through the sewage minefield, the five of us arrived at the entrances of the two shadowy tunnels at the opposite end of the cavern.

"I can go and check them out," said Kate, "but they look awfully dark. I'll either need the flashlight or-"

"I got it…" interrupted Nate, cracking his knuckles, "five orders of night vision eyeballs coming right up."

Within seconds, my eyes, along with everyone else's, adjusted to the low light.

"Mission accomplished, Nate…looks almost like daylight," said Kate, looking into the tunnels. "I'll be right back."

"Sounds good," said Little Red, clicking off her flashlight. "We'll just wait right here while you figure out what passage will lead us out of-"

"Done," grinned Kate, suddenly reappearing in front of Little Red.

Startled, Little Red jumped about a foot in the air. "Kate, you've got to warn someone before you suddenly appear in front…Wait…Did you just investigate *both* tunnels?" she asked.

"Yep," said Kate proudly, "both tunnels."

"If that truly is the case, then you're probably the fastest camper we've ever had at Crusader," replied Little Red excitedly. "Your speed is very impressive."

"Thank you, but apparently I'm not a very quick thinker," frowned Kate. "I should have been fast enough to stop Griffin and Dolores from getting away so easily."

"Don't be too hard on yourself. We were all caught off guard," said Little Red sympathetically, "besides, we can worry about all that later, but right now, we got to get out of here."

"Then we can focus on getting Anne and the amulet back, right?" asked Kate.

"Amulet Shmam-u-let," chuckled Nate.

"Don't you think maybe you could let us in on your little secret now?" asked Kate, placing her hands on her hips and scowling at Nate.

Nate narrowed his eyes and stared at Kate. "Nope, not yet," he replied. "Got to make sure you're not a shape shifter, too."

Kate crossed her arms in front of her chest and declared, "I'm not a shape shifter, you dork!"

Nate narrowed his eyes even further and moved in so close that his nose and Kate's nose were practically touching. "That's exactly what a no-good yellow-bellied, flea-bitten, shape shifter would say!" exclaimed Nate through his tiny eye slits.

"How about you just tell us which tunnel will lead us back to camp?" I asked.

"Fine," said Kate pointing to the left passage. "That one goes in the direction of the dining hall. There is a large grate in the ceiling of the passageway that appears to be right under the kitchen floor in the dining hall. Just beyond that, the passageway continues on to another outhouse towards the entrance of camp. The tunnel to the right branches off into two other tunnels, that I assume, lead to Crusader II. I didn't bother to follow either of those tunnels because I figured our best bet would be to get out through the kitchen floor."

"That's a good call, Kate...Let's get after it then," said Little Red walking off into the tunnel without saying another word.

With proper working night vision, we followed closely behind Little Red until we arrived directly under a large round metal grate that was dimly lit from above.

"That appears to be the dining hall kitchen up there, about ten feet up," said Kate pointing to the grating above our heads.

Logan cupped his hands behind his ears and whispered, "I hear something...coming from up there."

"I hear it too. It sounds like someone's listening to classical music," I confirmed, "maybe it's Frank."

"I'll just take a quick peak," replied Little Red, stretching her legs until she was tall enough to peer up through the heavy grating. "I can see underneath the kitchen sink," relayed Little Red, wrapping her fingers around the grating, "but this grate is pretty heavy and held down by some huge bolts from above."

"Maybe we should call for help," suggested Kate.

"Not so sure we should because you never know who may come running if we start screaming like banshees," replied Nate.

"Let me see if I can telepathically reach Frank," I suggested. "He may be willing to help us out without turning us into the town sheriff."

"Give it a try," replied Little Red, dropping down to her normal size. "Frank's actually a cool guy once you get to know him."

I half-closed my eyes and whispered, "Okay, let me give it a try."

Closing my eyes, I let the hazy light and soft music cover me like a warm blanket, my thoughts floated along with the sound of classical piano until they finally reached Frank, who was busily peeling potatoes in the back room.

"Frank, can you hear me?" I projected.

"Yes, I can...who's this in my head?" replied Frank, sounding uneasy.

"It's Tate, the boy that's in love with your mac and cheese."

"Ah, Tate. My favorite new camper! What can I do you for?"

"I kind of need your help right now."

"Is everything okay?"

"It will be if you can help us."

"Us?"

"Yes, there's a bunch of us below the dining hall kitchen sink?"

"Below the...what?"

"I can show you. Will you come over to the kitchen sink, please?"

"And take a break from peeling one hundred potatoes for breakfast? I'll have to think about that for a minute."

I waited anxiously until I could see Frank's body cast a long shadow over the metal grating high above.

"We're down below the sink?"

"What are you doing below my kitchen sink?"

"We're stuck in the cavern below the kitchen," I said nervously, fairly certain that Frank was going to run off and report us to Ms. Agatha.

After a few awkward moments of silence, we saw the glow of a flashlight and Frank's eye peering down at us. "Oh, you shouldn't be down there," said Frank uneasily. "You're going to get yourself into some serious trouble."

"We know, but right now we need your help," hollered Little Red. "I'll explain everything once we get up there."

"Hold on," replied Frank.

"Don't rat us out!" exclaimed Nate, just as Frank disappeared above.

After a few tense minutes, Frank finally returned with a socket wrench.

"I'll get this grating off in a jiffy," said Frank as he began to loosen the bolts.

"Thanks, Frank," said Little Red as Frank continued to work.

"Don't thank me yet because this last one's pretty stubborn," grunted Frank. "Not sure...I can...get it...to...budge!"

"Think strong," yelled Nate from down below.

"I'm trying..." grumbled Frank, continuing to struggle with the bolt. "The darn thing is completely rusted in place...it won't budge."

"Stronger, be stronger!" exclaimed Nate, "You can do it!"

"I'm...doing...the best...I..."

"BE STRONG!" roared Nate. "BE THE BEAST!"

From ten feet below, we heard a loud gasp and then the clicking sound of the socket wrench once again, as the bolt finally loosened. A few seconds later, Frank reach down and hoisted up the heavy metal grating with one hand, placing it to one side.

"I don't understand what just happened," said Frank looking down at us with a baffled expression. "That last bolt was completely rusted in place. There was no way I was going to get it off unless I sawed it off."

"Well, I guess your persistence paid off," replied Little Red.

"It's called grit," replied Logan, "and you got a lot of it, Frank."

"Maybe so, but suddenly I felt strong, real strong. Not only was I able to loosen that rusty bolt, but I picked up that hundred-pound grating like I was plucking a dandelion from my lawn."

"The power of suggestion," replied Little Red.

"The power of Nate," I quickly replied, "because he was the one doing all the suggesting."

Logan pushed up his glasses and asked, "Wouldn't it be extraordinary if we discovered that to be the case?"

"And all that can be figured out," added Little Red, "once we get out of here and back to our cabins."

Logan, Little Red, and Frank worked together as a team to lift us out of the dark cavern below. Sitting in stunned silence on the yellow tiled kitchen floor, Nate, Kate, Logan, and I watched as Little Red and Frank struggled to push the heavy metal grating back into place.

"See," grunted Frank, "I told you this thing is heavy."

"You're right," puffed Little Red, "It's even heavy for the two of us."

"You didn't go after the amulet, did you Red?" asked Frank as he re-bolted the grating and sat down next to us.

"Wha…What?" sputtered Kate. "You knew the amulet was down there all along?"

"You learn a lot of things when you work in one place for as long as I have," replied Frank.

Little Red reached over and patted Frank's shoulder. She took a long and deep breath and said, "What Griffin said about the Chaos Crew was true. Your mom, Alekzander, Nero, and Griffin's Mom were members…as was Frank."

"I was young…we were all young," said Frank looking at the clock on the wall, over our heads, as he spoke. "We thought we were going to save the world by making sure bad kids didn't have superpowers," said Frank clicking his tongue. "We were such idealists."

"But I'm still not convinced that it was a bad idea," said Logan. "This world would be a much better place without bad kids running around with super abilities."

Frank looked Logan in the eyes, grinned slightly, and said, "That's exactly what we thought all those years ago, but we were wrong."

"What do you mean?" asked Kate. "How were you wrong?"

"We forgot to take into consideration that people can change," replied Frank. "Just because someone makes bad choices early on in life doesn't necessarily mean that person will turn out to be bad later on. We didn't consider that sometimes the worst behaving kids turn out to be the best behaving adults."

"It's all part of learning and growing from your mistakes," replied Little Red, "because sometimes it's not always easy to figure out your path in life."

"No, it is not," whispered Frank, "and some kids have rougher starts than others."

"Which also means, we should be careful not to judge people too harshly, especially kids your age," replied Little Red.

"I kind of get what you're saying," replied Kate, "We had a whole social studies unit in class about walking a mile in someone else's shoes."

"Well, I'm not walking a mile in Dolores' stinky old shoes if that's what you want me to do!" exclaimed Nate squinching up his face.

"That's not what that saying means," replied Kate. "It means that we should try to be a little more understanding because we don't know what difficulties people have gone through."

"Does that mean we should be nice to the black-eyed beast because she has had a rough life and she's still figuring out her path?" asked Nate. "Because right now, I'd rather Dolores' path lead her off a very high cliff."

"That's a tough one because there's a delicate balance between trying to be understanding and being brave enough to stand up to a bully," replied Frank, "so don't be too hard on yourself, when you don't get it right. I mean just look at how Dolores pushed my buttons the other night. I completely lost my cool...and I'm an adult."

"I never once considered that Dolores could end up being a nice person somewhere down the road," said Logan.

"Yeah, maybe down a dead-end road surrounded by a pack of hungry hyenas," muttered Nate under his breath.

Kate reached out to smack Nate on top of his head, but he quickly dodged it.

"Well, I can't think of a better example of a kid that messed up early on, but has turned into one heck of an adult," grinned Little Red as she threw her arms around Frank's neck and pulling him in tight.

"But don't you miss your powers?" I asked Frank.

"Tate," glared Kate, "You don't ask someone that kind of question."

"It's okay. It's a legitimate question to ask," responded Frank, reaching over to give Little Red a pat on her shoulder as he stood up and brushed off his pants. "I do miss my super abilities from time to time, but you know something?"

"What?" I asked.

"I've become more powerful now that I'm powerless."

"That's an interesting notion," replied Logan, pushing up his glasses. "Please elaborate."

"I used to reply on my powers for everything like making new friends, impressing the girls, and of course fighting," replied Frank. "Because I grew up with super abilities, I always resorted to using my powers first, whenever I was in a tough spot."

"So, you're saying that you never had to think things through and solve problems on your own?" asked Kate.

"Rarely," replied Frank. "Losing my powers was one of the best things that happened to me. Being powerless has helped me discover that my brain is the most powerful ability I have. And since losing my powers, I've had plenty of time to use my gray matter to figure out how to be a better problem solver and make amends for my past mistakes."

"And you have," replied Little Red looking up at the clock, "but enough of the mushy stuff, I think it's time we get you all back to your cabins before someone becomes suspicious."

"Good idea," replied Kate.

Little Red reached down and extended her hand. "I'll drop off Kate to her cabin while you three boys hold hands all the way back to yours," she said pulling us up to our feet. "We can meet up at breakfast and figure out what our next steps are. In the meantime, Griffin or Dolores won't dare show their faces at camp any time soon, so we'll all be safe tonight."

I held tightly onto Logan's hand while Nate hung back for a moment to talk to Frank. I felt a sense of uneasiness as I watched Kate and Little Red disappear into the darkness.

The next morning, Nate, Logan, and I were first to sit down to a hot breakfast in the dining hall. Having hardly slept the night before, we were exhausted and bleary-eyed, but that didn't stop us piling our plates high with sausage links, silver dollar pancakes, and crispy homemade hash browns.

Nate shoved four sausage links into his mouth, his cheeks bulging out like a greedy hamster hoarding food. "Adventuring...makes me...so hungry," he mumbled.

"Hungry and tired," complained Logan. He took a giant swig of chocolate milk and then wiped the milk mustache off his top lip with a napkin.

"I hope we can locate Anne quickly so things can back to normal," said Nate forcing a fifth sausage into his mouth.

"Not sure what getting back to normal means once you've discovered you're a superhero," I replied, half looking around for Little Red and Kate as I dug into my hash browns.

"I'm just glad we're filling our bellies because it's really hard to think on an empty stom...AHHHCK!" sputtered Nate as a half-chewed sausage link shot from his mouth and landed on my plate.

"Hey!" I howled. "Why are you barfing all over my plate?"

Nate's eyes were practically bulging out of his head as he shot up out of his chair and jabbed his fork towards the end of the food line. "Her, her…" he mumbled.

"What now?" I asked nudging the half-chewed sausage off of my plate with my finger.

"Either my eyes are deceiving me, or the Black Eyed Banshee is standing right next to Scott in the food line, right now!" exclaimed Nate.

Looking over my shoulder, I couldn't believe my eyes when I saw Dolores standing right next to Scott, just twenty feet behind me.

"She's pretty brave coming to breakfast after pulling off a stunt like that last night," remarked Logan.

"That also means Griffin won't be far behind," I said. "We better watch our backs."

The three of us nervously watched as Dolores poured syrup on her hot cakes and then made her way to the far corner of the dining hall to sit with Scott and Lance.

Nate shoveled a syrup-soaked pancake into his mouth. "Shee's swoe cweepie," mumbled Nate, just as Kate plunked her chocolate chip muffin and cup of orange juice on our table and sat down.

"Who's cweepy?" asked Kate, "and has anyone seen Little Red yet?"

"Red's not in her usual spot," I replied looking over at the counselor's table.

"I was afraid of that," said Kate looking anxious. "She dropped by my cabin this morning in a big rush, saying she had somewhere important to go. She was acting all mysterious-like."

"Maybe she had to go to the bathroom," responded Nate between bites.

"She wouldn't have stopped by to tell me that," replied Kate.

"Maybe in the middle of the night, a rabid squirrel stuck an acorn up her left nostril, and she was on the way to see the woodland fairy doctor, but it was too late because a tree started growing out of her ears, so she went to the home-goods store to buy a tree trimmer, "suggested Nate.

"That's oddly specific," chuckled Logan, "and creative."

I picked up a warm sausage, using it to point over my left shoulder. "Maybe Dolores attacked her," I said grimacing.

Kate stood up, looked past me, and snarled, "What the heck is that tyrant doing here? Of all the nerve!"

"She's the cweepy one Nate was going on about!" I said pointing the sausage at Nate.

"What I actually said was, 'Shee's swoe cweepie,'" chuckled Nate, "and stop threatening me with that delicious sausage, Tate!"

Picking us his fork, Logan began to nervously tap it on the table. "Something about this whole situation isn't quite right. I say that if Little Red doesn't show up soon, we report everything to Ms. Agatha."

"And rat ourselves out?" asked Nate, "We broke about ten thousand camp rules. We'd be expelled from Crusader for sure."

"I think Logan's right," responded Kate. "We either find Anne and Little Red right away or we go straight to the top. "

"She's compromised," I said. "We can't be sure we would be dealing with the real Ms. Agatha."

"Then what should we do next?" asked Kate taking a bite of her muffin, "because we can't just sit around waiting for something to happen."

"I'm going to try and locate Little Red telepathically," I whispered as I shifted from my bottom to my knees.

"Ok, but be quick about it," whispered Kate.

"Can't rush perfection," I replied as I turned to look out the window next to me. Trying to calm my mind, I watched three playful squirrels scurry across the porch and then chase each other up the large tree in front of the dining hall. Closing my eyes, I slowed my breathing as I reached out with my thoughts.

"Little Red are you there?"

Nothing.

Just as I was about to try to reach out again, Nate used his elbow to nudge me out of my self-induced trance. "Oh, she looks furious!" he whispered in my ear.

"I was trying to locate Red," I muttered.

"Sorry," said Nate, "but maybe you should take a look at what's going on right in front of us."

Having just flung open the dining hall front door, Nurse Carter stomped straight over to the counselor's breakfast table.

"The nurse looks pretty irate today," commented Logan as Nurse Carter pointed her finger in Nicholas Knight's face with one hand and waved an envelope over her head with her other hand.

"Yeah, she's waving that envelope over her head like a crazy person," replied Nate.

"And it looks like Nick is trying hard not to cry," observed Kate.

Nick's face looked all puckered up like he had been sucking on a lemon as Nurse Carter reached over his breakfast plate and snatched the announcement bell out of his hands. Smoothing out her turquoise tee shirt embossed with the words You R.N. Good Hands, Nurse Carter marched to the middle of the dining hall and rang the announcement bell.

"I have something very important to share with you all," she said when the chatter finally died down. "However, I must warn you that some of you may be disturbed by what I am about to share. Especially, those of you that are fiercely loyal to Ms. Agatha," said Nurse Carter, looking back over her shoulder at Nicholas.

"She's probably holding a love letter from Dolores," snickered Nate under his breath. "That'd be very disturbing."

"Quiet," snapped Kate. "I'm trying to listen."

Nurse Carter held out the envelope in front of her, opened it up, and pulled out a lined sheet of paper. "I discovered this letter taped to my front door just this morning. I assure you that it has been written by Ms. Agatha Grimswood's own hand. This letter states that she and other individuals, whom I shall name shortly, have been extracting camper's abilities for reasons yet to be revealed," snarled Nurse Carter.

An audible gasp broke out, as campers stared at each other, dumbfounded.

"Because of these horrible revelations, I have contacted the N.H.B. They will be sending someone out tomorrow to investigate Ms. Agatha's improprieties over the past several days. The bad news is that before Ms. Agatha fled, she and her co-conspirators left behind yet another victim."

"But what does that mean for us?" asked Dante, one of the largest counselors at camp. "Are we safe?"

"You are," replied Nurse Carter. "We are holding tight until we either hear from Alekzander or receive direct orders from the bureau. In the meantime, I am in charge until that time occurs and it is my job to keep you all safe."

"Which camper lost their power?" blurted Frank from the kitchen.

Nurse Carter looked around the room as she cleared her throat.

Please don't be Anne...Please don't be Anne...Please don't be Anne," whispered Kate as she clasped her hands in front of her and bowed her head.

Nurse Carter looked long and hard at Kate. "I am currently treating Anne Adams in the infirmary," she said.

"I am in the middle of running tests, but it appears that she has succumbed to the same ill effects as the other campers."

I anxiously held my breath as Logan looked down at his breakfast plate.

Suddenly, Scott shot up from his chair, sending it skittering across the floor. "Nurse Boss Lady! I mean...Ms. New Director Nurse Boss Lady!" cried Scott as he bounded forward clutching a loose piece of paper.

"Yes, Scott?" asked Nurse Carter. "What seems to be the emergency?"

"I have evidence proving that Tate Larson is one of Ms. Agatha's accomplices. I think he and his siblings have been working with her the moment they arrived at Crusader."

Nurse Carter turned her head and looked over at our table as she spoke. "That is quite an accusation young man. What proof do you have?"

"I have this!" exclaimed Scott, shoving the piece of paper enthusiastically under Nurse Carter's nose. "I discovered a page from Ms. Agatha's clipboard under my pillow just this morning. The notes on the paper say that

Nate, Kate, and Tate Larson are related to Nero and that she has been using Tate to extract powers just like his uncle."

My face burned red hot and I felt like I was going to throw up as every camper in the room abruptly turned towards us.

Nurse Carter took the paper from Scott and read it to herself. "I can attest to the genuine nature of these notes. It does appear that the Larson children and Ms. Agatha have been working together," scowled Nurse Carter. "I guess now would be an ideal time to verify that I have discovered that Nicholas Knight is also a co-conspirator."

"What?" howled Nicholas from behind Nurse Carter. "I'm not involved in any of this!"

"I do not believe you," sneered Nurse Carter. "I have proof that you and those nasty Larson children have been plotting to overthrow this camp."

Nate popped up from his chair and slammed both of his palms down on the table. "Those are all lies! At least the part about us taking powers is."

Nurse Carter's eyes narrowed into small slits. "So, you admit you are related to that dastardly villain, Nero?" she asked coarsely.

Kate stood up next to Nate and yelped, "Someone just told us we were related to Nero, but we hadn't any idea until recently."

Nurse Carter looked up from the letter and asked, "Who told you this information?"

"Griffin told us," I said standing up next to Nate and Kate.

Nurse Carter turned around, looked at the counselor's dining table, and then turned back around to face us. "And now it just so happens that Griffin has gone missing just this morning," she said tapping her long pink fingernails on her chin. "Such a crazy coincidence, don't you think?"

"What'd you do with Griffin?" howled someone from behind us. "You better not have hurt him!"

"We didn't do anything to him," said Kate staring directly at Nurse Carter. "We haven't been in contact with him or Little Red since last night."

"You mean to tell me that both your counselors have seemingly disappeared into thin air? How very odd," replied Nurse Carter sarcastically.

"They must have taken Griffin and Red's powers!" yelled Dolores. "I knew they were no good the moment I laid eyes on them."

"And I knew it when Tate attacked me with his angry cow posse!" howled Scott over the commotion. "That family is rotten to the core, I tell you!"

"They have to be stopped!" hollered Lance. "Before they take all our powers!"

I covered my ears and clamped my eyes shut as campers hurled hurtful words at us.

"Somethings not right," I projected to Nate, Kate, and Logan over the clamor, *"How did Ms. Agatha's clipboard notes magically appear on Nurse Carter's door and under Scott's pillow because she constantly had them with her."*

"Griffin probably stole them off of Ms. Agatha's clipboard with the help of Dolores," replied Logan.

"It's a setup!" growled Nate.

"Of course it is, but we better come up with something quick," Kate replied.

"Please hurry...I'm too squishy to go to jail," Nate replied nervously.

Nurse Carter held up her hand and the roar quieted down to a low murmur.

"It has become quite apparent that I must take swift action before this gets any more out of hand," said Nurse Carter. "With that said, I will be escorting, the Larson siblings, Logan Lowry, and Nicholas Knight to my cabin so we may get down to the bottom of this. In the meantime, for everyone's safety, please finish your breakfast and stay locked down in your cabins until further notice."

"What?" howled Kate, "We haven't done anything wrong!"

Nurse Carter's face suddenly turned bright red. "I'll be the judge of that!" she shrieked furiously.

"I got this. I see some animal friends outside. I think they can help us, but you'll need to be ready to make a run for it," I projected, just seconds before Nurse Carter arrived at our table.

Crossing her arms in front of her chest, Nurse Carter glared at each one of us, the corner of her lips turned down in a hard, cold frown. "You will come with me to the nurse's cabin, right now, before this whole mess gets any messier," she snarled.

Nate replied, "But we are not responsible for any of this. Why don't you go ask Dolores about last night?"

"Nate!" yelped Kate, shooting him a dirty look.

"What about last night?" asked Nurse Carter curiously. "What were you four up to last night?"

Nate looked at me and mumbled, "We...uh...we."

Nurse Carter placed both of her hands on the table and loudly tapped her long pink fingernails as she scowled at Nate.

"Well, I'm waiting," sneered Nurse Carter.

"We haven't been up to much of anything Ma'am, just the usual superhero camp stuff," replied Logan under his breath.

"I doubt that," replied Nurse Carter baring her teeth. "I think maybe you were on the prowl last night."

Logan looked down at the table and whispered, "That's not true."

"I think your friend Anne was feeling just a teensy bit guilty about getting herself involved in all of this," hissed Nurse Carter leaning in closer, "and just as she was about to turn you all in, you pounced on her...that's what I think."

"It was the shapeshifter!" blurted Logan.

While Nurse Carter leaned in and examined Logan carefully, I quietly contacted the squirrels outside.

Shifting uncomfortably in his seat, Logan humbly said, "What I meant to say is that a shapeshifter has been hurting the campers...Ma'am."

"Oh, now I've heard it all!" roared Nurse Carter, "A mythical shapeshifter has been taking people's powers at Crusader...that's a laugh!"

"But the shapeshifter has!" I cried. "It took the place of Ms. Agatha while we were-"

"Enough lies!" howled Nurse Carter, "Haven't you done enough damage to our beloved camp already?"

Nate's chair flung backward as he jumped up. "But it's true!" he roared.

Nurse Carter slammed both of her hands down on the table and shrieked, "That's enough!"

The room suddenly grew quiet as everyone turned to look at us, no doubt anxiously waiting to see what horrible punishment Nurse Carter was about to dole out to us.

"We're not going quietly if that's what you want," I bravely whispered as I reached out with a spoon and tried to nudge Nurse Carter's twitching fingers off the table.

Like an enormous cheetah pouncing on a tiny unsuspecting gazelle, Nurse Carter snatched up my left arm. The spoon I once had in my hand clattered off the table and onto the floor as her long sharp fingernails pressed deep into my skin. "I won't allow you to use your powers to hurt me the same way you've hurt so many others," growled Nurse Carter angrily.

I frowned as I attempted to yank my arm away from Nurse Carter's tight grip. "You're hurting me," I gasped as Nurse Carter's sharp nails scratched my forearm, leaving three long streaks of blood in their wake.

Logan and Kate looked on in stunned silence as the blood dripped from my arm and pooled on the table.

"Let him go!" shouted Nate as he reached over and grabbed Nurse Carter's arm and tugged.

"Or what?" sneered Nurse Carter, "You'll take my powers, too?"

"I already told you, we didn't take anybody's powers!" roared Nate.

"Let go of my arm!" I projected.

Nurse Carter leaned over so our noses were practically touching. "You have five seconds to come with me or I will allow every camper to beat the truth out of you," she whispered through her clenched jaw.

"THAT WILL NEVER HAPPEN!" I thundered angrily, *"NEVER!!"*

Suddenly, Nurse Carter released my arm and staggered back from the table. "MY HEAD! MY HEAD!" she howled, grabbing her head, and bending over in pain.

"They hurt the nurse!" shrieked someone near the kitchen.

"Let's get 'em'!" roared Scott from the far side of the room.

Countless chairs and tables toppled over as angry campers leapt up, ready to pounce.

Nate howled, "We've got to get out of here!" as angry campers moved in closer, hurling threats at us.

"Were done for!" cried Logan.

"Yes, you are!" snarled Scott, standing at the head of the angry crowd, holding a chair over his head.

Looking desperately out the window, I pleaded to the animals outside, *"Now! Friends! Please...Now!"*

Within seconds, a sea of angry squirrels, opossums, and skunks flooded into the dining hall through the open windows and front door.

Caught off guard by the rodent tidal wave, campers dropped their chairs and leapt up on the tables, while a hundred rats poured down the chimney in a swell of frenzied fur.

"I-YEEE!" howled Nurse Carter as she tried to desperately bat away a pair of playful rats that were skittering up and down her legs.

"Let's get out of here," I projected to Kate, Nate, and Logan.

"Where to?" asked Logan anxiously.

"To Frank!" Kate shouted, pointing towards the kitchen.

"Back here!" yelled Frank, waving his arms above his head.

"You don't have to tell me twice!" exclaimed Nate, grabbing my hand. "Let's get out of here!"

Clambering over tables and chairs, we wrestled our way to the kitchen while the army of forest creatures kept everyone else busy.

Frank pulled us into the rear of the kitchen just as Nurse Carter and Lance tore out of the dining hall screaming their heads off as a small battalion of skunks pursued them.

"Well, that was interesting," said Frank grinning at me. "An army of furry critters, huh?"

"Sorry about the mess," I replied. "It was all I could think of in a pinch."

"Well, from the looks of you," said Frank, gently placing a clean dish towel on my forearm, "you were in more than a pinch."

"We were," said Kate anxiously.

"You mean *we are*," replied Nate, "because now every camper wants to beat us to a bloody pulp."

"You're going to need a place to lay low for the time being," Frank said, reaching into his pocket and holding out a green four-leaf clover keychain with a single key attached. "You four can take shelter in my cabin for the time being. It's at the far corner of the woods, the only cabin with a red roof, near the front of camp. You'll be safe there."

"We can't go out there right now," replied Logan anxiously. "Everyone's going to be on the lookout for us."

"That's an easy problem to resolve," replied Frank. "Tate can simply ask his frisky friends to keep everyone in their cabins for the time being. As long as you stay within the tree line, you'll be fine."

"Thank you, Frank, you're the best," I said smiling.

Frank looked down at me, smiled, and ruffled my hair.

"Glad to help. It's been many years since I've hung out with a bunch of rebels," chuckled Frank. "And good rebels to boot!"

Kate and Logan opened the back door, looked around, glanced back at us, and then disappeared through the doorway and into the tree line.

Nate reached out and gave Frank a high five. "Welcome to the team," he said grinning.

Frank patted Nate's shoulder. "Glad to be a part of it," he said, "but would you mind waiting outside for Tate? I need to talk to him privately for a minute."

"Sure thing," replied Nate, giving Frank a thumbs up before he leapt out the doorway and sprinted into the woods.

"I really am sorry about the dining hall if that's what you want to talk about," I said, still feeling guilty about the mess I caused.

"That's not why I wanted to talk to you," interrupted Frank.

Scurrying over to the refrigerator, Frank reached inside and took out a small squishy bag of yellowish-orange macaroni and cheese and shoved it into my chest.

"Take this," he ordered.

"I ate about ten minutes ago," I replied, "I'm not that hungry."

"This bag isn't for consumption," winked Frank, "but there is a special red glowing prize inside if you know what I mean."

I put both hands out in front of me and gently pushed the bag back towards Frank.

"I'd rather you hold on to it."

"Listen...Your brother asked me to keep it safe last night, but I really shouldn't have accepted it because I can't protect it. The best I can do, in an emergency, is to create a smokescreen with these things," said Frank flipping his wrists over so I could see the scars covering his mangled hands, "and from what I can tell, you're more than capable of keeping it safe."

"Okay," I replied, reluctantly grabbing the baggie.

"And keep this whole amulet business quiet for the time being," said Frank bending down and looking me straight in the eyes. "It sounds like this shapeshifter is a crafty one."

"Thank you...I will," I replied squishing the baggie deep down into my pocket.

"Now go," said Frank patting my shoulder tenderly, "and be safe."

I gave Frank a knuckle bump, leapt out the back door, and ran to join the others.

Together, the four of us stayed in the shadows of the thick tree line that ran behind the cabins. Once we arrived at the small white cabin with the red-tiled roof, we looked around, cautiously entered, and collapsed on the tattered brown sofa next to Frank's bed.

"What are we going to do next?" asked Kate, "The whole camp is after us thanks to Nurse Carter."

"She was acting very aggressive," said Logan, "It was a little unnerving."

"I wonder if that was the real nurse or the shapeshifter," I replied, "because she didn't seem like herself."

"It could have been," responded Logan.

"It would be a lot easier to take over camp with Ms. Agatha and Nurse Carter out of the way," replied Kate, "but all this craziness doesn't seem to add up."

Sitting up straighter on the sofa, Logan adjusted his glasses. "I may have pieced together a reasonable hypothesis about what's going on," he said looking over at Kate.

"That's great," replied Nate, "Because we are in desperate need of a hyper-thesis right now."

"It's called a hy-poth-e-sis," chuckled Logan, "It means an educated guess and I think I have a pretty good idea about what may be happening to the victims."

"Well, in that case," replied Kate, "Please share."

"Especially if your brilliant hyper-thesis came from an en-clo-pe-di-a," giggled Nate.

Logan chuckled, flashed Nate a quick smile, and then turned his head towards Kate. "When a shapeshifter assumes the identity of his or her victim, that person or creature becomes comatose during the time their identity is hijacked," he said.

"And how long does a victim remain in 'said coma' once their identity is no longer hijacked?" asked Kate.

"For maybe an hour afterward, two at the most."

"Which means, what?" asked Kate.

"Which means, if someone shapeshifted into Calder, Samantha, and Anne, even for a brief moment, they would be passed out when they were discovered," replied Logan. "Which might cause the adults at camp to initially assume that the victim's powers had been taken since that was what happened to those campers so many years ago. Many of the original victims were comatose for over a month before they woke up without their powers."

"But today's victims would only be knocked out for about an hour or two, right?" asked Kate. "Any reasonable adult would quickly figure out that the victims still had their special abilities once they woke up."

"And that is where my well-thought-out hyper-thesis goes off the rails," replied Logan. "I have no valid explanation as to why the victims have remained comatose for so long after the shapeshifter assumed their identities."

"Whatever is going on, it seems to have tricked Alekzander, Ms. Agatha, and Nurse Carter," I replied.

"Either way though, the only thing we have to do is stay put and protect the amulet until Alekzander shows up," replied Kate. She shifted her bottom on the sofa, so she was looking directly at Nate, "Unless of course, the amulet is currently not safely hidden."

"Take it easy Suspicious Pete," replied Nate. "It's in good hands."

I slowly slid my hand into my pocket to try and hide the fact that I was smuggling the amulet in a baggy of cold gooey macaroni and cheese deep within my front pocket.

"Very good hands!" chuckled Logan.

"Are you two going to tell me what's going on now or what?" asked Kate, standing up and throwing her hands high in the air, "because, unless I'm going crazy, I saw Griffin and Dolores grab Anne and the amulet, outside the vault, just last night."

"That was all part of the plan to deceive the deceivers," replied Logan.

"Would you two stop being so mysterious?" rumbled Kate. "What's that supposed to mean, deceiving the deceivers?"

Nate jumped up from the sofa like a jackrabbit, pointed at Logan, and said, "Fine, it was our hero, Logan, that single-handedly figured out that Anne had been replaced by that dastardly no good shapeshifter last night, so we made sure she didn't get the real amulet...and Logan's in love with Anne."

"That's already been established," sighed Kate.

Logan's cheeks turned bright red as he nervously pushed the glasses up the bridge of his nose over and over again. "I will not deny that I think Anne is brilliant," said Logan clearing his throat, "but love is a strong word."

"Okay, he strongly like-likes her," chuckled Nate as he reached down and smacked Logan on his knee and then flopped back down on the sofa next to me. "Either way, Logan and I made sure that Tate handed us the wrong ruby."

Logan continued, "Hoping the fake Anne would get a hold of it."

"And then I simply put the real amulet down the front of my pants and-"

"No, you didn't Nate...did you?" screeched Kate. "Down the front of your pants? Why not in your pocket...or somewhere, I don't know, less gross?"

"Because pockets are an obvious hiding place. I mean, who in their right mind is going to think I've got a magical glowing ruby, stashed in my undies?" chuckled Nate.

"As absurd as it sounds, he does have a point," interrupted Logan.

"But I hope you thoroughly sanitized it when you took it out." Kate's eyes suddenly grew large, "it's not...still down there...is it?"

"No, Frank's hiding it for us," replied Nate. "He's super trustworthy."

My face suddenly felt hot. I shifted on the sofa and looked around Frank's cabin, hoping nobody would notice the enormous bulge in my right pocket.

"So, then," asked Kate. "What's our next step brainiacs? I hope it includes hiding out here until Alekzander arrives."

"Nope...we start by paying Anne a little visit," replied Nate. "She'll be able to fill us in on what's going on."

"You mean *our* Anne? The one in the nurse's cabin?" asked Kate, shaking her head and making a sour face. "That would be completely reckless and-"

"And completely unexpected," finished Logan, "No one in their right mind would expect us to go there."

"I still think we should hang tight and wait for Alekzander or the authorities to show up," said Kate. "It's the logical next step."

"But the problem is, they aren't going to show up," I replied. "I was able to read a little bit of Nurse Carter's mind when she was talking to us."

"And?"

"And, she was lying," I replied. "No one is on their way to help us."

"So, we're on our own?" asked Kate.

"Not completely," I replied. "We could ask Nicholas Knight and Dolores Diablo to help us."

"Are you out of your crazy mind?" roared Nate, "You want the beast to join us? She's on the bad side, remember?"

"She's not," I replied. "We've been duped by Griffin. That wasn't her in the cave last night."

"And how do you know that?" asked Logan sitting up straighter on the sofa.

"Again...just bits and pieces, but Dolores honestly believes we are the ones taking people's powers. She's eager to turn us over to Alekzander. I know it's hard to imagine, but she actually likes coming to camp."

"Which means she's more than likely not involved in this whole mess," replied Logan. "A solid deduction."

"I still don't think she'd be helpful," said Nate shaking his head. "She's rude, she's mean, and-"

"And she would make the perfect double agent," I finished.

"I think it's a brilliant plan," said Logan. "We're kind of at the point of no return anyway."

"And who would ever expect that she was working with us," finished Kate.

"Well, good luck trying to convince her to help," replied Nate crossing his arms across his chest.

"Maybe she will if she knows Griffin's been using her as a scapegoat," said Kate.

"Well, that suits her because she smells like a goat," replied Nate. "A stinky one that eats rusty old cans and dirty socks."

"And you don't?" chuckled Kate.

Logan adjusted his glasses and said, "But she won't come willingly if she knows it's us."

"I can contact her. She'll come here if I pretend that I'm Blake Silverman from the Animo cabin," I replied. "I'll tell her that I accidentally stumbled upon some incriminating evidence that Frank is the real evil mastermind trying to ruin camp."

"Make sure to get Nicholas Knight out here as well," added Logan. "We could use his help, too."

Kate stood up and peeked through the curtain, "You better be very convincing and hurry up because it's getting close to eight-thirty and the rodent army looks like they're packing it in."

"Okay," I replied, "Here goes nothing."

Chapter Eleven

Caught in a Web of Lies

I tried using my telepathic ability to contact Nicholas Knight, but unlike Dolores, he was nowhere to be found. Leaving the door cracked open an inch, we waited patiently, hoping Dolores would be enticed enough to walk in on her own.

While Nate, Logan, and I quietly crouched behind the sofa, Kate hid behind the cabin door, ready to pounce if necessary. After agonizing for more than ten minutes, wondering if I'd blow our chance with Dolores, we finally saw a shadowy figure darken the doorway.

"Alright Blake, I'm here," whispered Dolores as she slowly pushed the cabin door open and stepped inside. "This better be good because I was just about to-"

Leaping out from behind the sofa, Nate, Logan, and I folded our arms across our chests and glared menacingly at Dolores as Kate slammed the door shut.

"Oh, it's you losers," Dolores said half-heartedly, brushing the dark hair out of her pitch-black eyes. "Where's Blake Silverman or have you vampires sucked him dry of his powers, too?"

"There is no Blake," I replied, stepping in front of Logan and Nate. "There never was. It's just us."

"Well, in that case, I'll be going now," said Dolores coolly. She turned around and glared at Kate who was standing with her hands on her hips, her back firmly pressed against the door.

"Not just yet," said Kate. "We need to talk to you."

"What if I'm not in the mood to talk?" growled Dolores.

"I think the four of us could persuade you," said Kate, a mischievous grin spread across her face.

"Don't be so sure," replied Dolores. She let her hair fall back over her eyes and cracked her knuckles. "I discovered my powers just this morning and I could kick all of your butts with one claw tied behind my back if I choose to."

Kate scowled at Dolores and Dolores probably scowled back at Kate, but it was hard to tell from behind the jet-black mop that was hanging down in front of her eyes.

"Move away from the door, now," ordered Dolores.

I leapt from my spot and nudged my way between Kate and Dolores. "Let her go, Kate," I said. "She's right about her newfound power. We're no match for her."

"What?" muttered Kate, "but, we just got her here-"

"Kate let her go."

"I told you she wouldn't listen, even if knew she was being set up," complained Kate as Dolores pushed past her. "She doesn't care about getting kicked out of camp because she hates Crusader that much."

Kate looked over at me and winked as Dolores froze in the doorway, her hand falling from the door handle to her side.

"Your lame reverse psychology won't work on me," said Dolores, her back still turned towards us. "I'm out of here."

"Well, go then!" blurted Nate angrily. "We didn't really want you around in the first place."

Dolores abruptly turned around, brushed the hair out of her eyes, and growled, "So, let me get this straight, dummy. You called me here because you didn't want me?"

The four of us just looked at each other, not sure what to say next as Dolores reached up and brushed her hair out of her eyes again.

"I'll give you two minutes," she said.

Nate flung himself on the sofa and mumbled, "You're so generous," as Dolores turned around and faced us.

"Griffin has been trying to pin diabolical acts on you," said Logan quickly.

Dolores let her hair fall back in front of her face and defiantly folded her arms across her chest. "I'm not so sure I believe you," she replied. "After all, you're criminals, and criminals would say just about anything to get themselves out of trouble."

"Griffin blamed you for kidnapping Anne and taking the amulet," I replied.

"Someone has the amulet?" asked Dolores sounding a bit more intrigued.

"Yes," I replied, "but it's kind of a long story."

Dolores stood still without saying a word for quite some time until she finally reached into her pocket and brought out a black hair tie. Tying her hair back into a ponytail, Dolores looked at us through her deep black irises.

"That may explain why Ms. Agatha and Nurse Carter have been probing me these last few days on the location of room A113."

"Why would they ask you?" asked Kate.

"Because my mother was head counselor at the time of the revolt. She was pivotal in scouting locations to hide the amulet once Nero was captured," replied Dolores.

"Do you know where the amulet ended up being hidden?" asked Logan.

"Of course not. Even my own mother didn't know, but she did compile a list, years later, from her memory. That list contained a dozen locations she scouted out that would be secure enough to hold the amulet."

"Did you give the potential locations to Ms. Agatha or Nurse Carter?" asked Kate.

"Are you kidding me? I wasn't about to divulge any well-kept Diablo Family secrets...At least not without being compensated," smirked Dolores.

Logan stepped up next to me and said, "Well, family secrets or not, we found room A113, and we found the amulet."

Dolores looked at us suspiciously. "Well then, where did you find it and where is the amulet now?" she asked.

"In a vault under the outhouses," replied Logan. "We were confronted by Griffin and an individual wearing a hood, which Griffin claimed was you."

"That individual took Anne, or at least the shapeshifter that looked like Anne, and the amulet before we had a chance to stop them," finished Kate.

"Which makes sense, since Griffin is Nero's nephew," replied Dolores, "and since he's also seeking revenge for his family bloodline, which just so happens to be your bloodline."

"What?" yelped Kate. "How'd you know all that?"

Dolores grinned, "I have my ways."

"We think Griffin is using you as a scapegoat to throw us off because he knew that we don't-" Logan paused.

"He knew you didn't like me," finished Dolores.

"Um…yes," replied Logan.

"That's fine because I still don't like any of you," said Dolores bluntly, "but, I resent the fact that Griffin is trying to frame me for being involved in nefarious camp activities. After all, I am perfectly capable of getting myself involved in questionable acts all on my own."

Logan looked Dolores squarely in the eyes. "So, what you're saying is, you'll assist us?" he asked hopefully.

Dolores looked at each of us with her intense black gaze. "What I'm saying is, I'll help you, but if any of you try snitch my powers, you'll be in for a world of hurt."

"Understood," said Logan flopping back down on the sofa. "Come and take a seat because we've already come up with a bare-bones plan."

"I was just about to offer my ability to Deep Link and donate my secret spy handcuffs to the mission," I said.

"You brought your handcuffs?" muttered Kate, "to camp?"

"Yep, but I was only going to use them for an occasion like this," I replied.

"But they weren't on the packing list," huffed Kate.

"Neither were voodoo doll supplies," smirked Dolores, "but I'm almost finished making a doll that looks just like you, Kate."

For the next hour, the five of us sat on Frank's sofa, eagerly discussing the specifics on rescuing Anne and saving the camp, while Kate kept a careful watch on Dolores out of the corner of her eye.

Crouching around the back corner of the nurse's cabin, Kate, Logan, and I waited patiently for Dolores to finish binding Nate's wrists with scratch brown twine.

"Checking coms," I projected to Nate. *"Can you read me?"*

"I can," replied Nate, hiding with Dolores in a clump of tall pine trees near the front of the cabin. *"We are almost ready to roll."*

"Then let Operation Save Crusader commence," I replied.

Hurriedly scurrying into place, Kate, Logan, and I each took our positions directly under a window at the back of the cabin as Dolores jabbed a stick in Nate's back and lead him out from behind the trees. Together, Nate and Dolores marched towards Nurse Carter's cabin door as I laid my back against the cabin wall and closed my eyes. Clearing my mind and focusing my thoughts only on Nate, I was able to initiate a Deep Link.

"Okay Nate, I'm all linked up," I said. *"I can now feel, hear, and see what's going on through you."*

"Perfect timing because we have arrived," responded Nate.

"Wait right here, loser," growled Dolores as she knocked loudly on the cabin door.

Within seconds, Nurse Carter flung open her cabin door and grinned eagerly down at Nate. *"Oh Dolores, how kind of you to bring me a gift, and all tied up in a neat little package,"* she cooed.

"Like a plump Thanksgiving turkey ready to be stuffed," chuckled Dolores.

Nurse Carter extended out her hand, running one long sharp fingernail under Nate's chin. *"How ever did you find him?"* she asked blissfully.

"He was outside my cabin spying on me. I think he was going to attack me when I came out."

Nate growled and pretended to struggle against the rope binding his hands in front of him. *"And I would have too, given the chance!"* rumbled Nate.

"I'm dropping him off to you so I can continue my search for the others," said Dolores, *"because none of us will be safe until we've caught every last one of these losers."*

"Go ahead and try to catch them!" exclaimed Nate, trying to wiggle free. *"They'll kick your keisters all the way to Antarctica before you can even-"*

"There'll be no keister kicking unless it's done by me," snapped Nurse Carter as she reached down and grabbed

the rope around Nate's hands and pulled him up close. *"Just leave him to me, Dear. I promise to take good care of him."*

"Do what you want with him, but whatever it is, make it really painful," grinned Dolores.

"I guarantee it," chuckled Nurse Carter as she yanked on Nate's bound hands and pulled him into the cabin.

Being careful to maintain the deep connection with Nate, I left my mind open just enough to broadcast a play-by-play to the rest of the team.

"Nate's in." I projected to Kate, Logan, and Dolores. *"Remember what we practiced back in Frank's cabin. Keep your thoughts at a minimum and don't talk too much because my brain gets pretty jumbled with everyone communicating through me all at once especially during a Deep Link."*

"Got it," replied Logan. *"I'll be sure to-"*

"She just pushed me into the backroom near you all," interrupted Nate, *"and she's in a pretty foul mood."*

Focusing my thoughts, I could see Nurse Carter through Nate's eyes. *"...and then you thought you could outsmart* me with your little rodent rampage..." sneered Nurse Carter, "but just look where that got you."

Nate replied, "That was my little brother's idea...He's the brains of the operation."

Placing both hands on Nate's shoulders, Nurse Carter forced him to sit down on a wooden stool in the middle of the room.

"Sit here," she ordered.

"Okay, okay, you don't have to be so rough," complained Nate.

"You don't even know what rough is, boy," Nurse Carter hissed, pulling a stool over for herself and sitting directly in front of Nate, "but you're about to find out."

"Oh, I know what rough is," replied Nate enthusiastically, "because one time my cat named Kitt licked my face. Have you ever had a cat lick your face? I mean, wow! I was lucky Kitt didn't lick my nose clean off my face because with a sandpaper tongue like that-"

"I didn't bring you back here to talk about your cat," rumbled Nurse Carter. "I want to know everything you know."

"Well," gulped Nate, *"Since you're so intimidating and I'm just a weak little boy, I'll tell you everything I know."*

"That's more like it," replied Nurse Carter, bending forward so her nose was almost touching Nate's nose. *"Then get on with it. Tell me everything you know."*

Nate took a long deep breath, sighed, and said, *"Okay here goes...Christopher Columbus sailed the ocean blue in 1492...A sloth can hold its breath longer than a dolphin...Your body produces enough saliva in a year that you could fill two bathtubs with it...A blue whale can create a fart bubble big enough for a horse to fit in...Researchers recently discovered that eating boogers may actually defend against stomach ulcers and may even be good for your teeth...Toe wrestling is a sport that first started in the United Kingdom in 1974 because-"*

Nurse Carter sat back in her chair and howled, *"Enough already! What are you going on about?"*

"You said to tell you everything I know."

"I didn't mean everything you know," groaned Nurse Carter.

"But you said to tell you everything I know'ed-"

Nurse Carter reached her hand up to her forehead and massaged her temples. *"Just forget what I said,"* she moaned.

"You don't look like you're feeling very well," replied Nate. *"Speaking of not feeling well, would you happen to have a snack because I never got to eat breakfast because a fat skunk ran off with my only piece of bacon...Who knew skunks liked bacon...Am I right?... I mean, did you know that skunks even liked breakfast foods because I had no clue that-"*

"Enough already!" bellowed Nurse Carter. *"You wouldn't be hungry if you and your retched siblings hadn't stuck your noses where they didn't belong."*

I suddenly felt my heart jump. ***"It sounds like she's going to reveal something Nate,"*** I whispered. ***"So, play along."***

Nate sat up taller on the stool and leaned forward just slightly. *"We couldn't help but stick our noses into what was going on,"* replied Nate confidently, *"because it was obvious from the start that you were the shapeshifter!"*

"What?" bellowed Kate in my brain. *"She's not the shapeshifter! No one thinks she's the shapeshifter, Nate!"*

"Quiet Kate!" I ordered. *"Stop talking and just listen because it's too late to go back now."*

I watched intently as Nurse Carter got up from the stool and walked over to a desk in the corner of the room. With her back still turned to Nate, Nurse Carter fumbled through a large stack of paper and asked, *"How long have you known? And don't you dare lie to me because I'll know if you do."*

"Lie," I whispered.

"Lie," Dolores whispered.

"Lie," Logan whispered.

"Lie," Kate whispered.

"Lie," Nate blurted out accidentally. *"Uh, I mean lie-k for a while now...We've known for a while...now,"* fibbed Nate.

"But how? Who double-crossed me?"

"Ms. Agatha," whispered Logan.

*"**Frank,**"* whispered Dolores.

*"**Dolores,**"* whispered Kate.

"Griffin," replied Nate. *"Griffin double-crossed you."*

*"**Good lie,**"* I whispered.

Nurse Carter puffed up her shoulders and then rolled her neck from side to side until it let out an audible 'crack.'

"I thought I just told you not to lie to me," hissed Nurse Carter.

"I'm not...lying," stammered Nate.

Walking over to her stool, Nurse Carter slowly pulled it underneath her, keeping her eyes on Nate the whole time as she sat down.

"I know you're lying," smirked Nurse Carter, *"because my own son would never rat me out."*

*"**Inconceivable!**"* blurted Logan.

Nate gulped, *"Your son?"*

"My son," said Nurse Carter narrowing her eyes.

Nate sighed, *"Well, in that case, it wasn't Griff-"*

Before Nate could react, Nurse Carter reached out and grabbed Nate by the neck, her long pointed fingernails digging into his skin.

"Hang tight!" I hollered anxiously. *"We're coming to rescue you."*

"No...Not yet..." gasped Nate.

I wanted to rush in and save Nate like he had saved me so many times before, but something told me that he hadn't quite reached the point where he needed saving.

"Let...me...go," sputtered Nate as Nurse Carter continued to squeeze his neck.

Releasing her grip, Nurse Carter hissed, *"Then start telling me the truth or the next breath you take will be your last."*

"Okay...okay," sputtered Nate as he wiped away a trickling drop of blood that was running down his neck.

Nurse Carter sat back on her stool and grinned. *"You may begin again,"* she said.

"Before I start, may I please have a...a snack?" stammered Nate· *"I really am very hungry. This won't be*

*a pleasant experience for anyone if my ADHD medication
ends up combining with low blood sugar. "*

"Then tell me quickly, " snarled Nurse Carter, *"and I
will see that you get what you have coming to you. "*

"But I really think-"

"Enough stalling! rumbled Nurse Carter.

"...Excuse me, " whispered Nate.

"Excuse me?" snarled Nurse Carter. *"Excuse you for
what?"*

"I just let a silent one go, " replied Nate sheepishly,
*"and my mom always told me to be polite when I fart, even
if someone is threatening to choke me to death. "*

"That...that stench came from...you?" stammered
Nurse Carter. *"I don't think...I've' ever smelled...anything
so horrid...in my life!"*

"I warned you! You should have given me a snack..."

"What's wrong with you boy?" cried Nurse Carter,
"That smell...It's...UGH!"

*"Lady, you better open up a window before it knocks us
both out!"* exclaimed Nate.

Logan, Kate, and I quickly scrambled out from under our assigned spots and hid around the corners of the cabin just seconds before Nurse Carter flung the window open, hung her head out, and gulped in large amounts of fresh air.

"UGH...OH, UGH! How on Earth...could...you..." coughed Nurse Carter.

"Oh No!" yelped Nate, *"I've got an even bigger one coming on! This one's gonna blow the roof off of the place!"*

Nurse Carter flew from the window with her hand covering her mouth and tears streaming down her cheeks. *"I can't...I can't...I can't,"* she muttered as she threw the bedroom door open and dashed out like her hair was on fire.

Nate rubbed his neck and sighed. ***"Good riddance,"*** he said as he walked over to the open window.

Reaching up through the window, Logan quickly untied Nate's wrists. Extending his hand down to each of us, Nate pulled us up and through the window. Once inside, we all set to work looking for clues.

"Wonder what's in there?" asked Logan, walking over to a closet door, and carefully opening it up.

"Looks like a really large medicine cabinet," whispered Nate over Logan's shoulder.

"See anything in there that could keep the victims knocked out for a long period of time?" I asked as we scanned hundreds of pill jars, glass vials, and syringes, all neatly organized on the shelves in front of us.

"Aspirin...no, Alfalfa...no, Benzoin...don't know what that is," mumbled Logan under his breath, "Bishop's Weed...no...so far none of these medicines look like anything she could use to keep her victims paralyzed for an extended amount of time."

"Just keep looking," whispered Kate as she carefully sifted through hundreds of loose-leaf papers and letters on the desk in the corner of the room, "since we're not exactly sure what we're looking for, let's just hope a clue will just pop right out and-"

"Speaking of popping, I'm popping out of here," interrupted Dolores. "It's obvious that we won't find any important clues in here."

Before anyone could stop her, Dolores opened up the bedroom door and walked out of the room as if it wasn't a big deal.

"Did she just do what I thought she did?" whispered Kate.

"If you think she just recklessly walked out of the room without a care in the world," I replied, "then yes."

Nate walked over to the bedroom door and looked down the hallway. "That girl is completely rash, reckless, and unpredictable."

"Just like someone else I know," replied Kate joining Nate at the door.

"Go and follow her," whispered Logan as he pushed his face deeper into the medicine cabinet. "I'll keep looking through this medicine for clues."

Nate, Kate, and I stepped out of the room and looked down the long hallway, but Dolores was nowhere to be seen.

"I think our double agent may be double-crossing us," I whispered.

"A double, double-crosser," frowned Nate, "and to think she was just starting to grow on me."

I slowed my pace, falling behind Nate and Kate, as we quietly snuck past a portrait of Charles Wildenbury on the wall. Just as Kate reached the open doorway, Nate turned around and gave me a strange look.

"Why'd you stop?" he asked.

I pointed to the floor as I slowly crept forward on top of a long green rug that partially ran down the hallway. Like a radio station out of tune, random fuzzy thoughts buzzed in and out of my head as I moved a few feet forward and then a few feet back across the rug.

"I think I've got something," I projected to Nate. *"Can you come back and give me a hand?"*

"Just a second," replied Nate.

I watched Nate silently tap Kate on the shoulder and then point back towards me. Kate nodded her head in agreement and then walked through the doorway while Nate joined me back down the hall.

"What's up Doc?" asked Nate looking at me with his head turned to the side like a confused puppy dog.

"I'm getting a jumble of weak thoughts from multiple people right about here," I said, bouncing up and down on my heels. "It sounds like faint cries for help."

"That doesn't make a whole lot of sense because we're standing in the middle of a hallway," whispered Nate. "Unless of course, this cabin is haunted."

"Maybe there's a hidden door along this wall," I replied. "Let's check."

Reaching out, we ran our fingers along the textured wall, trying to feel for anything unusual.

"Kate just found Dolores," I whispered as I closely examined the portrait frame. "She found her rummaging through the closet in that room, and she appears to have not ratted us out to Nurse Carter."

Nate plopped down on his hands and knees and began rolling up the carpet towards my feet. "Have they found anything yet?" he asked.

"Not yet," I replied. "I'm getting a little worried because we're quickly running out of-"

"Small hairy spiders!" exclaimed Nate below me.

"Small hairy spiders?" I asked, running my hand behind the portrait. "I wasn't aware we were running low on arachnids."

"Well, if we were then we'd be in great shape," replied Nate, "because I just found a gazillion of them."

Having rolled up a quarter of the carpet, Nate uncovered a hidden trap door built into the floor. Upon cracking the hatch to peer inside, a small army of hairy brown spiders poured out.

"It's a good thing I'm not afraid of them," whispered Nate as a dozen more spiders scurried across his hand, "but if Kate were here right now, she'd totally freak out."

"That's for sure," I whispered as I knelt and grabbed hold of the door. "Let me help you get that open."

A hundred more spiders skittered out of the opening once we managed to lift the trap door all the way open.

"There are people down there," I whispered to the pitch black below. "I can hear their thoughts. They're weak, but there are definitely people down below us."

"I've seen enough horror movies to know that there's also a bad guy down there with a chainsaw," said Nate anxiously. "So, I'd rather not-."

"But I think Calder, Anne, and all the others are down there," I interrupted. "We've got to get down there and rescue them before-"

"You get caught," boomed a deep familiar voice behind us.

"Forget what I just said about not being afraid of spiders," whimpered Nate as we slowly got to our feet and looked into what appeared to be glossy black spider eyes as large as dinner plates.

Grabbing Nate's hand, and then slowly backing away from the enormous hairy spider looming over us. "Griffin...is...is that you?" I stammered.

Thick saliva dripped from Griffin's razor-sharp fangs. "It is me...and you're just in time for breakfast," he snarled.

"We're not hungry, we already ate," mumbled Nate anxiously, "but thank you anyway."

"Not according to my mother," replied Griffin loudly snapping his jaws. "She said that you were starving just ten minutes ago."

Nate stuck out his belly and patted it. "I'm better now," he said, "See!"

"That's good," hissed Griffin. "I'll pass on the word to my mom, once she's done dealing with Logan."

"What'd you do with Logan?" I asked, anxiously looking over my shoulder towards the door behind us.

"It's a little late to worry about Logan," sneered Griffin as he extended his eight hairy legs outward, completely blocking the hallway between us, Kate, and Dolores. "He's already been dealt with, and your sister and Dolores are next. But don't worry about them either because I'll make their demise slow and painful."

"Actually, I'm more worried about turning into a giant spider, like you," said Nate, continuing to pull me backward by my hand. "How'd it happen? Were you bitten by a werespider or something?"

Griffin snapped his powerful jaws in our faces again and then roared, "It's my super ability, you halfwit!"

"But I thought your super ability was heightened senses?" I replied, trying to look through Griffin's legs to see if I could locate Kate and Dolores down the hall.

"I do have heightened senses. I just *accidentally* forget to tell you that I have heightened senses because I can transform into a giant spider," chuckled Griffin.

"So that's why you could see so well in Crusader Cave," I concluded, still trying to look past Griffin's enormous hairy body.

"And that's why you're so tired during the day," added Nate. "I just thought you were a lazy bum, but you're nocturnal."

"You've also been injecting venom into your victims after your mom, the shapeshifter knocks them out," I added. "That way they appear to have lost their superpowers."

"You two are smarter than you look," hissed Griffin.

"Sometimes," replied Nate.

Frustrated, because I still wasn't able to see behind Griffin, I decided to clue Kate and Dolores in on the little pest problem.

"Kate and Dolores!" I projected, *"There is an enormous spider in the hallway that goes by the name of Griffin."*

"Are you messing with me?" asked Kate sounding anxious.

"I'm not, but please come and help us, and be as quiet as possible. Spiders don't have necks, so he won't be able to see you unless he turns completely around."

"You better be messing with me," growled Kate.

"I wish I were," I said, abruptly cutting off the conversation because I could see Griffin was growing weary of Nate.

"So...just to get this straight, none of the campers have truly lost their powers," said Nate, rubbing his head, acting confused, "and...you did all this to get the amulet and to capture Tate?"

"Enough talking! Either Tate agrees to do what we say, or I'll devour both of you, right here, right now," hissed

Griffin as a long stream of sticky saliva dripped from the corner of his mouth and onto the floor.

As Nate and I continued to retreat towards the back room, I was finally able to catch a quick glimpse of Kate and Dolores between Griffin's thick hairy legs.

"Ack!" exclaimed Kate, sounding as if she were about to throw up, *"You weren't kidding!"*

"Don't worry…everything is going to be okay." I projected, trying to calm Kate's nerves.

"Okay? Okay?" yelped Kate. *"An enormous spider is taking up the whole hallway! There's nothing okay with that!"*

"Just remember it's only Griffin."

"I don't care who it is. You know how much I hate spiders!" groaned Kate.

"But we haven't much time…You've got to smack him, otherwise, he's going to eat Nate and me!" I projected. *"Just make him angry and I'll do the rest."*

"Are you insane? I can't even look at spiders and now you want me to smack a giant one?" grumbled Kate.

"Yes! Hard...Really, Really Hard!"

I caught a quick glimpse of Kate throwing her hands up in the air as she slipped back into the room with Dolores. A moment later, she and Dolores reappeared holding two large brooms, one in each hand.

Griffin roared, "I won't go over it again!" as four of his long hairy legs began to curl around us.

Grabbing Nate's hand, I pulled him back three steps and then planted my feet. "Fine, I'll go with you Griffin, but first you'll need to play a game," I said.

"I'm not playing any ridiculous game," snarled Griffin.

"Well, you kind of have to because...you're the game!" I exclaimed.

"Now!" I projected to Kate.

Kate closed her eyes and raised the broom over her head.

"HI-YAW!" yelled Kate as she and Dolores swung their brooms down with a solid thud on Griffin's back.

Stumbling forward under the assault, Griffin was unable to turn around because of the walloping he was receiving from Kate and Dolores. "Stop, stop!" bellowed Griffin, "or Tate will suffer...incredibly!"

Kate roared, "Leave my little brother alone!" seconds before she turned on her super speed, slamming the broom down on Griffin's body and legs, over and over and over again.

"Keep going!" I chirped happily. *"Smash him good!"*

"I can't...keep this up...much longer," projected Kate, beginning to sound weary.

"Just a little bit more," I begged as Griffin howled in pain.

"C'mon, Kate. You can do it," projected Nate.

"Too late. I'm all out of energy...I've got to take...a quick break," replied Kate as the assault suddenly came to an abrupt stop, giving Griffin just enough time to turn around and face her and Dolores.

"Now, you're mine!" roared Griffin, as Kate sunk to her knees completely exhausted.

"Leave them alone!" I yelled helplessly.

"I got this," replied Dolores as she threw her broom on the ground and bravely stepped between Kate and Griffin. "I don't think you want to mess with me," she snarled, brushing the hair out of her eyes.

"What's up with her eyeballs?" asked Nate. "They turned red."

"I don't know, but let's just go with it," I said grabbing Nate's hand and sprinting into the back room.

"Where are we going?" asked Nate. "Kate and Dolores may need our help."

"Listen," I said pulling Nate towards the far corner of the room. "I'll lead Griffin away from the cabin because he only wants me. That'll leave you, Dolores, and Kate behind to rescue Anne, Logan, and the others."

"So, you get to take on a giant poisonous spider and we get to rescue people," replied Nate. "That doesn't seem fair to you."

"It's my turn to be brave," I said, "besides, you'll also have to deal with Nurse Carter and her angry pink fingernails."

"Never mind..." sighed Nate, "it suddenly sounds fairer."

"Okay then. I'll lead Griffin away so you can take care of business."

"Just be careful, Bro," said Nate, sounding uneasy, "and let me know if you need help kicking Spiderboy's keister."

"Okay, but I got this," I replied, trying to sound braver than I felt at that moment.

Nate reached out and gave me a quick hug without saying another word.

"Thanks," I replied looking into Nate's eyes. "...Just make sure you stay hidden until I get Griffin out of here."

Nate gave me a thumbs up and then quickly retreated into the corner of the room as I ran back into the hall. "Hey, Griffin!" I yelled, "Your only chance to release Uncle Nero is leaving the building!"

"What?" snarled Griffin as I quickly turned around, sprinted back into the bedroom, enthusiastically dove out the cabin window, and landed with a hard thud on my stomach.

"NO!" roared Griffin in my head.

"Nate, stay hidden. He's coming through!" I groaned, struggling to get to my feet.

Glancing back through the window, I watched in horror as Griffin burst into the bedroom, seconds later. "Let me out!" he snarled, trying to stuff his enormous body and eight hairy legs through the tiny window, shattering the glass into a million pieces.

"Come and get me!" I projected, dashing off towards the thick pine forest.

"You're mine!" roared Griffin in my head.

"I got this...I got this...I got this," I repeated to myself, running hard until I stopped for a moment at the edge of the forest to catch my breath.

"He's smashing the back wall to bits, and he's almost out!" said Nate.

"Okay," I replied, stepping further into the dark shadows, my mind racing as I desperately looked around for my next move.

"You can run, but you can't hide!" bellowed Griffin, finally squeezing through the large hole in the back wall of the cabin.

Kicking it into high gear, only a minute ahead of Griffin, I frantically zigzagged my way between tree after tree until I finally came to an enormous fallen pine blocking my path. Leaping over the log, I ducked my head low, laid my back against the fallen tree, and pulled my legs up to my chin, only seconds before Griffin exploded into the forest.

"I'm going to find you," echoed Griffin's raspy voice in the otherwise silent forest.

Trying to slow my pounding heart, I closed my eyes and laid my head back on the decaying tree. After what seemed to be a lifetime of deafening silence, I slowly opened my eyes but left my head resting on the log. "What the?" I whispered as a smokey yellow wasp appeared from a small gash in the log only a few inches from my face. Laying my chin on the log, I leaned in closer and projected an image of Griffin to the inquisitive wasp. Cocking its head to the side, the wasp briefly fluttered its wings and then nodded its head before it disappeared back into the log.

"Your sister just got taken out of commission by my mom," hissed Griffin from somewhere nearby. "It's time you surrendered before we have to take this any further."

Thinking about Kate, knocked unconscious somewhere back at camp, made me sick to my stomach but I stayed put, knowing that Griffin was trying to draw me out of my hiding spot.

"If you don't come out, Nate will be next!" roared Griffin nastily, "and I will hurt him real good."

Hot anger boiled within me as I placed my hands down on the dry needles blanketing the forest floor. Quietly flipping onto my knees, I reached out and snatched up a long thick stick and held it tightly against my pounding chest.

"And then we will move on to your worthless mother!" howled Griffin. "I will make her beg for mercy!"

"Leave my family alone!" I shrieked, leaping up on the log, unable to tamp down the rage inside me anymore.

Caught off guard, Griffin momentarily shrunk back when I suddenly appeared on the log only a few feet in front of him.

"Go away!" I ordered bravely, pointing the sharp stick directly in Griffin's face.

Without warning, Griffin stretched out his eight powerful arms and leapt towards me, easily swatting the stick out of my hand. "You're mine!" roared Griffin as two of his legs struck me in the middle of my chest, sending me hurtling backward through the air. Landing hard on my back, I gasped as all of the air left my lungs. Not able to breathe, I clutched my chest and thrashed my legs wildly about as tears filled my eyes and streamed down my cheeks.

Not wasting any time, Griffin crawled over me, his legs surrounding me like thick hairy prison bars. "Last chance," he hissed, his hot breath puffing into my face as I frantically tried to coax air into my lungs.

"Help Me!" I projected to anyone or anything that would listen, *"I can't breathe!"*

"Looks like you lost, little man," replied Griffin as he lowered his head so close to mine that warm saliva dripped onto my face. "This truly is your last chance," he hissed.

"I...I...won't-" I gasped as the air suddenly rushed back into my lungs.

Before I could take another breath, Griffin lashed out, sinking his razor-sharp fangs into my flesh. Searing hot pain exploded in my shoulder as I felt his fangs hit my collar bone and inject venom into my body.

I cried out in agony as Griffin stood back on his hind legs to admire his handiwork.

"I quite enjoyed that," grinned Griffin. "Let's do it one *final* time!"

I closed my eyes and pulled my knees up and into my stomach, whimpering under the intense pain.

"Please," I whispered almost inaudibly, lying helpless on the forest floor.

As I waited for the final blow, my thoughts turned to my family. I struggled to remember the last time I showed them how much they meant to me. And now, lying in the bleak shadows of the forest, it was unbearable to think that they would never know how much I truly loved them.

"Goodbye, I love you," I feebly projected as I silenced my thoughts and gave into my fate.

Chapter Twelve

Standing Tall

Quieting my mind, waiting for Griffin to strike again, I heard a gentle breeze whistling through the treetops, the sounds of birds chirping high above, and of bees buzzing nearby. It wasn't until the buzzing sound grew louder that I realized Griffin hadn't delivered a final lethal blow. Wiping the tears out of my eyes, I looked up and saw an enormous haze of wasps swarming between me and a recoiling Griffin.

"Go away, pests!" roared Griffin.

Lying on the ground, I whispered painfully, "Show no mercy..."

The swarm of angry wasps shrouded Griffin's entire body, stinging him over and over again.

"Stop! Stop! Stop!" wailed Griffin as he wildly thrashed all eight of his arms in the air to no avail. Unable to defend himself against the powerful swarm, Griffin ran off into the woods with the gray cloud of wasps relentlessly pursuing him.

"Spider bites aren't usually as bad as snake bites...I still have some time," I whispered as I rolled over and slowly pulled myself to my feet. "Of course, most spiders aren't six feet tall either," I chuckled painfully.

Carefully placing my numb right arm against my chest, I slowly staggered out of the shadows and into the warm morning sunlight at the edge of the forest.

"I'm coming Nate," I projected as I stumbled across the open field to the nurse's cabin, stopping directly in front of what remained of the shattered back wall. I reached out with my left arm, unsure how I was going to pull myself up into the cabin, but I was desperate to find Nate and Kate.

Suddenly, Nate appeared in front of me. "Tate, Get Down!" he screeched from the hole in the wall.

My brain didn't have time to process what was going on before Nate recklessly jumped out of the window, tackling me to the ground.

"Cover your head!" yelped Nate just as an enormous black dragon exploded through the roof of the nurse's cabin.

Countless pieces of shattered wood, glass, and insulation rained down on us as we rolled onto our stomachs and covered our heads.

"What the heck's going on?" I asked Nate as the dust began to settle around us.

"A dragon," replied Nate.

"I can see that!" I exclaimed, rolling onto my back and looking up at the enormous black dragon with thick jagged scales, red glowing eyes, and savagely sharp claws, standing almost as tall as a two-story building.

"That's Dolores," Nate continued. "Nurse Carter showed up and she assumed Kate's identity and now Dolores is taking her on."

"Is Kate okay?"

"She's fine, but she got knocked out, so I stashed her down in the cellar with the other people," replied Nate. "I figured she'd be safer there."

"Who else was down there?"

"Anne, Ms. Agatha, Samantha, and all the other victims. I think I even saw Frank in the dark down there."

"How'd Nurse Carter capture Frank?"

"I don't know, but he was down there, knocked out and tied up with spider webs and everything," replied Nate.

"But Dolores is wreaking havoc on the cabin, right now! She's going to crush them to death!" I exclaimed.

Dolores suddenly tilted her head back and roared, shaking the ground beneath our feet. In awe, Nate and I watched as Dolores slowly stomped her way forward, demolishing the front of the cabin like a giant lizard ravaging Tokyo.

Nate hopped up and brushed off the seat of his pants. "It's fine, that cellar is like a cement fortress...super thick walls," he replied, reaching down and grabbing my injured right arm.

"Not that arm," I said wincing in pain.

Nate's eyes grew wide as he examined me from top to bottom. "I knew I should've followed you," said Nate uneasily. "What happened between you and Griffin in the forest?"

I slowly reached my left hand across my chest and up to my shirt collar. Pulling my collar down, Nate winced when he saw the swollen, bloody puncture wounds on my shoulder.

"He bit you?" asked Nate, "Did he-"

"Yes, he injected venom," I replied.

"Are you sure?"

"My shoulder felt like it was on fire and now my whole right side is going numb," I replied, "so yes, I'm sure."

"Then we've got to get you to a nurse," replied Nate uneasily.

I rolled over onto my side and slowly stood up to face Nate. "Look around," I said nodding to the demolished cabin in front of us. "If you haven't noticed, the only nurse at camp is an evil one...I'll take my chances with the venom."

"Don't be dumb!" exclaimed Nate. "You'll die if you don't get help soon."

"I've got time," I replied. "It's not that bad-"

"Yet!" exclaimed Nate.

I looked away from Nate when I saw tears welling up in his eyes.

"Listen," said Nate half looking at me, "you won't be much help-"

"Because I'm not as strong and brave as you or Kate are?" I growled.

"I didn't say that," whispered Nate, turning his head away from me.

"You didn't have to," I replied. "You and Kate have been standing up and protecting me my whole life."

Nate sputtered, "But, you needed us…"

"You've always thought of me as your little baby brother, not as your equal, even though I was born three minutes before you," I replied.

Nate looked down at his feet and didn't say another word.

"A lot of this has been my fault," I continued. "I've allowed you and Kate to look after me because I'm not as brave as either of you, but I think it's time I stop being so scared all the time. That's why I wanted to deal with Griffin on my own."

"I understand," whispered Nate.

"And we need to finish what we started," I continued, "so, how about you use your power and help me 'imagine' that I'm feeling better so I can stand up and be braver this time around?"

Nate blinked, sending tears rolling down his cheeks.

Nate reluctantly wiped the tears away with the back of his hand and sputtered, "But...if we don't finish this thing quick, then I'm going to take you somewhere to get help."

"It's a deal," I replied quickly.

Nate gently placed his hand on my aching shoulder and exhaled slowly through his mouth.

Closing my eyes, I felt the pain slowly drain from my arm, shoulder, and back until it was completely gone. "Thanks," I whispered. "I'm feeling a whole lot better."

Nate smiled weakly as he grabbed my hand and lead me away from what remained of the Nurse's cabin. "Please remember, that poison is still in your system, so we have a time limit," he whispered.

"I won't forget," I replied, "besides, I'm sure-"

"POOF!"

My heart almost jumped out of my chest when Nicholas Knight suddenly appeared in a puff of gray smoke directly in front of us.

"I'm ready to catch me a couple of villains, Texas-style," smirked Nick, holding a long scratchy rope in his hand.

"What's he doing here?" I asked Nate, "and what villains is he talking about because Griffin already took off into the forest. He's long gone."

"Nick joined our team while you were busy in the woods playing with the giant spider," replied Nate, "and the two villains he's referring to are Nurse Carter and Lance Phillips."

"Sassy Pants Lance is helping out Nurse Carter?" I asked as the three of us walked to an enormous pine tree growing in front of a large gray boulder, just to the left of what remained of the nurse's cabin.

"And where'd Dolores just disappear to?" I asked looking around the immediate area. "It's not very easy to lose a fifty-foot dragon."

"She's behind that clump of trees. It looks like she's heading toward the proving ground tower," replied Nick.

"And I think Nurse Carter and Lance are hiding in the shadows right over there," Nate said pointing towards the clump of pine trees near the front of the smoldering nurse's cabin. "Preparing to pounce on Dolores at any moment, no doubt."

"The last thing we need is Nurse Carter shapeshifting into Dolores," Nick replied as he carefully wrapped the thick rope around his hand.

"Absolutely," agreed Nate. "Nick, you'll lasso Nurse Carter and I'll take down Lance."

"Which one of them do I get to help capture?" I asked pointing towards Lance and Nurse Carter.

"None of them, but not because I don't think you can," Nate quickly replied.

"If you don't doubt me, then why can't I go?"

"You're our emergency backup in case one of us gets into trouble," he replied. "We don't need your heart rate going up right now because that'll just make the poison spread quicker."

I scowled at Nate. "But...I-"

"Please don't argue with me," pleaded Nate.

"Fine..." I replied reaching down into my back pocket to fish out my secret spy handcuffs, "then take these just in case."

Nate grabbed the handcuffs. "Gladly!" he replied, happily opening and closing them over and over again. "Sheriff Nate's on the job and he's about to kick some-."

Before Nate could finish, Dolores let out an ear-shattering roar that shook the ground under my feet.

"Up there!" exclaimed Nick. He pointed at Dolores who had stopped midway between the crumbling nurse's cabin and the proving ground tower. "It looks like Lance and Nurse Carter just teleported onto her!"

"We got to go now!" yelled Nate, just as Dolores opened her powerful jaws and spewed a stream of hot blue flame towards Lance and Nurse Carter.

"She missed them!" I yelled, the blistering flame incinerating a small patch of pine trees on the ground.

"Nick, teleport me up there!" roared Nate. "I'm going to arrest Sassy Pants!"

"You got it!" replied Nick.

Before I could say another word, Nate grabbed Nick's hand, and they disappeared in a cloud of gray smoke.

"POOF!"

"So much for a covert operation," I projected as I watched a large crowd of nervous campers gather behind the dining hall.

"Yep, a little late for that," replied Nate as I reestablished a deep link with him.

"Just be careful," I projected, as I anxiously watched Nate snap one handcuff onto his wrist before he silently crept across Dolores's neck and popped up directly in front of Lance.

"You're under arrest for being the biggest jerk at camp!" exclaimed Nate as he clamped the other handcuff onto Lance's wrist.

"Let go of me!" yelped Lance, frantically yanking his handcuffed wrist away from Nate.

Nate grabbed hold of Lance's hand and replied, *"No way, dude. I've been saving up a super smelly treat just for you!"*

"You wouldn't dare!" sneered Lance.

"You obviously don't know me very well!" bellowed Nate joyfully. *"One order of fresh, hot, steamy dog poo, coming right up!"*

Lance used his free hand to cover his nose and mouth, but it didn't appear to be doing him any good.

"UUGH…I can't…I can't…breathe!" sputtered Lance.

"I got a lot more where that came from," giggled Nate. *"A whole lot more!"*

"Get away from me, freak!" exclaimed Lance, struggling to free himself.

"I'm not going anywhere, Mister Sassy Pants Lance!" chirped Nate.

"We'll see about that!" roared Lance as he attempted to teleport away from Nate even though they were still attached at the wrist.

" POOF! "

I caught sight of Nate and Lance, still attached at the wrist, as a wisp of smoke appeared on the top of the dining hall in the distance. *"SUPER STINKY UNDERWEAR!"* bellowed Nate. *"Enjoy the smell!"*

Lance placed his hand over his mouth and turned away from Nate, looking a little green.

"Enough! Enough!" coughed Lance, right before they teleported again.

" POOF! "

Nate and Lance suddenly reappeared, balancing precariously, on top of the proving ground tower.

"SLIMY RACOON VOMIT!" howled Nate, *"WITH CHUNKS!"*

Lance shrieked in horror as he and Nate disappeared again, this time, completely out of sight.

" POOF! "

"I guess that fancy superhero academy didn't teach Lance how to handle someone like Nate," I chuckled to myself.

Suddenly, Dolores let out an ear-shattering roar that made my bones rattle. Shielding my eyes from the sun, I anxiously looked upward and saw Nurse Carter holding Nick's limp body in one hand and the rope in the other, just as the searing pain returned to my body with a vengeance.

Wincing in pain, I slowly pulled up my shirt and looked down at my belly. I held my breath as I lightly touched an enormous red patch of swollen skin that ran from the top of my hip all the way up to my neck. Unable to move my right arm or even stand up straight anymore, I leaned back on the boulder for support, watching helplessly as Dolores let out another soul-shattering roar.

"I'm disconnected from Nate and his powers," I whispered painfully as Nurse Carter let go of Nick's limp body and laid her hand on Dolores' neck.

Tilting her head forward, Dolores unleashed a gigantic blue fireball towards the dining hall, sending campers scattering in every direction. Within seconds, the ball of fire walloped the dining hall. Intense flames quickly consumed the building and then viciously clawed their way towards the treetops. Bursting into action, campers beat back the flames in an attempt to keep the inferno at bay as Dolores roared weakly, one final time far across the field.

"This can't be happening," I muttered as Dolores' glossy black skin suddenly turned to a dull gray and withered to the ground like a giant deflating parade balloon.

I dragged myself behind the large boulder to gain some cover and sat on the ground just as Nurse Carter reinflated into a massive fierce dragon.

"Why did we come here?" I sobbed as I slowly pulled my knees up to my chest. "Why did I have to have these stupid powers in the first place?"

I felt the ground around me rumble as I weakly watched three more fireballs soar overhead, on their way towards Crusader II.

"Nate's right, I'm not capable of defeating anyone, especially a fifty-foot dragon," I whispered miserably as a light breeze blew across the field and tousled my hair. I took a slow deep breath and then painfully turned my body towards the pile of smoldering rubble that once was the nurse's cabin. Tears filled my eyes when I thought about Kate, trapped in the dark basement, still needing to be rescued.

The wind abruptly swept across the field again, this time blowing my hair back. "Be brave child..." whispered the wind, its gentle voice suddenly sounding familiar.

"Ms. Agatha?" I whispered. "Is that you?"

"You have to be the one," whispered the wind. "Save us..."

I closed my eyes and felt the cool breeze blow across my warm skin. "It's just me this time," I groaned as I slowly pulled myself to my feet, my body feeling weaker every passing moment. "I have to be the one to do something."

Leaning back on the boulder, I carefully reached deep into my front pocket, pulled out the macaroni and cheese baggie, opened it, and tipped the amulet into my hand. Even though it was covered in sticky orange cheese sauce, I could feel the power of the ruby tingling in my palm.

"There's a lot of power in this thing," I muttered as I raised the amulet to my face and thought about Frank, "but I think I'm going to need to use something more powerful than the amulet to get me out of this mess."

Suddenly, the ground shook under my feet as the dragon roared, "Hand over the amulet...the real amulet!"

"What? How'd you…"

"How'd I know?" snorted Nurse Carter. *"Silly boy… You're not the only mind reader at camp. I have many allies at Crusader."*

"Well, I'm not handing the amulet over to you!"

"I guess I'll just have to burn you out, then!" growled the dragon.

Suddenly, the air around me grew stifling hot as the tree, directly in front of the boulder, erupted in an intense inferno. *"Leave me alone!"* I projected as the boulder sizzled red hot, the flame scorching the earth all around me.

"Not until you do as I ask."

"Why do you want me to release Nero so badly?"

"I don't want you to release Nero," hissed Nurse Carter. *"Why would I want to resurrect a man that chose your worthless mother, over me?"*

"Don't talk about my mom that way...besides I'm sure Nero intended to-"

"Who cares about intentions," snuffed the dragon. *"He can rot in that rock for all eternity for all I care."*

"Then what do you want?"

"I want you to release the powers that rightfully belong to me...I want immortality. Isn't that what anyone ever really wants, to be immortal and live forever?"

"I just want to be a kid," I replied.

"And that's precisely why powers are wasted on fools and cowards like you," snarled the dragon.

"I'm not a fool or a coward!" I bellowed painfully.

"Then prove it by coming out," hissed the black dragon angrily. *"Before I lose my patience."*

With a half-formed plan swimming around my head, I used the boulder as a crutch to straighten myself up the best I could. I knew that if my idea was going to work, I had to not let on how injured I really was.

"Fine!" I exclaimed from behind the boulder, *"but you have to promise not to hurt my family anymore."*

"Done."

"And you'll have to shapeshift into me to release the powers from the amulet because Nate will call me a baby for surrendering to you without a fight."

"Gladly."

"And don't broil me to a crisp when I come out with my hands up."

"You being dead will do me no good."

"Then I am ready," I replied from behind the boulder, my body shuddering in absolute agony.

"Come out now, but no tricks," snarled Nurse Carter.

"I'm coming," I replied, trying not to sound completely exhausted even though every movement was horrifyingly painful as I stepped out from behind the boulder.

On the verge of collapsing, I bit my lip and pushed on, using every last ounce of strength to drag myself across the ash-covered ground until I finally stood at the feet of the mighty black dragon.

"I give up," I whispered, bowing my head as the enormous dragon lowered hers.

"Silly boy," hissed the dragon. "You should have helped me because once I become you, I will use the amulet to steal your powers for myself and you will be back to being just an ordinary boy."

"I'm tired of feeling different," I whispered, staring at the ground. "Just do what you need to do."

I fell to my knees, bowed my pounding head, closed my eyes, and helplessly dropped the amulet onto the ground in front of me.

"So be it," snarled Nurse Carter as she lifted her heavy claw and placed it on my shoulder. "May this be truly painful."

The air around me grew thinner and thinner as Nurse Carter began to assume my identity. The last thing I heard before losing my balance and blacking out was Nurse Carter screeching, "What have you done boy? What have you done…"

Chapter Thirteen

The Beginning

"T...a...te...T...a...te...Can you hear me?"

Even though my brain and body were begging me to stay asleep for a couple more hours, I slowly opened my eyes anyway, wondering who was calling my name.

"There you are," said Grandpa, his huge face smiling down at me through his thick glasses. "Pretty tired still, Li'l Buck-a-roo?"

"Yes," I muttered. "I feel like I could sleep for a week."

Grandpa grinned down at me. "That's how I feel most mornings," he chuckled.

"Did I dream all of this up?" I asked, concentrating hard to keep his face in focus.

"You mean about what happened at camp?" asked Grandpa.

"Yes, what happened at Crusader."

"Yep, it all was a big dream and if you don't believe me then you can go ask the tin man, the scarecrow, and the cowardly lion. In fact, I'm wearing the ruby slippers, right now!" chuckled Grandpa, gently patting my leg. "Of course it wasn't a dream, kiddo!"

I took a deep breath, rolled over onto my side, and slowly sat up in my bunk.

"Where'd my shirt go?" I asked looking down at my bare belly.

"Alekzander brought a couple of doctors back with him to camp, and they fixed you right up," announced Nate, walking through the cabin door, and tossing me my tee shirt. "They sucked the shirt and the poison right out of ya!"

I let out a sigh as I gently ran my palm over my chest, side, and neck, relieved to see that the swollen red poison patch was no longer invading my body.

"So, what happened, exactly?" I asked as I put my shirt on, "because I don't remember a thing after I walked out from behind the boulder and faced the dragon."

Nate and Grandpa sat down on the bunk directly across from me.

"Well...Lance and I reappeared back at camp just moments after you allowed Nurse Carter to shapeshift into you," replied Nate. "Lance was all tuckered out from trying to ditch me...I'd say we teleported at least a hundred times."

"Wow, a hundred times," I said weakly.

"Yep, we teleported all over Colorado," replied Nate, "and just so you know, we were right, that washing machine museum was pretty lame, but the Sasquatch Outpost was cool."

The cabin door squeaked open again. This time, Kate, Logan, and Anne peaked their heads through.

"Come in, Young'uns," said Grandpa licking his lips. "The wizard just returned from Oz."

Logan and Anne followed Kate into the room. The three of them sat down on the bed next to Grandpa and Nate.

Kate leaned forward, looked me square in the eyes, and said, "You really took care of Nurse Carter. She was down for the count after shapeshifting into you."

"She was out cold!" exclaimed Nate.

"I have Logan to thank for that," I replied. "He's the one that told us about how shapeshifters not only take the physical appearance of their victims but their energy level as well. With all that poison in my body and no one else around to shapeshift into, I figured she'd not only save my life but capture herself as well."

"And since she'd already shape-shifted into Kate and Dolores, then she probably wouldn't have enough energy to shapeshift again anyway," concluded Logan.

"I hoped it would work," I replied.

"It was a brilliant idea that definitely paid off!" exclaimed Logan, reaching over and giving me a fist bump.

"And it goes to show you that it pays to have a nerd on our team," said Nate reaching over and putting his arm around Logan's neck. "I mean, where would we be without Logan's amazing brain and his outstanding hyper-thesises?"

"I guess I'll take that as a compliment," chuckled Logan.

"Sounds like a wonderful compliment to me," grinned Anne from behind her hand.

Logan adjusted his glasses and flashed Anne a huge smile. "Well, in that case, compliment accepted."

"I extend my compliments to all of you," said Alekzander suddenly appearing in the doorway "because from what I understand, you did a great job working together as a team to solve our little problem at camp."

"Who told you that?" asked Kate.

"Both Red and Frank," replied Alekzander, grabbing a chair and sitting down at the head of my bunk. "They gave you all glowing reviews."

"Red was awesome too," replied Kate. "You're both lucky to have each other."

"Yes, we are," grinned Alekzander, "very lucky indeed."

"But where'd Red disappear to and where have you been?" I asked scooting to the edge of my bunk. "You missed all the fun."

"Unfortunately, Nurse Carter had me convinced that she and Ms. Agatha had everything at camp well in hand," he said running his fingers through his long gray peppered hair. "I didn't find out what was truly going on at Crusader until Red tracked me down at the N.H.B. just this morning. We would have been here hours ago, but when Red and I tried to teleport into camp, some unexplained force stopped us from doing so."

"So, how'd you get here then?" I asked.

"Your grandpa drove us," said Alekzander with a smirk.

"If you can call what he does, driving!" chuckled Nate. "You're lucky to be alive."

"Hey," grumbled Grandpa, "I think I drove pretty good for someone who's legally blind and over a hundred fifty years old!"

"You're eighty-one and you can see perfectly well," laughed Nate. "You're just a bad driver."

"Correction," chuckled Grandpa, "adventurous driver."

"Anyhow," said Alekzander with a grin. "We have Nurse Carter and Lance in custody, but we are still scouring the forest for Griffin. We also recovered the amulet by what is now being called, Charred Rock, by the campers."

"So, none of us are in trouble?" I asked hesitantly.

"Not in the slightest," smirked Alekzander, "but I would have preferred that my nurse's cabin and dining hall weren't completely destroyed in the process of saving camp."

"Sorry," whispered Anne.

"It's okay," smiled Alekzander, "besides, there truly is only one person to blame for this whole mess."

Nate sprung up from the bunk bed like a rocket. "Not me!" he exclaimed. "None of this mess is my fault!"

"Not all of it, anyway," winked Alekzander, "but if you all wouldn't mind, I'd like to speak to Tate alone for a couple of minutes if you please."

Alekzander held out his hand, beckoning me to stand up while Nate, Kate, Logan, Anne, and Grandpa left the cabin.

Carefully leading me over to a chair to sit, Alekzander sat down next to me and said, "It's good you're up and around because you had us all pretty worried."

"I'm feeling a bit weak still, but much better than before," I said letting out a long sigh and slumping in the chair.

"I'm told that's fairly typical of how someone feels after they've been injected with venom by a six-foot Wolfsbane Spider."

"I didn't even know such huge spiders existed until I ran into Griffin."

"They are quite rare," replied Alekzander. "In all my years at camp, I've seen a giant cockroach, banana slug, and praying mantis, but never a Wolfsbane spider."

"I guess I was just lucky again," I replied.

Alekzander reached over and placed his hand on my shoulder and looked me straight in the eyes. "That was a smart and brave thing you did out there today, you should be proud of yourself."

"It's the first time I've stood up to somebody in my whole life," I said looking down at my bare feet. "I'm not used to being brave."

"That's not what I heard," replied Alekzander, running his fingers through his beard. "According to Frank and Red, you stood up to Scott, Griffin, and Nurse Carter a couple of times since you've been at Crusader."

"But I had people, animals, and insects to back me up," I replied. "I wouldn't necessarily call that being brave."

"Not everyone is born brave," grinned Alekzander, "In fact, most of the time, bravery takes encouragement, practice, and sometimes...a little back up."

"Makes sense, I guess, but is that why Mom and Dad didn't send us to camp before now...because they thought I wasn't going to be brave enough?"

Alekzander turned and nodded his head towards the door, "Why don't you just ask her yourself?"

"Mom!" I happily shouted when I saw her smiling at me from the doorway.

"Hi, sweetie," replied Mom, walking into the room, and sweeping me up into her arms. "I missed you so much..." she said hugging me tightly, her warm cheek pressing against mine.

"I missed you, too," I replied as tears filled my eyes and then rolled down my cheeks.

"I'm so sorry," she whispered over and over again as I buried my face into her long brown hair.

"It's okay," I whispered.

"It's not okay, really," she replied. "I should have been honest with you, Kate, and Nate, years ago."

"Your mom and dad were convinced that they should hide everything from you because they wanted you three to grow up and lead normal lives," said Alekzander.

"That's because sometimes being a superhero and trying to hold down a full-time job can be stressful and overwhelming. Dad and I didn't want you kids to be burdened with those extra responsibilities," continued Mom.

"They were so concerned about you, Kate, and Nate," added Alekzander. "It took quite some time for them to accept things as they are, not how they hoped they would be."

Mom kissed me on the cheek and then lowered me down on the chair as she sat on the bed across from me.

"With your dad constantly gone on top-secret assignments, both Alekzander and your N.H.B. therapist finally convinced me to send you to camp," frowned mom, "but I'm kind of second-guessing that decision right now."

"We were hoping you'd have a nice calm first year at Crusader," mumbled Alekzander. "We never intended you three to get mixed up in all of this."

"And we never dreamed all of our past mistakes would come back and haunt us again," finished Mom.

"It's okay because I think I finally get it," I said half smiling.

"What do you get?" asked Mom.

"That sometimes, kids start out life kind of rough, like you and Alekzander did, but most people are able to eventually turn things around and make changes for the better."

"That's a very wise perspective," replied Mom. "Coming from a nine-year-old boy."

"Nine and a half," I said, "and most of it was Frank's perspective."

"Oh, sorry," grinned Mom. "Nine and a half."

"And you know something," I said, "Frank was right about people changing."

"How so?" asked Alekzander.

"Well, take Dolores Diablo, for example," I replied, "she changed."

Alekzander glanced out the window, looking dumbfounded. "Huh...A Diablo child making good decisions for once. That is very interesting."

"And I think she *still* may be on the good side," I replied, "...possibly."

Alekzander patted my shoulder again, stood up, and flashed Mom a quick smile. "If you'll excuse me," said Alekzander. "I have some camp business to take care of."

"What kind of business?" I asked curiously.

"Ms. Agatha and I have some boring paperwork to fill out for the N.H.B. and our insurance company but first I'll need to check on Nickolas Knight and his two broken legs."

"I'm glad he'll be okay," I said. "He was a hero."

"Yes, he was," replied Alekzander, "and so were all of you."

I sat up a little straighter and said, "And now I think I'm ready to start trying to be a little braver each day from here on out."

Alekzander reached over and ruffled my hair, "Then you're definitely in the right place for that."

"Definitely," replied Mom, "most definitely."

Book One

The End

Made in the USA
Las Vegas, NV
28 September 2021